THE
LOW NOTES

A WEXLEY FALLS NOVEL

KATE ROTH

Debbie,
Thank you for always
being an amazing friend!
I love you,

PRAISE FOR
THE LOW NOTES

"Kate Roth leaves no emotional stone unturned in this enjoyable, sexy read with an ending that will surprise you!"

    —Caitlyn Duffy, author of *The Rock Star's Daughter* and *The Believer's Daughter*

"I absolutely loved this book! Kate Roth spins an enthralling story."

    —Britni Hill, author of *Tears in the Rubble*

"The story of Nina and Kevin is a must read for anyone who loves a juicy forbidden love."

    —Julie Young, author of *Fifteen Minutes of Fame*

"A wonderful love story but not your standard tale of boy meets girl."

    —Lisa J. Hobman, author of *Through the Glass* and *The Girl Before Eve*

CHAPTER ONE

AUGUST

The house was a sea of brown cardboard boxes as he slowly unpacked his life. There was something truly strange about moving back into your childhood home as an adult. Putting each book on a shelf, each dish in a cabinet, felt odd. The last time he'd spent a night in the house he was seven years old. Sitting on the living room floor was for playing with matchbox cars, making elaborate roadways and tunnels out of pillows and the lines of the old shag rug, not something so mundane as organizing DVDs. It wasn't until the reading of the will a few weeks ago that Kevin even knew his father had held on to the house. It had been looked after by his Aunt Margot over the years. She made sure it was kept clean and checked that everything was still in working order.

So with no place else to go, nothing keeping him in Michigan, Kevin decided to move back to Wexley Falls, where he'd been born, to be near the only family he had left. And yet he couldn't quite figure out if he felt comfort from the home he grew up in or haunted by it.

There was a quick knock at the door and Kevin's cousin Jeff and his wife Jennifer walked in. They were greeted by Sasha, Kevin's large Irish Setter. They each gave her an automatic pat on the head and made their way into the living room, checking out Kevin's progress.

"How goes the unpacking?" Jeff asked, clapping his cousin on the back. Kevin stood up amidst the boxes and some of their strewn about contents.

He made a face. "It sucks so far."

"Well, can we help in any way?" Jennifer asked, looking around unenthusiastically at the huge job to be done. Kevin didn't know Jennifer that well but he did know that tone in her voice. It was a courtesy offer, not a real one. He shared a knowing glance with Jeff and replied. "That's sweet, Jen, but I think I got it. Could wind up being cathartic, you know?"

"Before we leave I have a quick favor …" Jennifer said with a coy grin.

Oh no, Kevin thought, *she didn't.* Shouldn't he be the one asking favors?

"My dear friend Lynn is dying to meet you so I told her you guys could meet up at this little piano bar down the street tomorrow. Have some dinner, listen to music. Jeff and I go there a lot. It's just a quick walk up the street in that cute little arts district. You'll love her. She's so sweet and she's very pretty. So tomorrow night at The Black Jewel at seven. She'll meet you there."

Not a favor but a done deal already, he thought to himself.

Again, Jeff looked at Kevin quickly, an apology wrapped in an 'I owe you'. Kevin wasn't mad, just annoyed. The last thing he wanted was a date. He'd just buried his father, now he was moved into a vaguely familiar town without a clue what to do with himself and no job yet to speak of. He didn't need a blind date to be the sour cherry on top. But Jennifer had already made it known it was her mission to find someone for Kevin. She had some sort of fantasy of double dates and raising kids together that couldn't be shaken even by Kevin telling her to her face that he wasn't ready to date.

"Great, I'm sure she's great. I'll meet her there," he said.

They said their goodbyes and Kevin was back to unpacking, feeling more alone than he had before. The past four weeks had been a whirlwind. It was more than any twenty-six year old man should have to deal with. He tried to push it from his mind and forget the worst of it for a moment. Losing his father was something he'd never counted on happening. He'd lost his mother so young, it had never occurred to him that he could be orphaned well before thirty. Kevin was nearly over the anger that had sprung up soon after the funeral. Every now and again though he was overcome. It would flood him when he thought of how quickly his father declined, how there was no stopping the disease and how he'd had no one to help him. No mother, sibling or even girlfriend to lean on.

He tried to shake the feeling and gave Sasha a quick rub behind her ear before he got back to his boxes. The sooner the house felt like home the sooner he could rebuild his life. *Hell*, he thought, *the sooner I can start my life*. It was only days after his college graduation that he realized he needed to move in with his dad. The Alzheimer's had crept up heartbreakingly fast. It was only a matter of time before his condition deteriorated. Five years went by in a long aching blink and then he was gone.

Sitting amongst the pile of books he'd been unpacking, Kevin sighed. He would get through it. He would move on. He would find a way to start over and be happy. Maybe the blind date wouldn't be so bad. He could very well be meeting the woman of his dreams tomorrow night.

"Have you ever been here before?" Lynn asked, raising the thin-stemmed glass of white wine to her lips. Kevin forced a smile. "No, I just got into town two nights ago. This is my first time venturing anywhere other than the grocery store."

"Oh right, I forgot. Well, it's really nice here. Kind of different," she said, looking around the restaurant. It was nice. It was a large, dimly lit space with a stage up front and a bar in the back. Small round tables with no more than four seats at any one were placed all around. It was certainly set up to be a romantic space.

Lynn was a tall, athletically built woman with long, strawberry blonde hair that she wore pin straight. She was slightly over-dressed for the atmosphere in a black mini dress, heels and chunky jewelry. She seemed nice enough but Kevin's mind was elsewhere. He was silently cursing Jen for her brilliant plan of sending him on a blind date before he even had a job. He was thinking about bills, bank statements and job searches all while Lynn was flipping her hair trying to keep the conversation going.

What did Kevin actually have to talk about? Probably best to leave out the past five years of his life, specifically the last month. Nothing brings a date down like funeral talk. He covertly breathed deep, trying to relax. If he could just get through this one date then maybe he could hold Jen off for a few weeks.

Their dinner arrived and he ordered another glass of wine for himself. "So have you found work yet?" Lynn asked. Again, he gave a slightly pained smile. Just what he wanted to talk about.

"Unfortunately, no. That's tomorrow's adventure. I was working at a bank back in Michigan so I guess I'll start there. I have a teaching license I've never used so maybe I'll put in for some substitute jobs at the local schools," he replied.

"I'm sure it will all work out for the best," Lynn offered. It barely sounded like she'd heard him let alone that she was interested. He knew being unemployed wasn't exactly the most desirable thing in a man his age but it was the hard truth. And it was more complicated than she could understand.

Just then he noticed a young woman stepping onto the stage. She was stunning in a simple black dress. It was somehow fancier yet more appropriate for the venue than Lynn's outfit. The rest of the patrons gave a soft applause. She took a seat at the large black piano that had been played just a few minutes before by an older man. He'd played standards and easy listening stuff and while it was nice, for whatever reason, Kevin was dying to know what this girl was about to play. She wore no jewelry and only a hint of makeup. Her skin was flawless, pale with a nervous blush tinting her cheeks. Her hair was cut in a shiny black bob, hanging just above her shoulders. The young woman's eyes squinted at the spotlight at first then as she put her lips near the microphone, her shoulders rolled back and she looked at ease.

"Good evening. I'm Nina Jordan," she said before the keys began to send out beautiful notes.

Her sultry voice slipped out over the crowd like a silk sheet. After just the first verse of her rendition of "Save Your Love For Me", the audience was enthralled. Especially Kevin. Her voice had the haunting sweetness of a Norah Jones but the sometimes raspy delivery of a Stevie Nicks.

The server came over to the table. "More wine?" he asked quietly.

Kevin hadn't heard him. He was too busy watching the young songstress on stage. He could feel Lynn's eyes on him but it was as if he physically couldn't look away. He was feeling each word that flowed out of the young woman hit him like a ton of bricks. His lips were parted as he watched her in awe. Her voice proved just as stunning as her beauty. There was just something about her.

"Kevin?" Lynn whispered.

He didn't hear her or he chose not to anyway. He only heard the forceful belts, the evocative words, and the song that seemed to be singing out only to him. Was it the way she looked? She was gorgeous, yes, but it was more than that. There was something to the way she sat at the piano. The way she looked perfectly at ease there.

"Kevin." Lynn raised her voice and he turned to her but his eyes were still distracted.

"The wine?" she asked. Kevin shook his head and waved his hand off to the waiter. He let his eyes wander back to the stage. The moment her song ended, a girlish grin spread over her face at the applause she received. He felt goose bumps seeing her smile. Taking her bow and smiling at the crowd one last time, she made her way off the stage. The older gentleman came back and continued on with a vaguely familiar Sinatra song and Kevin went back to eating his dinner. Lynn was staring at him in disbelief.

"Wow," Kevin muttered under his breath, glancing back at the stage like he expected to see her up there again.

"It was nice meeting you but I think I'm gonna take off," Lynn said icily, picking up her purse and turning to leave.

Kevin stood up, half-heartedly concerned for her reaction. "Um, are you sure? Did I do something wrong?" he asked innocently.

She pursed her lips and Kevin thought he saw her jaw clench before she opened her mouth to speak again. "I'm looking for something serious and I can spot a man who isn't. Goodnight, Kevin."

She flipped her hair over her shoulder one last time as she turned and walked out of the restaurant. Kevin's eyebrows were still raised in amazement. He'd never been jilted on a blind date before. He figured it was better this way but he hated to be that kind of guy. The asshole that wasted her time. Maybe the failed date would keep Jen off his back for a while. Calling the waiter over, he asked for the check.

Kevin waited patiently, nibbling on what remained of his dinner. He finished his glass of wine in one big swig. The waiter cruised by his table and placed the bill down without a word; his section was filling up quickly. Kevin wasn't offended by the move. He just wanted to get out of there, leaving behind the uncomfortable memories.

Out of the corner of his eye, he spotted the singer from earlier walking his way. She'd changed her clothes. Now she was in a long gray cardigan over a white tank top and dark, slim jeans. He was finishing off Lynn's glass of wine now, settling his nerves while contemplating talking to her before she was gone. His eyes were slow and precise as they moved up her body from where she stood next to his table. She was beautiful and he just couldn't suppress the urge to want to speak to her. "Excuse me, miss? Nina?" he started, barely reaching out to touch her arm. She stopped and turned to him, raising her eyebrows timidly.

"I just wanted to say how much I enjoyed your performance. You've got an amazing voice. Really. Quite extraordinary," he said with a slight quiver. Was it the wine going to his head? He wasn't usually mystified by women but this one had him baffled from the moment she'd taken the stage.

She let out a breathy, bashful laugh. "Oh, um, thank you. Goodnight."

Her voice was just as sweet spoken as it was sung and Kevin felt something in him he barely recognized. As she turned to walk toward the door, he reached out to her once more, overcome with a strange confidence. "What I mean to say is—I managed to botch a blind date tonight and right now I'm thinking that the only good thing I'm going to remember about this evening is that beautiful song," Kevin finished. She smiled at him sweetly, her eyes softening. He couldn't stop staring at her pink lips stretched across her perfect, white teeth. She came around the side of the table and took Lynn's empty seat.

"Sorry about your date," she said, absently thumbing the corner of the tablecloth. Kevin was taking the moment to examine her. Her porcelain face was touched with just the slightest hint of pink. Her eyelashes were so long they nearly brushed her cheeks when she blinked.

"Would you want to help me make up for it sometime?" he asked before pressing his lips together as if to silence himself. Kevin immediately regretted asking. He wouldn't know what to do when she rejected him. His unforeseen bravery in the last few moments had already put his stomach in knots. He wished his mouth would stop listening to his head.

"Maybe," Nina replied, looking up at him, those long, dark eyelashes opening wide letting Kevin see the light gray eyes he hadn't yet been able to get a good glimpse of. Kevin was speechless. Her smile was lighting up the room and keeping him at a loss for words. Finally, so as not to let her see him make even more of a fool of himself, he thought of a response.

"How about coffee?" he suggested.

She bit her lip. "I don't really do coffee."

Damn, he thought.

"Drinks then," he tried again.

"I don't drink …" Her voice trailed off into an innocuous laugh.

Jesus, don't blow this Kevin, he thought to himself.

"Dinner?" It was his last try and all he had left. When he went out for his blind date he wasn't planning on trying to make *another* date with *another* woman at the end of the night.

"Dinner works," she stated. She started to get up from the table when she looked down at him again, her coy grin taking him by surprise. Kevin mimicked her and stood up on his side of the table as Nina rose.

"Great! There's a nice looking place right across the street. Does tomorrow work?" he asked, damning himself for being so bold. He shoved a few twenty dollar bills into the leather book that his check sat in.

"Meet you there. Six-thirty. But under one condition," she said as they walked out into the warm night air together. Kevin still felt slightly buzzed from the wine and from the head rush he'd been given by Nina. He stopped and gave her a momentary look. She playfully put her hand on his arm, holding back a chuckle.

"You're going to have to tell me your name," she said.

A gush of air escaped Kevin's lips as he bashfully lowered his head and began shaking it back and forth. "I'm an idiot. *Kevin* the idiot. Kevin Reed," he said, jutting out his hand to her.

She shook his hand and shrugged her shoulders. "Until tomorrow, Kevin the idiot," she said with a laugh. He laughed at himself watching stagnantly as she walked to her car. Breaking himself from the trance, he headed home.

CHAPTER TWO

Home for Kevin was just two blocks away from The Black Jewel. He took his time on his walk feeling the summer air rush around him. Wexley Falls was proving to be more interesting than he'd imagined. Especially after tonight with one ruined date exchanged for the promise of a better one. He walked inside and called out as he locked the door behind him. "Sasha! I'm home!"

She padded down the wooden stairs, careful with her steps. Kevin could tell she'd just woken up. Her long, dark red waves swished as she finally made it to the last step. Her eyes lit up when she saw him standing by the door and as he bent down to run his hand over her head, her tail began to wag.

"Sasha, you're the only woman I can count on," he said, scratching under her chin. Her face was beginning to show her age—speckled with white, eyes beginning to cloud. She wasn't too spry these days but she was still just as sweet as the day he picked her up from the shelter, hoping she might ease his father's pain.

Kevin went into the kitchen and found a soda in the refrigerator, popped it open and took a swig before scooping some food into Sasha's bowl. His phone vibrated in his pocket and he pulled it out to see the alert on the main screen stating Jeff had left a voicemail while Kevin had been talking to Nina.

"Heeeey Kevin, it's Jeff. Lynn just called Jennifer. What happened bro? Call me back." Jeff's voice sounded forced and just before the message ended Kevin heard Jennifer in the background. "He *should* be calling Lynn to apologize for being an ass."

Kevin rubbed his forehead in anguish and tapped the screen again. "Hello?"

Shit, he thought. *Jennifer.*

"Hi Jen. Can I speak with Jeff?" he asked tightly.

She scoffed before her voice sounded far away. He could hear some kind of argument, no doubt about him, but he couldn't make out their exact words. "Hey man," Jeff said, finally speaking clearly into the phone.

"Are you sleeping on the couch tonight because of me?" Kevin asked lightheartedly.

Jeff chuckled. "No. Not yet anyway. What happened dude?"

Kevin expelled a sigh. "I'm not really sure. We were having a nice dinner. Small talk. You know, first date stuff. Then this girl came out on stage and she was amazing. Maybe I stopped paying attention to Lynn for a second but for whatever reason she got pissed and bolted. She said she could tell I didn't want anything serious."

"Pretty observant for her to see the *obvious* fact you don't want anything serious," Jeff said facetiously. Kevin heard Jennifer yelling at Jeff from the background again and laughed.

"Anyway, I got a second date out of it," Kevin said.

"Yeah?"

"I wanted to tell the singer she was great and I ended up asking her out. I'll admit I had a little liquid courage. You should see this girl, Jeff. Amazing," Kevin said as he let his mind wander back to seeing her up on the stage, the white light bathing her, highlighting her shiny black hair and her pink lips. Kevin snapped out of it as Jeff started talking again.

"Well cousin, I'll live vicariously through you and your adventures of dating hot chicks."

"We'll see. I'll talk to you later, man," Kevin said before Jeff said goodbye and they each hung up.

His feet took him to the living room with his mind set on one thing. Scanning the built in bookshelves behind the sofa, he finally spotted it. Kevin pulled the CD from the shelf and slid the disc into the stereo. It was the first track and though it wasn't the voice he wanted to hear, it would do.

Kevin thumbed the volume knob until Nancy Wilson's *Save Your Love For Me* was echoing through his home. The saxophone and soft hits on the cymbals led in her powerful voice. The piano came in and it was all coming back to him. He pictured Nina up on the stage putting her own subtle spin on the standard.

It was the first time he'd ever listened to the CD but he knew it was part of his collection. Now that his father's music collection had become his own. John Reed, Kevin's father, was a complicated man. Kevin knew as much. As close as they'd been, there was still a lot about his father that was a mystery to him but there were two things he knew for sure.

John loved Jazz. More than that, John loved a good torch singer. Etta James, Julie London, Sarah Vaughn and of course, Nancy Wilson. Kevin had always been more of a rock and roll guy. He was used to his music equating women to being 'fast machines' or 'terminally pretty'. These women—these torch singers—could crack your soul open with an "ooh" or a "baby." He remembered his dad telling him a lady who could sing like that was trouble. *The good kind of trouble.* Nina could sing like that. She had the same way of dragging out the notes and the words with a sexy sigh. You could tell she was digging deep within to croon the enchanting song. Yet demurely, she sat at the piano instead of caressing the microphone in a full length gown.

Kevin leaned back against the sofa and stared at the ceiling. His head told him he wasn't in any way equipped to be the dating kind right now. But his heart and his eyes—*her eyes*—told him different. *You're just the unemployed new guy in town with way too much baggage*, he thought. Nina would figure it out before too long and he'd be back where he started.

Alone. A sigh rolled out of him as he lifted his head and stared out his front window toward the street. What if she didn't figure it out? What if somehow she could see past it? The thought of having someone in his life was tempting. He'd been so isolated for the past few years. It had been hell taking care of his father and living away from his only other family, Jeff.

He thought about how nice it could be to have someone to come home to who might have a smile for him. Someone to wrap his arms around and kiss goodnight. Someone to talk to and to be completely real with. He might finally be able to unload the burden of his challenging young adulthood just by having someone like that in his life. Not only would he have someone to lean on, he'd have someone who could lean on him. In fact, he liked the idea of tending to a woman.

Kevin thought of how his father doted on his mother before she became ill. There was always coffee at her bedside each morning and he was sure to bring flowers on any old Tuesday. They shared a bottle of wine each anniversary and toasted to one hundred years of marriage. Kevin wanted that. Romanticizing their love affair always made his parents seem like the perfect example. Truthfully, he knew relationships were hard and his mother and father no doubt had their problems. But he wanted a love like that, problems and all.

This enticing idea was clouding his head and suddenly the most enticing thought of all came creeping in. This someone could be Nina.

CHAPTER THREE

Nina walked inside and slipped her shoes off near the door. Her feet were killing her. As she was silently reminding herself to bring a change of shoes the next time she went to The Black Jewel, a note on the mirror in the foyer caught her eye.

Out with Blake, call Dad. -Greta

She let out a sigh of relief, thankful her sister wasn't home. Though Greta was only five years older than Nina, they shared little in common and Nina always felt at odds with her. In fact, Nina was convinced Greta hated her and blamed her for their mother leaving when Nina was five.

Nina always wondered about her mother and yet she didn't really miss her. Her leaving was sudden and still unexplained. From what she could remember about her mother, she wasn't the Suzy Homemaker every girl wanted waiting in the kitchen with milk and cookies when she came home from school. She didn't braid her hair or cuddle and read books. She was uninterested and how that could've possibly been Nina's fault she wasn't sure. Greta never said that was how she felt but Nina sensed it in her stare, as if she was constantly seeing her sister as the five year old brat who scared their mother away.

Nina crumpled up the paper with her sister's handwriting on it and headed to her room. She hung her black dress next to a few others she'd impulsively purchased in the past year.

When she walked in to The Black Jewel for the first time, she never imagined they would let her on stage. But after a few weeks of begging and a handful of times dropping in on the owner to play for him, trying to convince him to give her a shot, he finally agreed. She got one song tonight and before she left David told her he would be happy to have her any time. Nina was ecstatic. It was what she'd been waiting for. Being on that stage had been more than she could've ever imagined. She couldn't wait to do it again.

But to Nina, that wasn't even the best part of the night. Kevin the idiot, as she was lovingly referring to him in her mind, was the highlight. He'd been a complete surprise. Good looking and with that sweet, bumbling, shy kind of thing. He was adorable. He had a strong jaw, dark hair, dark eyes and a little bit of scruff. The real tall, dark, and handsome type.

He was older though. She could tell as much from the fact he had a glass of wine on his table. She could also see it in his eyes. Not wrinkles but just enough of those tiny lines that showed he'd seen more days than her. She told herself it wouldn't be an issue. Tomorrow would be great. She'd even convinced herself that a *don't ask, don't tell* policy for the evening would be in her best interest.

Nina dug in her purse for her cell phone, tapping her father's number to dial. The phone rang and rang and finally her father's voice picked up. "You've reached Harold Jordan. I'm unable to answer my phone so please leave a message and I'll return your call."

Of course, she thought. He hadn't answered one of her calls in the past four days, why would he now? "Hi Dad. It's Nina. I'm in for the night. I sang tonight at that place I told you about. Anyway … I guess I'll talk to you sometime. Goodnight," Nina said, hanging up with a sigh.

Her father had left for London for work about a week ago and was planning on staying there for almost four months. His exact words before stepping through the door had chilled her. *"I'll do my best to come home a few weekends but eight hour flights are getting tough on your old man."* His meaning—don't bet on it, kiddo.

For the past week he'd been gone it'd been like living alone. Of course Greta didn't have any trouble showing how irritated she was by the new living arrangement. If their father knew Greta spent almost every night at her boyfriend's house, leaving Nina with the house to herself, he'd flip. This certainly wasn't her dad's first business trip, but it was the longest on record and by now Nina had grown accustomed to caring for herself with all of his traveling. She could stock the groceries, clean the house and make herself meals. Sometimes it felt unfair and sometimes she got lonely but then she remembered she felt just as lonely when her family was with her. Why not make the most of her freedom starting with a date? For now, a good night's sleep was all she wanted. Maybe she'd dream of that handsome face she'd be seeing tomorrow night.

CHAPTER FOUR

She was early and cursing herself for rushing to the restaurant. It was just so exciting. It felt like her first date. Nina tried to keep her cool and she found a bench near the front doors of Ambrose, the little bistro where they'd decided to meet. But Nina's nerves were starting to get the better of her and she tried not to fidget.

The summer weather was nearly flawless and this evening was no exception. The balmy air felt wonderful on her bare shoulders. She was in a green linen sundress with thin straps and white ballet flats. A slender green headband pushed her hair, which hung perfectly above her shoulders, away from her face. She started picking at her fingernails anxiously as her mind began to race. *What if he doesn't show up? What if he hates the color green? Am I supposed to pay or let him pay?* Just as she felt one of her signature worry-induced red splotches start to form on her neck, she saw him in the distance.

He was nearly to her when he started to smile and with that, her stress melted away. His eyes said he definitely didn't hate green and Nina stood as he approached.

"Hi," he said, his grin growing.

"Hey." She tried to be nonchalant but was sure it wasn't working.

She walked past him as he held open the door to the restaurant, breathing in the scent of his cologne. It was, as she imagined, quite sexy. The restaurant was quant with little square tables, each with a candle and a single white rose. The walls were painted a deep maroon making it dark on the inside but warm as well. After Kevin held up two fingers the hostess quickly led them to the smallest of the tables set for two near the back.

Nina was taking in their surroundings when she glanced at Kevin. He was holding out a chair for her. She was sure her grin was goofy and girlish but she was impressed. It was exactly what she would expect of an older guy. "Have you been here?" He asked.

"No, it's nice though," she replied. One corner of his mouth turned up and he nodded and she felt herself growing hot under his stare. It was going to be a feat concentrating with this handsome man's eyes on her. Before they had time to jump into conversation, a tall broadly built man introduced himself as Gary and asked for their drink orders.

"Would you like some wine," Kevin asked.

Her heart thudded in her chest as she thought about how to answer. Kevin shook his head and gave an embarrassed laugh. "Sorry. I forgot. You said you don't drink. Never mind." He turned to the waiter and told him he'd have water. The pounding of her heart waned and she found her voice to chime in. "Same for me."

The waiter scurried off and they were alone again. There weren't many people in the restaurant and the quiet was making Nina's thoughts seem loud. She took a moment to take in Kevin's face and noticed he seemed fine with the silence between them. There was no hint of apprehension in his chocolate brown eyes or the slightest bit of worry in his brow. He merely held her gaze.

"Can I ask you something?" he said coolly.

"Sure," Nina replied.

"What the hell are you doing singing at a place like The Black Jewel?"

Nina tensed momentarily. "What do you mean?"

"You're amazing."

Nina's eyes shot up and for a second they just stared at each other.

Kevin cleared his throat. "Your voice. You're an amazing singer. You could have an album, win a reality show. Is that what you do for a living?"

"I'm lucky to have a place like that to perform. I'm going to start filling in for Louis, the old guy who plays piano. It's easy work and if they'll let me sing then I can't complain. I'm living with my sister right now until I get things figured out. I've been looking at colleges," she said.

Kevin nodded. "That's great. You want to study music?"

She lowered her eyes. "Maybe. I'm not sure right now. It's kind of up in the air."

"I hope you do. Maybe you don't realize how talented you really are."

With her eyes still down, Nina pretended to read the menu but she was really avoiding his stare. He was something else. No one had ever given her such genuine compliments. She'd believed in herself enough to get on that stage and she craved it again but something about his words put a fire in her. She wanted to make him right. "What about you, what do you do?" she asked.

"I just moved here this week so I'm kind of ... between jobs. I guess I call myself a writer but I'm not sure what I'm gonna find here in Wexley," he said.

"A writer! What have you written?" she asked eagerly.

"Nothing you've read I'm sure. I used to do freelance work for a financial magazine. Not that exciting. But I'm writing this thing about my father's life. I have his journals and I did a series of interviews with him before he died so ..." He drew out his last word into a whisper and stopped. His eyes flitted around the room after he spoke.

"I'm really sorry," Nina said, reaching out, gingerly laying her hand on his. It was the first time they'd touched all night. She felt electricity between them when he found her eyes with his. In a little more than twenty four hours, she'd managed to feel the kind of compassion for this man she barely felt for anyone in her own family. She cared about him in a way that confused her but eased her at the same time. Finally Kevin smiled and nodded a 'thank you'.

From then they couldn't stop talking. From books they loved to Kevin giving her pointers on how to incorporate songwriting into her repertoire. It was as if they'd always been friends. Nina stopped wondering how old he was, stopped caring about the details and just allowed herself to laugh. To flirt.

Kevin didn't say anything else about his father or the circumstances of how he moved to town but Nina figured his move was determined by his father's passing. He talked about how hard it was not knowing anyone. He worried about making friends and fitting in.

"Well, you know me now," she said, her eyes glittering.

Kevin beamed. "I won't forget it." He grabbed the bill and quickly paid as Nina tried to object, offering to chip in.

"Of course not, it's my pleasure," he said, shooing her hand away. She thanked him a few times, a girlish grin still painted on her face. They walked outside together, neither saying a word. For a while they just enjoyed the warm breeze and the faintly blue night sky. Then Nina saw Kevin's face fall a bit as he looked at her.

"Look, Nina," he started and her heart clenched. It seemed too perfect. What was he about to say? She wished for an instant he would stop right there and kiss her goodnight so the evening could end just as wonderful as it had been. But he continued.

"I wasn't planning on dating right now. Not last night on that blind date and I certainly wasn't counting on meeting anyone as great as you. I've had a rough few months and I just feel like I need to get adjusted first, you know. But I …" His voice cut off and he ran a hand through his chestnut hair. "I really like you," he said with a grin.

Nina smiled back, biting her lip, trying to conceal it. She looked down at her hands and realized she was absently wringing them, pulling at her fingertips. She smoothed her hands down the front of her dress and tried to steady herself.

"Can I call you? When I feel like I have it a little more together?" he asked.

It wasn't exactly what she wanted to hear but she couldn't blame him for wanting some time to find a job, maybe unpack his house. She smiled and asked for his phone. Kevin slowly handed over the cell from his pocket with a confused face.

"I'm putting my number in here so you don't forget about me," she said. She opened the main screen and saw an alert message. "You, uh, missed a call and have a voicemail."

Kevin frowned and shook his head as if he didn't know who it could be. She typed her name and number into his contacts list and then turned the phone around and snapped a picture of herself. Kevin chuckled taking the device from her. "How could I ever forget that face?" he mused.

She twisted her lips bashfully before feeling her nerves kick in. She didn't want to say goodbye. What if she never saw him again? Fear was getting the better of her. For it to end like this after a beautiful evening just seemed unfair.

"So I guess this is goodnight?" he said softly.

"Yeah. I had a really nice time. See ya, Kevin," she said, trying to hide the quiver in her voice. She gave a little wave, turned and started walking to her car. She got to the door and began digging in her purse to find her keys when she heard her cell phone chirp. She pulled it out and took a glance at the text message.

Screw it. You free next Saturday?

Her head whipped up to see Kevin where she'd left him with his phone in hand and a Cheshire grin plastered on his face. He shrugged. A giggle escaped her lips and she strode toward him swiftly. She was now closer to him than when they'd initially said goodbye and when she inhaled his sweet smell again, she felt herself going dizzy.

They were smiling at each other like fools until Kevin's hand slowly rose to tilt her chin up. Nina's breath was ragged and her skin burned under his touch. Kevin's eyes looked carefully at her face as she waited for him to move. With one simple motion, as though he'd done it a thousand times, he shifted forward and placed his lips softly against hers.

Nina's lips parted at the feeling of his mouth and she waited for the kiss to turn deep and passionate. The kind of kiss she'd always dreamed of. But she was denied. Kevin pulled back and drew in a deep breath.

"Goodnight, Nina," he whispered.

CHAPTER FIVE

"Nina! You're going to be late," Greta screamed from the bottom of the stairs. Nina heard the shrill noise and paid it no attention. She pulled a brush through her hair over and over again until it was just how she wanted. She glossed her lips quickly and popped in a pair of silver hoop earrings.

It was Monday morning, the first day of her senior year at Wexley Falls High School. Though the excitement of this day was greatly due to the thought of it being the beginning of the end of her school career, she had another thing on her mind. *Kevin.* From the moment she arrived home after their date, she hadn't stopped replaying it. She remembered his boyish grin, the way his eyes lowered in vulnerability when he spoke of his late father. Her body tried to remember the feeling of her hand on his and his lips against hers.

"Nina, I'm serious!" Greta yelled again. Nina was already on her way down the steps and she breezed past her sister with a forced smile. She picked up her bag and snatched her keys from the table in the entryway.

"Goodbye Greta," she said in a sing-song tone as she raced out to her car and headed to school.

She couldn't help but let the guilty feeling creep in during her drive to school. She should've told Kevin she was only seventeen. But she hadn't and she couldn't take it back now. She couldn't take back the date, the laughing, the flirting—or that kiss. What was done was done. But what would next Saturday hold? She asked herself whether or not she could keep the lie of omission going any longer but it was a question she honestly felt like putting off, at least for the first day of school.

When she arrived in the student parking lot, she spotted the one person she'd been dying to talk to. James Dalton was Nina's best friend. He would call her his soul mate and Nina often felt his words were true. He'd been out of town for the last two weeks of summer vacation, but before that they'd been inseparable. The pair had grown up together given their father's were old college buddies.

It wasn't until eighth grade that Nina knew James was the brother she never had. When he came out to her he dashed her dreams of ever marrying him and having babies with his green eyes. He was grateful for her support and even more, her lack of reaction. It didn't faze Nina one bit. He said the words, *I'm gay,* and she replied with, *okay, what movie are we seeing this weekend?* He was her family, the one person she could always be herself with.

Nina parked and ran over to James who was standing by his car.

"God, I missed you!" Nina said, finally releasing him from her tight embrace. "Where have you been? I'm scared we're going to be late," he said anxiously. Nina was shocked. James had never cared about school before now. He was happy to be late and often did it on purpose.

"What's with you?" Nina asked as they made their way into the building and headed toward the auditorium.

"There's a surprise in there for you and I'm dying to see your face!" he exclaimed. Nina groaned. No surprise on her first day of high school could be a good one.

"So, what did you do without me these past two weeks?" James asked as they stepped inside the doorway they'd been dreading to come back to for the entire summer. Nina took a moment to glance around at the rush of students coming in all around her before turning back to James.

"I sang at the Black Jewel," she stated nonchalantly, but her confession came as quite an explosion. Nina had been talking about singing there for years.

"You wait until I'm in the Bahamas to sing there! How was it?!"

Nina sighed. "It was kind of ... perfect." She reminisced about the evening for a split second before thinking of Kevin's face. They climbed up a flight of stairs and crossed over through the gymnasium before finally making their way to the auditorium. Students were flooding in and their chatter was bouncing off the high ceiling causing an echo of voices to resonate where Nina and James stood. James grabbed Nina by the shoulders and turned her away from the auditorium's doorway forcefully. She looked at him as if he had lost his mind.

"The parentals asked me last year if the school needed any kind of improvements. You know dear old dad, he felt like throwing money at something. I told him what I thought and that I also thought your dad might be interested in helping. So, my sweet Nina. I give you," he turned her back to face the doors. "The Dalton-Jordan Auditorium."

Nina stared with her mouth hanging open at the new words above the entryway of the auditorium. Her name and her best friend's right next to one another, gracing the school as though they owned the place. She felt a sting in her stomach taking in the steel block letters. It was a classic move by her father. He couldn't answer a phone call but he had thousands of dollars to show as a grandiose gesture. Of course James loved it, he liked the attention. She didn't. She knew she was a hard puzzle to solve sometimes, but this wasn't the kind of attention Nina particularly liked. Applause from strangers at The Black Jewel was different from the entire school looking at her like she was a spoiled rich girl who just *had* to have her name thrown up on some wall. She tried to hide her indifference. James was giddy at the sight and she didn't want to bring him down.

"Does this make you want to sing at the senior concert? I don't want to beg you, but I will. You're way too good to just be playing the piano," James said.

Of course his ulterior motive would come out sooner or later. Nina laughed and linked her arm with his before leading him into their auditorium. Students were grabbing empty seats and as Nina's view became less and less obscured, she saw the extent of the renovation. She looked at James in disbelief and then back at the stage. James started in a whisper. "This girl once told me that with a red velvet curtain and gold scroll trim, a stage could transform into anything and could transform *anyone.*"

Nina looked at the stage that had grown in size and design. The gold-painted wooden structures that graced the top and sides of the alcove were stunning. Pulled apart on either side was a thick, red velvet curtain. She didn't think about her father looking at the space. She knew it was all James. He must have told his parents about her dream stage and the night they stayed up late talking about the things they wanted most in life. Nina told him she wanted to stand on a huge stage with a red velvet curtain drawn back against gold scrolls, singing her heart out. She sighed and pulled him to her tightly, speaking into his neck. "I love you, James. Thank you."

He just smiled and pointed out two seats they could take.

The obligatory reminder about proper school conduct had already taken place and schedules were being handing out. Nina and James compared papers trying to figure out when they'd be in class with each other and when they could walk together. For the past three years, they always had at least one class together and always found time to meet up in the halls. They had a few other friends but no one that came close to sharing the kind of bond they had.

"Choir second period and Economics seventh period," James read from their papers. Nina laughed at the joy in his voice as the warning bell rang and the mad dash for the doors began. Senior year had officially begun and Nina was off to her first class, Creative Writing. She'd been waiting since she was a freshman to take the course. It was only offered to seniors and it was only a semester long, but she was excited that it would be the start to her day, at least for a little while.

Nina stopped by her locker and grabbed one of seven new notebooks she'd bought for herself the day before. She checked her makeup in the mirror that hung inside the blue metal door. She stared into her own eyes and imagined they were Kevin's. She couldn't control her thoughts of him. *Kevin. Kevin, the idiot. Kevin Reed.* She snapped herself out of her trance and got back to the task at hand. She smoothed out her white button-down top with her hands and slammed the locker closed. Glancing at her schedule, she looked only at the room number, B100.

She found B100 and entered the opened door. Students were still jockeying for seats and the class was a little out of order at the moment. She found a seat near the back and started arranging her desk, all while wondering where the teacher was. The bell rang just as she heard his voice.

"Sorry I'm late. I'm so glad to have seniors first thing in the morning. You guys can handle me being late. I have a feeling Freshman English will be the death of me. Uh, I realize I'm not Mrs. Oliver. You might have heard she's out on maternity leave and I'm taking over. I'm Mr. Reed," he said, turning his back to the class, writing his name on the dry erase board.

The sting in her stomach was back but it felt more like a fireball now. Her mind was blank, her mouth gaping as she stared at his back for another moment, praying he wouldn't turn around. She didn't have time to run. She didn't have time to think. In what seemed like slow motion, Kevin turned to face the class with a beaming smile and tears started to well up in Nina's eyes.

He caught her stare and for a moment his smile grew until he took in the sight of her. She was sitting in a desk in his high school classroom, notebook out ready to write, book bag on the floor beside her. Nina watched in horror as his face fell.

Chapter Six

Their eyes locked for only a moment and yet he felt like time had stopped. He saw from across the room her eyes were glistening with the threat of tears. Kevin winced at the realization he was trying to avoid. He looked down and shuffled his papers finding his first period class list. There, on the middle of the page, the letters jumped out at him. *Nina Jordan.*

It took all of his might to hold in the rage he felt building inside of him. He slid his tongue behind his teeth nervously as he tried to block out thoughts of exactly what this situation was. Then he became aware that the students were quietly waiting for him to continue.

He figured the first day of school was always the easiest for teachers and students alike. He'd run through the scenario in his head the previous night before going to bed, only to dream of Nina lying next to him. *Hand out the syllabus, go over the rules, get everyone's contact information and end the class,* he thought as his palms started to sweat. It would have been as simple as that had his date not walked through his door, school books in hand.

He gathered his papers and began walking down the aisles, handing out the semester's syllabus. He started on the opposite side of the room from where Nina sat, avoiding her gaze. "This syllabus was Mrs. Oliver's. If I make any changes, I'll let you know by the end of this week," he said, handing each student the papers.

Finally, he was at the last desk in the last row staring right into

Nina's young face. He took a moment to look at her. Her eyes were bloodshot and he saw streaks down her face where her makeup had been washed off by tears. He took a slow hand and slapped the paper down on top of her desk, watching her flinch in her seat. Then he made his way back up to the front of the room to continue the longest class of his life.

A little less than an hour later, the bell rang and the students shuffled out the door with their newly acquired text books in tow. Kevin took a seat at his desk and glanced over at Nina. She hadn't stood up to leave. He hadn't thought she would. Anxiety was swamping him as he began dreading their impending conversation.

Kevin sighed, desperately trying to get a grip on his anger. "If you don't have anything to say for yourself, you should just leave," he snapped in a whisper.

She rolled her eyes and stood up, grabbing her things. "You didn't say anything about being a teacher."

Kevin stood up fast, placing his hands firmly on his desk, and growled. "Oh, I'm sorry. I didn't think that fact would matter seeing how I'm not in the habit of dating teenagers."

"I'm just saying, you kind of glazed over the fact you teach here at Wexley," her voice trembled.

Kevin tried to regain some composure. "You kind of glazed over the fact you *attend* here. And if you must know, the call I missed on our date was this job offer." His breath was ragged, the word *date* stuck in his throat. His hands were shaking and his eyes darted around the room, looking anywhere but her beautiful face. If he looked into her eyes, he'd no doubt have to look away. The betrayal was more than he could take and yet it was sadness that filled him more than anything. He was faced with having to mourn something he didn't yet know was real.

"I didn't mean to hurt you," she whispered as she headed toward the door. Kevin winced, feeling the immense grief in her voice as it penetrated his heart.

"Nina," he called out, stopping her before she walked into the hallway. Nina turned on her heels and looked him square in the eye.

"I know. It's over," she said softly.

"It has to be," he muttered. When he saw tears wetting her eyes again, he stifled the urge to run to her and pull her close. He struggled, wanting to stroke her hair and tell her it would be all right but he knew he couldn't.

Kevin straightened as he saw Jennifer headed toward his classroom. "Hey, Mr. Reed! How's your first day going?" she asked excitedly.

"Jennifer, uh, I mean Mrs. Benson. Things are going fine," he said. Actually things were terrible and Jennifer was the last person he had wanted to see. Jennifer looked over at Nina standing in the door way. "You have Nina in class? She's one of my favorite students. You're going to *love* her, Kevin. In fact, I think I have you next period, right? You'd better get going," she rambled with the giddiness of a child as Kevin stared at Nina, waiting for her to leave.

"Yeah, Mrs. Benson, I'll see you in there," Nina said, glancing over her shoulder at Kevin before walking into the bustling hall.

"Seriously, how's it been so far?" Jennifer asked again and Kevin though he'd die. He was on the brink of a breakdown and holding it together for his cousin's wife was the hardest thing he could imagine being tasked with at the moment. He had to be appreciative, though. She was the one who got him the job. But at this particular point in time, he would've preferred to still be unemployed and happy with his thoughts of Nina. After all, ignorance is bliss.

"Good. No problems so far," he said through clenched teeth.

Jennifer smiled. "Well, I should get going. The kids are probably already in the auditorium admiring the renovations. Oh, Jeff said something about a new girl you're dating. She cool?"

Kevin felt like screaming, but instead he answered the best he could in effort to get her to leave. "I'm not sure that's going to work out after all."

Jennifer threw a patronizing frown his direction and said something about him having better luck with a more stable woman like Lynn before disappearing into the hall. The minute she cleared the room, he stood up and shut his door. Putting his back against it, he started pounding his head back on to the wood. He wanted to run. And the next thought that crossed his mind was that he wanted to ask Nina to go with him. Damn him and his disloyal mind.

She'd tricked him. Played him like the piano she loved so much. He'd been fooled by the way she looked, the way she walked and the way she kissed. High school girls hadn't been like that when he was younger. There wasn't a Nina in sight when he was a senior.

He'd spent the rest of his weekend after their date scrambling to prepare for the job he'd been offered. He remembered thinking it was all falling into place. He had a job and he had a second date on the calendar. She'd made him feel something he hadn't felt in a long time and she'd done it way too easily. And then with a snap it was taken away.

CHAPTER SEVEN

The girls bathroom was surprisingly empty as Nina entered, throwing her bag down onto the floor. She moved swiftly to the sinks and wet a few paper towels to hold against her cheeks. She wanted all evidence of her tears to be gone. The cool water seeped from the rough, brown paper and rolled down her chin and neck.

Overwhelmed by thoughts that continued to race through her mind, Nina slumped to the floor and burst into another fit of sobs. The moment he walked into that classroom, she felt her heart shatter. Seeing Kevin's face fall when he realized she wasn't who she claimed to be was the worst way she could've pictured the truth coming out.

Nina picked herself up off the floor knowing she had to hurry out of the restroom and down to the auditorium. Pushing her thoughts into the farthest corner of her mind, it was all she could do to keep herself from feeling sick.

"Nina! Over here," James yelled as she took a seat next to him quickly. "How was English? I heard there's a hot new teacher."

Nina held back another outburst. "Yeah … I guess he was kind of cute."

The rest of the day flew by in a blur. It was all course outlines, grading scales and grabbing a textbook or two. After Nina and James' seventh period class together, she hurried back to her locker and threw all of her new books inside, a hint of anger behind the action.

"Are we walking out together?" James asked. Nina shook her head then flipped her locker door back and glanced in the mirror. The shame she felt now looking into her eyes was unbearable.

"I've got to meet with Mrs. Benson about some things so I'm staying late. I'll see you tomorrow," she lied.

James put his hand on top of her head lovingly and smiled before running off to meet up with a small group of friends who were waiting for him. Nina wasn't meeting with Mrs. Benson. She was going to talk to Kevin. She wanted to see if she could do anything to fix the mess she'd made. As she rushed back to B100, she saw that the door was closed and the lights were off and she was just about to walk away when she peeked inside the window on his door. He was just standing there in the dark. She turned the handle slowly and walked inside.

He was posed among the desks in the back row. The last desk, the one where she'd sat that morning. His head was hanging low and his fingers were pressed firmly against the pale laminate. She closed the door behind her and with the noise, Kevin's head jerked up to see her with her back to the door.

"You shouldn't be here," he said in a barely audible tone. Nina stepped toward him and he stepped back though they were still feet apart.

"I *need* to apologize, Kevin," Nina said, staying put as she spoke. She saw his eyes shut as he heard her speak his name.

"It's my fault. I was stupid." His voice was slow and rigid.

She couldn't let him take the blame. She came at him again, not caring if he was uncomfortable with her standing too close. Then he turned to her with fury in his eyes.

"God dammit, Nina! High school? Do you even understand what

you've done? How you've made me feel?" he barked, his eyes piercing her.

"I should have told you. But I didn't tell you because I ..."

"No. Don't say anything else. This needs to be resolved so we can move on as teacher and student." The words seemed to choke him. She'd been waiting all day to talk to him again, but now that it was really happening, she wished she'd bolted out to her car the minute the final bell blared.

"Please," she whispered.

"Just get out," he said through his teeth.

Nina accepted her defeat and walked slowly out of his classroom. She held in anything else she wanted to say, her hands balled into fists at her sides. Breathing in his scent one last time before she took her final step out into the hallway, Nina filled with regret. The fairy tale was wrecked and she didn't see any other way to fix the damage but to walk away.

CHAPTER EIGHT

SEPTEMBER

The first two weeks of school went by in an excruciatingly slow blink. Nina managed to skip Kevin's class every day after the first. She came to school on time and ducked into the library while every other student went to their first class. She didn't want to face him even though her thoughts were always fixed on him. Different versions of apologies ran through her head like a news station crawl at the bottom of a television screen. Thinking of him hating her was the worst part yet she could understand if he did.

Nina made her way to her second period music class with James at her side. He was completely oblivious to her skipping habit.

"I think Mrs. Benson is going to talk about the senior concert today," James said with a joyful anxiousness in his voice. Nina smiled at him, her mind elsewhere as they arrived at the auditorium and found their usual seats.

"Okay people, it's time to start planning the senior concert!" Mrs. Benson's voice echoed in the nearly empty theater. "You know the drill. You've seen it every year. First act is group performances and solos chosen by me and act two is the traditional choral performance by the entire senior choir."

After Mrs. Benson informed everyone that auditions would be held the following week, the students started to chatter, grabbing onto each other claiming groups and throwing out ideas for song choices. Nina just sat quietly next to James. Though she was technically considered part of the choir and had been since freshman year, Nina never sang. She was Mrs. Benson's assistant pianist. She played for every concert and even in the classroom. She'd been asked to sing a few times but Nina never had the desire to audition for a real spot in the choir. Nina sighed absently, lost in thought amongst the babbling hum of the class.

"Honey, what's wrong?" James whispered. Nina turned to him and James' eyes urged her to confess. She looked down at her paper and considered telling her best friend the truth. But if anyone other than him heard her, it would be catastrophic to both she and Kevin. Plus, she thought about how James might think of her. She didn't think he'd gossip about her, but he'd certainly take the situation the wrong way. He'd make up this version of a wildly scandalous sex affair between teacher and student and he'd never let her hear the end of it.

"I met someone while you were gone over the summer. He was—he is wonderful and sweet and funny." Her words spilled out with ease as she thought of Kevin and their night together.

"Then why are you so sad, sweetie?" James asked.

"He's older than me and it wasn't until after I knew something great could happen between us he realized how old *I* was. He's … angry. He's all I can think about, but he hates me for being seventeen." Nina's breath quivered as she sighed at the horrible truth.

Her heart had been aching for the past two weeks, thinking of Kevin thinking of her with such disdain. Every night she dreamt up the right thing to say to him that might change his mind. She knew it was against the rules and that a secret relationship between the two of them had the potential to break their hearts. But Nina's heart was already broken having lost their chance.

James grimaced at her sympathetically. He was just as inexperienced in love as she was and as such, he had little advice for her. He put a careful hand on her leg and patted her sweetly. He didn't have to say anything.

CHAPTER NINE

Kevin shoved a stack of papers into his black leather satchel paying no mind to the students from his last period class who were still pushing their way out into the hall, the sounds of slamming lockers and booming voices ricocheting into his classroom. He put the last assignment into his bag and let his eyes sweep over the room for anything he might have forgotten. His eyes lingered on the last desk in the last row. It was Nina's empty seat. The seat she hadn't been in for nine days.

It was his job as her teacher to fix the issue of her skipping class but it was his guilt as a man that made him wary of approaching her. He hadn't seen her since she walked out of his room, silently crushed. He looked for her in the halls and even scanned the lunchroom a few times to try to get a glimpse of her. He wondered if she was skipping all of her classes. He wondered if something happened to her, if she wasn't coming back. The thought made his stomach twist miserably.

He flipped off the lights and closed the door behind him and headed toward the exit. The sky was still crystal clear and the breeze smelled of sweet summer scents just as it had the evening he and Nina spent together. The teacher's lot was adjacent to the senior parking lot. It was a special privilege for twelfth graders to park closest to the school and avoid the trek underclassmen were forced to make every day from the far parking lot to the school.

Kevin dug in his bag for his keys as he leaned against his car door, his impatience taking over as he slammed the bag on the hood of his trunk to get another angle for his search. Finally he saw the glint of silver inside the black abyss. He grabbed the keys and looked up just in time to see her walking out of the building. She was alone. She was beautiful. *Nina.*

His breath caught in his chest seeing her stroll to her car. He noticed a thin white wire coming down around her slender neck. She was oblivious to her surroundings as she listened to a song Kevin could only imagine. In a daze, he took a few brisk steps across the pavement in her direction. Nina glanced up from her purse and Kevin was in front of her in an instant. He watched as she pulled her earphones out and stared at him blankly.

Kevin drew in a deep breath before he spoke. "Hello, Nina." It was all he could manage to think of at the moment. Just seeing her face made him dizzy. He cursed himself for still wanting her. He should be the one with the grimace, not her. He noticed Nina shut her eyes for a moment, maybe in effort to make him disappear.

"Do you want me to talk to the dean about putting you in another English class?" he asked delicately.

Nina's grey eyes flew wide open and she began shaking her head vigorously. "No! Why would you—? No," she blurted.

"Well, how exactly should I grade someone who doesn't attend my class?" Kevin retorted, his anger pushing its way out of him.

She sighed and turned her face from him. "I'll be there Monday morning, okay?" she whispered.

Kevin nodded and turned quickly to walk back to his car before he let himself say or do something he might regret. He felt his breath quickening thinking about how easy it would have been to reach out and touch her.

"Kev- Mr. Reed?" Nina called out, correcting herself halfway through.

He spun around to see her again, a vision of grace and beauty. She stood biting her lip primly, starring out at him across the lot.

"I'm singing at The Black Jewel tonight."

Her statement was simple and true, but the implications her words held were clear to Kevin. He imagined himself running to her, closing the distance between them, sweeping her up in his arms and crushing his lips against hers but he stopped his thoughts dead in their tracks. He nodded at her once more, careful to not coax any more information from her. He was back to his car promptly and, simply to torture himself, he glanced back. Nina stood outside of her car door, watching him. Time was stopped, the two of them gazing at each other through the sea of people. Kevin's eyes smoothed over the curves of her face, the one he'd been dreaming of. Her pink lips parted and her tongue slipped out to wet them. Kevin knew the gravity of what was happening. He knew the depths of the consequences that could arise and yet he was blinded by attraction, letting all rationale escape him. Things were only going to get more complicated.

"What time?" Kevin shouted out.

Chapter Ten

Kevin glanced at the clock for the fourth time in twenty minutes then looked at Jeff, sprawled out on the couch with his hand grasping the remote. He was staring at the television like a drone. He hadn't said a word in close to an hour. Jeff and Kevin had taken the night to hang out, though Kevin was ready for him to leave so he could get to The Black Jewel on time.

"Well, man, maybe we should call it a night …" Kevin's voice trailed off in effort to insinuate it was time for Jeff to go.

Jeff stretched his arms above his head and sat up from the indent he'd left in Kevin's sofa. "Yeah, the wife probably wants me home."

Kevin was glad it was going to be that easy to get rid of him. He still needed to shower and find something else to wear before heading down the block to see Nina perform. Every time Kevin thought of what he was doing, his stomach twisted into knots. He was changing his mind every few minutes. He *wouldn't* go because it was inappropriate and he didn't want to lead her on. He *would* go because he was only going to take in some live music, nothing more. He *wouldn't* go because he was still angry with her and there was no changing that. *Yeah right,* he thought.

Jeff started slipping his shoes on near the front door.

"How did you know Jen was the one?" Kevin stumbled over his words.

Jeff shot him a look. While the two had been so close growing up, like most men, they rarely made mention of the really serious stuff. Jeff had been the shoulder Kevin cried on when grappling with hospital and funeral decisions for his dad, but they hadn't really talked about women in anything more than a joking manner since high school.

"Why?" Jeff asked, his eyes tight on Kevin.

Kevin sighed. "That girl from the restaurant. She … things didn't work out. And I don't think they ever could. But I can't stop thinking about her."

"I knew Jen was the one when I realized I cared more about what happened to her than I cared about myself," Jeff said pointedly.

Mulling over his cousin's statement, Kevin tried not to think about it in terms of Nina. It was too soon, too painful.

"You're not gonna go see her sing again are you?" Jeff asked.

Kevin let out a laugh. All their years of scheming as teenagers had given them a somewhat psychic ability with one another.

"Come on man. If you wanna feel like shit, listen to the sappy love songs in the comfort of your own home. Preferably with scotch on hand," Jeff chided.

He was right. It would be torture to sit in the darkened restaurant and hear her sweet voice wrap around him. If she saw him there, she might think he was there to rekindle their romance and Kevin was forcing himself to believe that wasn't what he wanted.

Jeff grabbed his keys and clapped Kevin hard on the shoulder. "Resist the torture."

Kevin chuckled. "I will."

With that, Jeff was off into the street and on his way home. Alone with his thoughts, Kevin's mind flipped through every image he had of Nina. Burned into his brain, was the picture of perfection he'd first glanced upon. Black dress, black hair, pink lips. That was the order in which he'd first seen her. And then there was the intangible beauty of her voice. The velvet sweetness flowing out of her in a captivating song. Kevin opened his eyes and realized he was still standing in the open doorway and his eyes flitted down the street in the direction of where he knew Nina was. He took a second to look down and examine his clothing. His snap decision made, Kevin shut the door and started walking down the sidewalk toward the restaurant.

He *would* go because … well, he just would.

CHAPTER ELEVEN

Nina peeked out around the thin black curtain on the side of The Black Jewel's small stage. The room wasn't very crowded and she didn't recognize anyone, making her feel at ease and discouraged all at once. She saw Louis playing the black baby grand that would be hers in just a few minutes. It was nine o'clock, a later time slot than last week which meant there was a different group to perform for.

Walking back to the women's restroom, she shut the door and took in the image of herself in the mirror. Her blue dress dipped into a V at her neckline and in the back as well showing a bit more skin than the black one she donned last week. She was wearing the dress for Kevin though she'd never say that truth out loud. Her hands smoothed down the sides of the satin bodice and she let her eyes linger in the mirror. *He's not coming,* she thought. Her heart sank. It was better to come to terms with it now than in an hour.

Nina walked out of the ladies room and passed Louis in the hall. He was a slender man about seventy years old. White hair and large wire-rimmed glasses framed his sweet but aged face.

"You're up, Cookie," he said, walking by without looking at her. Nina gave a little laugh and pushed her way through the black curtain to the stage. She loved the sound her heels made as they clicked against the hardwood floor. She loved the scene that was laid out before her as she stood there looking into the crowd. Candles were lit on every table and there was a sprinkling of romantic couples and mysterious loners. She took a seat on the shiny black bench and scanned the room in one fluid look.

"Thank you," she said softly at the minimal applause she received. She played the starting notes of "I Fall to Pieces" and drew in her first breath when she saw the front door open slowly. Kevin breezed in just as Nina sang out her first line of the classic country song set to her own slower, jazz arrangement. Kevin stopped just inside the door and stared as Nina continued on with her song, not missing a beat though her heart had all but stopped at the sight of him. She turned her head back to the keys, breaking the gaze held so intently between them. As he moved to the bar, Nina felt a chill run up her spine.

Watching him in the back of the dark room as he stood listening to her, she couldn't help the sadness that coated the words she sang out. He started moving back from where he came and when his hand touched the door, the moment between them was nearly lost. Turning back to meet her eyes one last time before vanishing, her lips formed the words that were all too true for the both of them. Nina finished her song feeling each phrase dig into her heart, leaving gaping holes filled with sorrow. Every song she heard, every song she sang, would always be about him from then on … one way or another.

The crowd gave a light applause and she was off the stage in a flash. Nina jogged in her heels back to the ladies room and shut the door firmly behind her sliding down to the floor pulling her knees to her chest.

He walked in and walked out. How could he have been so cruel? Was it out of spite? Walk in to show her he could and walk out to show her he didn't really want to be there? A lump formed in her throat, the kind that warned her tears were on the way. She breathed in deeply through her nose and blew out a huge gust from her mouth. She repeated it again and again and still the moisture started to build in the lower rim of her eyes. When a light knock sounded at the door, she shot up to open it, her tears subsiding. It was David, the manager of The Black Jewel.

"You okay, Nina? I thought we decided you were going to do a whole set tonight and not just the one song," his voice trailed off in question.

Nina nodded and smoothed her hands over her cheeks then ran them through her hair.

"Sorry. I felt sick for a second. I'm fine, though. I'll be right out," Nina said, fidgeting with her hemline, waiting for David to leave. He smiled cautiously and made his way back out to the restaurant. Nina drew in one more ragged breath and went back to the stage, leaving her emotions at the door.

CHAPTER TWELVE

Paper was littered out before him, a mess of un-graded work and a slew of sketchily written notes on his own lesson plans. Kevin shuffled through the pile absently. He put assignments in one stack and tiny scraps of paper in another then threw them into separate folders. He was still adjusting to the job. Despite his stress, it seemed like he was getting the hang of it. With the exception of the two senior creative writing classes he had first and second period, his other classes were all freshman English.

He was still arranging the notes when he opened his lower left-hand drawer and saw a stack of pastel colored index cards. He grabbed the stack and began thumbing through them. On the first day of school each student had written down their full name, address, parent's names, phone number and a personal email address. As he flipped through the stack, her name jumped out at him.

Kevin pulled the blue card out from the rest and stared at it closely feeling his heart wrench reading her card for the first time. He took the information from his students as a formality, a precautionary rule set by the school. Kevin wondered if Nina purposefully made her handwriting so elegant. Her words were scripted in perfect cursive giving the entire card a fluid look.

Nina Maureen Jordan lived at 56 Victor Boulevard with her parent Harold Jordan. Kevin scanned the words and felt an ache in his heart as he pictured Nina going home after their date. The bedroom she slept in that night would one day be what she called her childhood bedroom. His eyes lingered on her phone number. His thoughts tempted him, reminding him he already had that number stored in his cell phone. He imagined being able to talk freely with her just to get to know her better. There would be no schoolmates or fellow faculty to answer to, no age difference or face to face tension. Just the two of them having a conversation.

The warning bell rang, disrupting his wandering mind. Students began staggering in through the door and he waited impatiently for Nina. She told him she'd be coming back to his class but that was before they exchanged glances at The Black Jewel.

When he walked in that night after wrestling with his choice to hear her sing, he wasn't expecting to feel the way he had. It had all been like a dream to him. First, he was walking down the street. Then a bit more swiftly. Then nearly in a full jog. By the time he could see her car in the parking lot, he was running toward the door like a mad man. He collected himself and opened the door smoothly, letting the stagnant air from the restaurant waft over him as he entered. He glanced to the stage not expecting her to be there as she was. She was stunning. Her dress showed him just enough to keep his dreams interesting for the next few weeks. Then as their eyes met from across the room, she sang words that seemed written only for them. Kevin tried to just listen and enjoy her voice as a patron. But it was far too difficult.

He saw her squinting from the stage, looking into the darkness to the back where he stood. She was searching for him as she sang the truth and he felt as though one more lyric, one more instance of seeing her slender hand caress the ivory keys, might have him running to the stage. Instead, he turned and walked out. Though his stomach felt like emptying and his eyes felt like watering, he walked out and left Nina alone with her song.

His memory of Friday night set him in a trance that was broken by the very thing occupying his mind. The bell rang loudly and he flinched. Kevin's eyes moved slowly upwards as he realized someone was standing in front of his desk. He saw her milky white arms holding books tightly to her chest and he forced his eyes to reach hers quickly. Nina peered down at him and scoffed looking at the card he held in his hand.

Kevin was startled by her presence. He was still amazed by the affect she had on him. He glanced down at her information card, realizing she'd seen him staring intently at it and he quickly folded it up and shoved it in his pocket.

He offered a stack of handouts from the classes she missed and struggled to find words to explain to her what she needed to make up. She glared at him and he opened his mouth to speak. With his mouth gaping open, he ran his eyes over her face quickly.

"Just do the reading and look at the handouts. Don't worry about making up the assignments, I'll take care of it," he said, lowering his voice, noticing how quiet the class had gotten since the final bell.

Her face softened and she nodded slowly before taking her seat as Kevin stood and made his way to the front of the class. Looking out at his students and seeing Nina tucked in the back row as she had been on that first tumultuous day, Kevin felt a sigh of relief roll through him. He was glad she was back in class.

Chapter Thirteen

She tried to be angry with him. She tried to hold on to the pain she felt seeing him waltz in and back out of The Black Jewel, toying with her, but she couldn't. His boyish bumbling as she caught him staring at something as pitiful as her student information card made her heart swell. It was as if that card had been her picture in a beautiful gold frame and he was looking longingly into her face.

The class wasn't as horribly awkward as she expected. It wasn't the same as it had been the first day. Now that they knew the truth about each other and had some time to process it, the tension was lessening. It was still hard for her to look at him though. He stood at the front of the room, lectured, and wrote on the board like any other teacher but to Nina he wasn't Mr. Reed. He was Kevin. *Kevin the idiot.*

"This is the first big assignment. I want to see really good work. Poems are due Wednesday. Impress me," he said, wiping his notes from the board as students packed their bags before the bell rang out. Nina waited in the back, watching Kevin closely as he cleaned the white board. The last remaining student stepped out into the hall and then it was just the two of them sitting in the starkly lit room.

"You know, I can do the make-up work," she started then smiled seeing Kevin jump at the sound of her voice. Their eyes met and they both let out a nervous laugh.

"You scared me," Kevin said. Nina stood up smiling widely.

"D-don't worry about it, Nina," he stuttered and slowed to say her name softly. She nodded and her smile faded as she approached him at the front of the class.

"Nina," he whispered as a warning to her as she stepped closer to him. It was the closest she'd been since the moment they kissed at the end of their date. She looked up at him and heard him sigh quietly as he in turn looked down at her.

"No, I need to say this. I'm sorry. I really am. I've never been more sorry for anything in my whole life. The thought of hurting you—it's just …" Nina's voice trailed off and she averted her eyes. She thought she heard him sigh again but she didn't dare look. Not with her emotions so exposed in this moment. She pulled her bottom lip in her mouth and bit down on it lightly, keeping any risk of tears away before going on.

"There are so many things I wish for. I wish I was older, or that you were younger. I wish you hadn't found out the way you did. I wish I would've told you the truth in the first place. I wish none of it mattered. But mostly, I wish you and I could talk. Just have a conversation. I wish we could've had the chance to get to know each other better so we'd know if what's between us would be worth all the trouble. Worth fighting for, you know?" Nina said.

She adjusted her book bag and shrugged with a crooked smile before turning and walking out.

In the hall she glanced down at her hands, watching as they trembled. The night before she'd practiced those words in the mirror, making sure he would realize she was starting the conversation she wanted so desperately to have with him.

"Nina!" she heard James call out from behind her. The thumping of his feet grew louder as he reached her with a loud *thwack*. His face popped into her peripheral view and she could see he was wearing a huge grin.

"Oh my God! I just saw your English teacher. Meow!" he said, huffing out a breath, slowing his pace to match hers. Nina's heart thumped at the mere mention of Kevin, her hands still jittering from nerves. She forced a smile as they walked to the auditorium. Her mind was swimming with thoughts of what she'd done, what she'd said.

Nina wanted to tell James the truth. She wanted to tell anyone. Her frustration with the feelings growing inside her was coming to its peak. Fear built up in her mind about James' tendency to blow surprises and spread gossip. But would he really do that to his best friend?

"Are you okay?" James asked as they reached their class.

She turned to him, forcing the same fake smile she'd worn for days. "Fine."

James made a frown at her and patted her on the top of her head playfully. Pressing her lips together, Nina felt a hint of guilt for the lies piling up between her and James. She took the time to let her mind wander as she played the boring notes of the vocal exercises for the class. Kevin's face was the first thing to enter her thoughts. Strong jaw and dark eyes, the softest lips she'd ever touched and the thin lines crossing his brow ...

Her mind strayed all day through math and physics, through study hall and on to lunch. Then school ended without warning and she realized her entire day had been consumed by Kevin. Going home, she wondered exactly when it would all stop and when she'd be able to think of something other than her English teacher.

CHAPTER FOURTEEN

After dinner and a lazy hour of television, Nina slinked upstairs to her bedroom. With her mind clouded all day by thoughts of Kevin, she was starting to feel accustomed to having his face burned behind her eyes each time she shut them. Sitting at her desk, she pulled out the handouts he'd given her and began reading over them.

She tried to move onto to her math homework afterward but she was too fidgety. Nina closed the weighty calculus book and tossed it on the bed watching it bounce. She reached for her cell phone after hearing the delightful ding as a voicemail popped onto her screen.

"Hello darling, hope all is well. You'd better be studying. Only kidding, have a good night, sweetheart. Sorry we keep missing each other. Love you." Her father's voice sounded so unfamiliar. Her eyes rolled by reflex and she deleted the message without giving it a second thought.

Another chime came from the phone and a new text message took over the screen.

Hi.

It was a two letter word from a phone number she'd seen only once before. Thank God she'd saved the number. She'd forgotten she'd done it until that very moment. Maybe it was a mistake. Maybe she saved the number wrong and this was a stranger. If it were really from him ...

Nina breathed in sharply, realizing she'd been holding her breath as she stared at the word. She glanced around her empty bedroom, irrationally paranoid of someone reading over her shoulder even though she knew her sister was asleep down the hall. With butterflies filling her stomach, she looked at it again.

The most difficult part was deciding whether to believe it was real or not. Had Kevin actually hit send? Did he expect a response? If she didn't respond, what would class be like the next day? There were so many complications. She was angry their romance had been stolen from her before it even began. The thought that it was all her fault and Kevin somehow hated her ate her up inside. Still, seeing his face in class, in the halls—in her dreams even—gave her a thrill. The idea of waiting until her first period class cleared out—the two of them alone in the room— gave way to fantasies she was too embarrassed to even write in a journal.

His rough hands gripping her waist, the click of the door handle as she pushed in the lock. Each time she saw him, her mind went straight to visions of him clearing his desk with one swift sweep of his arm and laying her down upon it. Nina shook away the thoughts; her head spinning when the phone hummed in her hand, another chime ringing out.

This is a terrible idea. But ... conversation started.

Her hand was trembling and her heart was beating loud in her ears. She no longer cared about it being a terrible idea. She didn't care about the consequences or the complications. She simply started tapping away on the screen.

Chapter Fifteen

The walk from Kevin's kitchen to the living room was roughly fifteen steps. He'd been counting as he walked into the kitchen to get a beer then back to the living room to see if Nina had replied to his text. He'd already taken three trips and cracked open three beers, his mind reeling from the notion of what he'd just done. He knew it might've been the biggest mistake of his life but he didn't care. Her words earlier gave him the strangest feeling. As if her apology made it all okay again. It wasn't true; he still wrestled with the right and wrong of the whole mess. But when he got home and reached into his pocket, pulling out the pale blue card he'd been daydreaming over hours before, it dawned on him fate might have a hand in all of this.

He tried to think of the reasons not to follow his heart. The job wasn't that important to him. He might not even get hired on full time. It was a temporary thing. He was waiting on responses from three agents who had his manuscript and though he knew he couldn't get rich off of the book, it could end up being comparable to his teacher's salary for half a year. In fact, subconsciously, he was getting up and going to work each day not for the money but for Nina.

Seeing her smile as she walked to her car with her friends in the afternoon, that's what he wanted. Did she know he waited for her in the parking lot? Had she seen him passing by the lunchroom nonchalantly, peering in through the smudged glass walls at her? Did Nina know when they passed each other in the hallway he was strongly compelled to whisk her into the nearest empty classroom and put his hands on her?

The refrigerator had been standing open for several minutes and he stared into it as if it were a black hole. He wasn't hungry. He was anxious. He closed the stainless steel door and leaned against the island that stood in the middle of the kitchen, staring at the gleaming appliance. Glancing down to his feet, he saw Sasha asleep on the hardwood floor next to her food dish. He smiled, watching her lips and whiskers twitch as she dreamt.

From the living room came a quiet noise Kevin recognized immediately—the glorious *ding* of a text message. His stomach fluttered as he slowly took the fifteen steps. He bounced toward the coffee table in two giant leaps and clicked to open the message.

Shutting his eyes for a moment, he breathed in and prepared himself for the possible outcomes. She could hate him, think he was creep, or she could really want to have the conversation she mentioned earlier. Oddly, he didn't know which of the three would be the worst.

He read the message. **OK. How are you?**

Nervous, he typed back, worried she wouldn't keep responding.

The thought barely had time to form before he heard another ding.

Me too. How is this supposed to work?

Kevin heaved a sigh. *Good question, Nina*, he thought. He'd never experienced the kind of angst he was filled with now. *All over a teenage girl*, he thought with a laugh. It couldn't work. Could it? What was *this* anyhow? A relationship, a friendship, a secret?

He sighed again and read the text one last time before calling out to Sasha to join him upstairs. Surely sleeping on it would help. But as Kevin drifted off to sleep, the torment followed him into his dreams.

The vision of Nina on an enormous stage with powder blue lights painting her skin seemed more than real. She wore a tight fitting red top and a short Catholic school girl's skirt. He watched her as she opened her mouth to let out a note. Nothing happened. The seats of the venue were empty in front of him. He sat in the back row on the far right side. His eyes frantically squinted to see her as he realized how far he was from her. She was gasping for air, unable to speak, sing or breathe. He tried to stand to help her and suddenly the stage was at the front of his classroom and the students were all in their seats with him at his desk. She glanced at him with a smirk before holding up a book to show the class.

"I did my book report on *Lolita* by Vladimir Nabokov," she giggled, looking at him again. Each student turned to stare at him simultaneously and he felt his face grow red. Nina walked back to her seat in the back row on the far right side and fixed her eyes to him as well, letting the pencil she was holding sit delicately between her lips. Booming laughter came from the gallery of students before him.

Kevin sat straight up, covered in sweat. He glanced at the clock just as it flipped to six o'clock a.m. and his alarm began to buzz horribly. Sasha sat up slowly from her pillow bed on the floor and looked at him sweetly. Kevin swung his legs over the edge of the bed, feeling his body trembling. Drawing in deep breaths, he settled his nerves before throwing on his clothes and heading downstairs to hook Sasha onto her leash for their ritualistic walk.

The breeze was cool and dewy as the pair took a trip around the block, waking them both for the day. Kevin tried to push the memory of his dream out of his head. All he wanted was to see Nina again, no matter what his dream implied.

CHAPTER SIXTEEN

Slamming her locker shut, Nina began walking briskly toward her first class. She'd been up too late waiting on a response from Kevin. She'd finally fallen asleep with her math book splayed across her chest and very little of her homework done.

The bell rang as she scooted into room B100 just in the nick of time then she saw him. She held back a laugh as she realized they had matching dark circles under their eyes. Clearly he'd suffered a long night as well. Class started and Nina listened intently to Kevin's voice as he lectured them on the tools of poetry. Nina felt herself sigh each time his eyes met hers. She was truly a schoolgirl with a crush. When Kevin made a joke the whole class thought was funny, he laughed with a beaming smile and looked right at Nina. For the briefest of moments, neither of them broke the gaze.

"Here's the list of terms that'll be on an upcoming poetry quiz. Keep this paper. You can have the rest of class to work on your assignment for tomorrow," Kevin said as he began sending around the stack of papers.

The girl who sat in front of Nina took a paper then turned to her. "That was the last one. He forgot you," she said before turning back to the front of the class. Nina caught Kevin's eye as he finished a soapbox speech to a boy in the front row about the romance of language. She knew he hadn't forgotten her. In fact, she figured he'd been quite deliberate in his paper count. She slowly raised her hand and waited to be called on.

"Yes, Nina," he said.

"I didn't get a worksheet," she replied.

His head cocked to one side. "My mistake. Here," he said as he grabbed a paper from the stack on the podium and began walking back to her. Nina's hands were lying on the top of her desk as he reached her. Slowly, he set the paper down and without hesitation he let his index finger slide off the page and up into the curve of her thumb before heading easily back to his desk.

Nina's skin tingled so much that she'd yet to move her hand from that place, reveling in the energy of his touch. The bell rang, causing her to jump slightly then she peered over at Kevin, leaning back comfortably. Again, she made the effort to look as though she was packing up her things until the last student was out the door. Standing and slinging her bag over her shoulder, Nina stopped in her tracks, overtaken by a huge yawn escaping her lips.

Kevin chuckled. "Let me guess, bad dreams?"

Nina looked at him starkly. "No. Waiting by the phone."

She smirked before walking out, intentionally glancing over her shoulder at him as she reached the hall.

For the first time since seeing her on stage at The Black Jewel, Kevin took in the glorious sight of her legs. Covered in dark blue jeans, the curves didn't lie and he imagined her creamy white skin underneath. A chill ran up his spine seeing her pass by his door and out of sight. He couldn't believe he'd been so bold. Letting the simplest touch happen between them was electrifying. It could've been an accident and he wondered if she thought it had been.

The mystery of Nina was part of what gave him chills. He wanted to know more about her. He wanted to know how she'd gotten to be the way she was. Mature but still full of youth and seemingly self-aware. *Seventeen.*

Kevin's second period students were starting to arrive when something caught his eye. Against the royal blue carpeting near the desk he'd come to consider Nina's, there was a glint of light bouncing off something. He squinted as he neared the tiny object on the floor. Reaching down to pick up the glittering bauble, he smiled realizing who the earring belonged to. His smile lingered as he thought about seeing her again to return it. It was the gentlemanly thing to do, after all.

CHAPTER SEVENTEEN

The lunchroom was crowded as Nina made her way to the salad bar, fixing herself a bowl. James was close behind, indulging in the standard rectangle pizza. He slid his tray next to hers on the steel tracks of the buffet and peered at her through her thick wall of dark hair that hung next to her face.

"Are you *smiling* to yourself?" James asked, craning his head to get a better look at her. Nina whipped her head around and grinned coyly.

"Maybe," she said, letting her eyebrows raise.

She saw James roll his eyes. He knew he wouldn't get an explanation from her. They made their way to an empty table but when James glanced at Nina again, the same absent smile was fixed on her lips.

"I've been meaning to ask you something," James' voice trailed off as he took his first bite of the plastic looking pizza. "Oh my God, this is so good," he said interrupting himself, joyfully.

Nina laughed. "What do you need to ask me?"

James' face fell a bit and he took a deep breath. "Don't get mad, but have you talked to Todd recently? I mean, I know you said you went out with that guy over the summer so I'm assuming you and Todd aren't really together but, like, what the hell is going on? I can't believe we haven't talked about this. It's like we haven't said more than two words to each other since school started." James rambled on until Nina put her hands up in effort to stop his monologue.

He was right. Nina's mind had been so preoccupied with thoughts of Kevin she had little else to talk about. She'd contemplated telling James the truth so many times but she was still so unsure of what she even had with Kevin. She didn't know what to name it. How could she put that into words? For now, Kevin was her secret to keep. It didn't feel like a lie.

Todd. Now that was a subject she'd left untouched for quite some time. If not for James and his grilling, she might have forgotten about Todd altogether. Nina sighed, tucking a few strands of her hair behind her ear. When she opened her mouth to speak but was hushed by James quickly.

"Oh honey, you lost an earring. I like it though. It's very eighties," James clearly saw the annoyed look in Nina's eye as she stared at him, absently reaching up to feel her naked earlobe. "Carry on," James added before continuing to eat his lunch.

"I haven't talked to Todd since he left. Since the first of June," she said casually, biting off a fork-full of salad. James' eyes went wide and his hands slapped the table.

"What?" he exclaimed.

Nina shrugged. "We didn't exactly break up before he left but I'm certainly not going to be dating someone who hasn't made the time to call or write me for three months. You know how he is. Selfish," Nina said as she stabbed at the pile of lettuce and vegetables mindlessly.

She was avoiding James' eyes, knowing he found her reaction suspect. Finally she spoke again, after mulling over her feelings about what happened with Todd for the first time.

"We had an okay relationship but it's over and who's to say I won't find some other guy?" Nina said, smiling to herself again, letting Kevin's face creep back into her mind.

"It's pretty clear you already have a guy, Nina." Her head snapped up to see James eyeing her blankly. The irrational paranoia filled her once again as she ran through her actions of the previous night in a split second.

A smile spread on James' face. "Me. Duh. You've got me. Now that I know you two are Splitsville, I can say this. Todd Dawson is a complete tool."

Nina burst out laughing. Relief swept over her hearing his joke instead of an accusation. "Not that I entirely disagree with you, but why do you say that?" she asked through fits of giggles.

James rolled his eyes at her. "Oh, you know! Todd thought he was better than the entire town of Wexley Falls. And you and I both know that's not the case. He was an okay guy for a starter boyfriend. But you need someone who's more mature and genuinely nice. And hotter. Too bad things with that other guy didn't work out. I can see you with someone older." James washed down his rant with a gulp of soda and smiled at Nina before they were interrupted by the bell.

The pair hopped up and headed for their lockers in the next hall over where Nina opened her locker and exchanged a few books from her bag, grabbing the notebooks and folders she needed for the second half of her day. Before she was finished, James was done gathering what he needed and back at her side. He leaned his shoulders against the pale blue metal, watching her impatiently as she primped in her mirror. Her fingers ran through her already smooth, dark hair. She checked her face for any imperfection as James continued to huff. He glared at Nina until he saw something that pulled his interest from her.

"Nina!" he said in an excited whisper. Nina groaned, her lips currently being coated with shimmering gloss.

"Hottie English teacher alert and he's coming right for us," he exclaimed, his tone still hushed. Nina's ears perked at that. She gave herself one more examination before closing her locker, seeing Kevin in the distance.

The hall seemed to go dim and each student slowly disappeared from her view, their voices diminished. She saw only Kevin walking to a soundtrack in her mind. He walked toward her in slow motion, his hand rising to push through his thick chestnut hair. Their eyes locked and as he got closer, a smile crept onto his lips.

She heard James' voice, sounding miles away in her ears, mutter a sentence containing the words *Jesus* and *gorgeous*. He approached and the lights went back up and the thunderous voices in the hall grew loud again. She stood before him stunned, a blank look gracing her face.

"Hey, Nina," Kevin said. She breathed in the intoxicating scent of him, knowing James no doubt was doing the same.

"Hi." The single word fell out of her unceremoniously. His smile was as bright as it was the night he stumbled over his words, trying to make her acquaintance. She hadn't been this weak in his class or even on their date. But just minutes prior, as James unknowingly mentioned his positive thoughts of her with an older man, she felt a truth sink in to her heart.

She was ready to fall for Kevin Reed.

His hand jutted out in front of her, fist closed, palm facing up. She and James both gave him puzzling looks and his smile spread wider. He chuckled as his hand opened to Nina slowly. James let out a quiet gasp as he recognized the sparkling jewel sitting in Kevin's palm.

"This was under your desk," Kevin rasped. Silently and unabashed, she let her fingers dip into the cup his hand had formed to retrieve her earring. Her fingertips grazed his skin deliberately. She pulled away and pinned the earring back on before smiling at him.

"Mr. Reed, that was really sweet of you. Thank you," Nina gushed, putting her hand on his arm for only a second.

His fingers repeated the motion of running through his dark brown hair. Nina suspected he was nervous and it filled her with a blissful sense of excitement, a tingling tremor low in her abdomen. Kevin glanced at James who was staring at him, nearly drooling. Kevin nodded at both of them and timidly smiled before walking away without as much as a goodbye.

Nina felt her heart beating wildly in her chest and tried to control her breathing. Kevin had most certainly put a spell on her that wouldn't be easily broken if they kept playing this game. Nina adjusted her bag on her shoulder and looked at James to see if he was ready.

"You've *got* to be kidding me," James said, his face stunned.

"What?" Nina asked naively.

"He is *so* in love with you. And it's hilarious because you barely know he exists. You said he was just *kinda* cute? What planet are you living on?" James was spewing his words out between scoffs as they walked through the halls, seemingly baffled by her, thinking she was clueless about Kevin's affections. Maybe keeping James in the dark would be easier than she thought.

"He's not in love with me, James. He's my teacher," Nina said, smiling to herself once more, careful not to let James see the truth.

CHAPTER EIGHTEEN

The muted thud her Physics book made as it shut was music to Nina's ears. Her homework was finished and now she was free to do as she pleased. As she wrote out her assignments and read her textbooks, her eyes shifted every few minutes to her cell phone. It sat on her white wooden desk on silent mode so as to not be too tempting, but she knew what might be waiting for her. She was hopeful Kevin would reach out her after what happened between them in the hall. She let her lips curl into a grin thinking dreamily about the simplicity of her fingertips smoothing the curve of his palm.

Twice that day they'd touched. Twice that day they'd exchanged smiles and stolen quick glances only they were privy to. She laid back on her bed, sighing at the memory of his boyish grin as he walked down the crowded hall. His sole intention had been to return her earring. It was so romantic. He recognized her missing gem and made a point to escort it back to her in person.

Nina wondered about what James had said. He hadn't clued in to the fact she was awe-stricken by Kevin so how could his assessment of Kevin's feelings be accurate? Maybe he was just better at reading men.

All of her rationale flew out the window each time Kevin's eyes connected with hers, making her weak. She knew the repercussions of a relationship like the one she longed for with him. It meant trouble for both of them but reality was becoming fuzzy in Nina's mind, her thoughts clouded by her emotions.

She sat up and slid over to her desk and took a moment to glance over her shoulder and then she was staring at her text message inbox. His name stood out in bold, the way anyone's did when she had an unread message. Her breath caught in her throat as she read his words on the backlit screen.

Sorry I kept you waiting last night. Is this too weird?

No. Just the right amount of weird. She tapped *send* and laughed to herself.

Nina tried to picture him sitting somewhere with his phone in hand when his next message popped up.

Can I assume by the way your friend looked at me today that he isn't your boyfriend?

Nina let out a hearty chuckle. Her hands trembled slightly as she thought out her response before sending it quickly.

If I said he was, would you be jealous?

Her pulse thumped in her ears as the seconds ticked by in slow motion. *Too bold*, she thought. Whatever was happening between them was more delicate than she could handle. Nina barely knew anything about dating, let alone whatever *this* was. The phone lit up and vibrated in her palm.

Maybe.

Nina's heart swelled and her panic subsided. Clearly she hadn't been too bold. She explained who James was and teased Kevin by telling him how good looking James thought he was. It got easier to talk and they were responding quicker each time. It was as easy as the way they talked at Ambrose that August night. She learned that Mrs. Benson was his cousin's wife and got the whole story of how he'd gotten the last minute job at the high school. She told him about her frustrations with her father and how it had been weeks since they'd actually spoken. Two hours later, Nina let out a yawn and finally became conscious of how long they'd been texting.

It's late. I should go to bed, his message read.

A second message came immediately after. *You better have your poem done for tomorrow, young lady.*

Nina smiled to herself. Oh, it was done. That part was easy. But handing it in might prove to be the challenge. She tapped send with a sigh, not wanting the conversation to end.

Goodnight Kevin.

She hopped up and headed to the bathroom to brush her teeth and wash her face, the house silent aside from her footsteps and the running water. Her body felt relaxed, completely at ease. It was a total difference from the first week of school when anger, fear and regret filled her to the point of agony. Heading back into her bedroom, she flipped off the lights and climbed under the covers with an absent smile. She reached over to plug her cell phone into its charger when she saw his message across the screen.

Sweet dreams, Nina.

They would be.

CHAPTER NINETEEN

"I'm pretty excited to see what you all have come up with," Kevin said to his morning class, flapping the stack of papers the students had just handed in. "Friday is the quiz on poetry terms and tools. Don't forget," he added, hearing them groan at the notion.

He finished just as the bell blared and the students stood up almost in unison with the exception of one. Kevin let a smile linger on his face as his gaze drifted to Nina. It was becoming a habit for the two of them to play out the same scene each day. Nina would wait, pretending to pack up her things or ask him a question. Kevin would pay her no attention until they were alone and then—they'd have their moment. Some days Kevin felt like all he wanted was to breathe next to her. As if that made him more alive.

The last student was gone and Nina's eyes flitted up from her desk and fixed on Kevin at the whiteboard. Her teeth sunk into her bottom lip in effort to hide her grin, a look he was beginning to recognize as her signature. He turned to face the board and waited, trying to be patient, as he heard her step behind him and out of the sightline of the hallway.

"I'm glad we got to talk last night," he whispered with his back to her.

A light laugh escaped her and he imagined her tucking one side of her hair behind one ear.

"I'm not even sure what I said at this point," she replied.

Kevin turned. Before he spoke, he took in the sight of her.

Imagining her was far less amazing as the real vision of her beauty. A smile formed on his face as he realized she had in fact tucked her hair back.

Closing the gap between them, he heard the subtle change in her breathing as he got closer. Kevin's mind was no longer in charge. His heart however, had full access and control of his body. Slowly, his eyes grazed over the curves of her face and the perfect lines of her neck and on down the length of her.

"Why is it so easy for me to talk to you?" he whispered. He stepped even closer to her, an unsafe distance for the way he was feeling.

Shamelessly and obviously without rational thought, he reached out a hand and twisted his fingers around a tendril of her black hair that hung near her porcelain face. He sighed, looking into her gray eyes, wide and filled with a mix of worry and longing. Nina tilted her head, leaning into his hand, allowing his fingers to brush her cheek.

"Kevin …" her voice came out, barely a breath.

"Mmm?" He had no strength to speak, only to continue examining her face, etching it into his mind.

Nina reached her hand up and gripped his fingers, still intertwined in a lock of her hair.

Just as Kevin moved to pull her in for a daring embrace, he heard the shuffle of students entering the room. His hand jerked back from her with the near speed of light and they each stepped back away from the other. Startled by the interruption, they stared at each other in horror, having been so close to being caught—and for what? For something as innocent as Kevin's hand in her hair to be their undoing would be insulting to their hearts.

"Thanks again, Mr. Reed. I'd better go or I'll be late for auditions," Nina forced the words out, eyeing him. Three perfect lines grew deep in his forehead as he kept his eyes on her.

"Auditions. Right. Well, b-break a leg," he said as more and more students sulked into the classroom, finding their seats.

"Can't wait to read your poem," he said cheerily as she turned to leave.

Nina craned her head back at him and smiled brightly, her eyes rolling in a teasing way as she slipped out the door. Their secret was still theirs and it filled Kevin with the kind of thrill a person could easily get too wrapped up in. But Kevin loved it when his heart beat fast from a simple smile Nina gave him.

He watched as she walked into the hall and blended with the other students. His palms were clammy and his mind was racing. He would spend yet another day distracted because of her.

Nina scurried down the hall and into the auditorium, struggling as she ran. She yanked the sheet music from her bag and just made it when the bell rang. She spotted James in the third row and he gave her a questioning look as she slipped in. Mrs. Benson walked on stage and the class hushed for her to speak.

"I'll call you in order of the sign-up sheet for your audition. I expect everyone to be respectful of all the performances. That means be quiet and encourage your fellow students. Hannah Bruckheimer, you're up first. Nina, I need you on piano," she said.

"What made you so late? You're all red. Are you freaking out?" James asked as Nina passed him. He was picking at the edge of the sheet music sitting in his lap. Nina could tell he was nervous about his audition. He and two other boys from their class were going to do a group piece and James had the lead.

"I left my sheet music in my locker. Just lagging today. My mind is …" She made a flitting gesture with her hands and huffed.

"*Your* sheet music? You're singing?" he mouthed at her excitedly.

Nina smirked and took a seat at the piano. She played fourteen songs. Some for groups like James' and some for solos like Hannah. Her normally nimble fingers were starting to feel stiff from playing so much. Then Mrs. Benson stood from her seat in the front row of the auditorium and addressed the class again.

"Great job everyone! We only have room for six performances in act one and it's going to be a tough decision for me after all of these fine auditions. You have the rest of class to do what you want while I start narrowing it down. Just behave, okay?" she said.

Nina stood up from the piano bench, shaking slightly.

"Mrs. Benson? If it's not too late … I'd like to audition, too." Her words sounded strange in her own head. She couldn't believe she was actually doing it. Mrs. Benson beamed at her from below stage level.

"Nina, of course! I've been waiting four years for you to sing for me. I know you've got a voice in there," she teased.

Nina smiled shyly. "Would you play for me? I've written an original piece but I just want to sing it. I—I want to stand at the microphone."

In a flash her teacher hopped up the stairs and crossed to Nina. Nina listened to the sound of her own shoes clicking against the wooden stage as she stepped to the microphone. It was her first time standing on the new stage, staring out into the wide sea of seats with thick red velvet hanging on either side of her. She handed the papers to Mrs. Benson who was smiling from ear to ear as she took a seat at the piano.

The music she'd written in her head in a dream began to play and Nina waited for her cue. Before the words rang out she heard Kevin's voice in her head and a smile as well as a sudden burst of confidence shone out of her as she started.

Chapter Twenty

The school was clearing out at the end of the day and Kevin saw Nina down the long corridor of the senior hallway sifting through a mass of papers in her locker, her best friend James was nowhere in sight. She was shoving papers, folders and books into her bag when he reached her and put a light hand on her shoulder.

"How'd it go?" Kevin asked, his eyes shifting around the halls.

Nina stood slowly from her bended stance and came up almost against his chest. Her eyes mimicked Kevin's cautious scan of the hall. The few lingering students and teachers were all in their own worlds. Would no one notice the sparks flying between them as they had a seemingly innocent conversation as teacher and pupil?

He tried not to care, pushing the salacious connotations out of his thoughts. A smile shaped Nina's lips and a sparkle was in her eyes as Kevin peered down at her face.

"I got it. I'm going to close to the first act of the senior concert. Pretty surreal," Nina said before slamming her locker shut and slinging her bag over one shoulder. For an instant Kevin felt foolish just standing, staring at her with a grin.

"That's great! But high school concerts are small time when you're the shining star of The Black Jewel, right?" he teased.

"Oh yeah, I'm only doing it for my legions of fans," Nina replied as a girlish grin spread on her face.

Silence fell between them and they came to an unspoken conclusion as they began walking the length of the hall. They stayed at arm's length, careful to put off the appearance of a harmless friendship.

"You're just headed home then?" Kevin asked as they made their way to the exit near the gym. Nina hoisted her bag up higher onto her shoulder, the weight of it causing it to slip with each step she took. Kevin swiftly took the bag from her shoulder and slung it over his own with ease.

"Thanks," she said. "Yeah, I'm going home. The twenty pounds of homework in that bag should keep me pretty busy." A laugh slipped out of her and Kevin let out a chuckle, too.

"I need to run into my classroom for a minute, do you mind waiting?" he asked. They were right outside B100, his hand already on the door. Nina shook her head and followed him in. Kevin scrambled to gather his work off of his desk while Nina leisurely propped herself up onto a desk to wait for him.

As he grabbed at assignment notebooks strewn out on his desk, he continued letting his eyes wander to Nina. She was swinging her legs and looking around the room. His heart sped up at the mere sight of her. He was losing his grip on reality. Kevin knew he was spending too much time with her and it was clouding his judgment on what was reasonable behavior.

The more time he spent with her, the more he thought of her when they were apart. The more he thought of her, the easier it was for him to convince himself things could be somewhat normal for them. However, these thoughts only came to him when he was alone. When he was near her he could only think of the next way he might be able to meet her again, making it look coincidental. A lost earring, a walk to the parking lot, those were easy enough. But how much longer would he be able to play the game of convenient meetings?

"Is your father still out of town?" he asked. He hung both his bag and Nina's over his shoulder and gestured toward the door.

Nina hopped down and they were back on their way to their cars. "Yep," she answered.

"Still staying with your sister?" Kevin asked.

"My living arrangements haven't changed since last night. What are you getting at?" Nina replied quickly. He stared at her, scrutinizing her face. Each line, a tiny scar, every shade of pink. What was he getting at?

'You could come to my place,' he thought impulsively.

'We could run away,' his mind was firing sparks.

'We could live happily ever ...' He was interrupted by Nina clearing her throat. He realized they'd been standing in the parking lot, his thoughts racing while Nina waited. Nina was glaring at him incredulously. She was undoubtedly waiting for a response that wasn't imagined.

"Uh, Mr. Reed?" she said after clearing her throat once more.

His face twisted horribly. "Don't call me that," he snarled.

Nina blinked after being scolded by him. Before Kevin could say anything, the concrete around them was swarming with teenage boys, all in sweaty black and gold uniforms. Kevin still couldn't decipher soccer from softball at this school but either way these boys were some kind of Wexley Falls team and their path was the same area where Kevin and Nina were stopped. Kevin looked around frantically as the boys jogged by them and gave them both confused glares.

What the hell was he thinking? The realization of all of the people that could have seen this odd exchange between them had him frazzled. He was letting things get way too far out of hand. He had to stop it while he still could.

"Goodnight," he muttered as he turned toward the teacher's parking lot, making his way unceremoniously to his car, leaving Nina standing wide-eyed and jilted without a clue as to why. It was the last thing he wanted to do to her but he simply had to get away from her.

CHAPTER TWENTY-ONE

The door opened with its usual creak and Nina breezed through, dropping her keys onto the table just inside the foyer. Her drive home had been noiseless. Her racing thoughts were keeping her so preoccupied she didn't so much as touch the radio. She went over the day in her mind on the drive, trying hard to figure out exactly what happened that made everything so bizarre.

"Nina! You want dinner?" Greta shrieked from the kitchen, startling Nina as she closed the front door behind her. She took a deep breath, annoyed that her sister was home, let alone speaking to her.

Greta stood with one foot tucked high onto her thigh in some sort of flamingo yoga pose as she stirred a simmering pot of something. She muttered about needing to add butter as Nina opened the refrigerator, rolling her eyes. Greta hadn't even looked at her. She felt her cell phone vibrating in her pocket and she yanked it out and hit the answer button before glancing at the name or number.

"Hello?" she asked, browsing the metal shelves for the tub of butter.

"Hi, Nina."

A coughing fit overcame her and in one fluid motion, she slammed the stainless steel door shut and scurried to the stairs.

"Kevin? What the hell are you doing calling me?" she asked in a hush. Her steps were loud thuds as she tore up the staircase to her room, praying her sister hadn't noticed.

"I'm sorry but I have your bag," Kevin said softly.

Dear Lord. She'd been too stunned by the way he ran off to notice or to remember to get it back.

"Shit," she breathed. It was the only expression she could muster. She had too much homework to wait until tomorrow when she would see him again. Her grades were already slipping as it was.

"Can I come get it from you?" she asked. She didn't want to pursue any more time with Kevin but if it meant getting a few more A's during the week rather than the C's and D's she'd been pulling in, so be it. Kevin agreed and gave her his address before she quickly hung up the phone. Nina knew exactly where his house was once she heard the street name. He was just a few blocks from The Black Jewel, within walking distance even.

Her mind floated back to the other night when he wandered in while she sang. It felt like a year ago. That night crushed her heart and the next day she mooned over him even more. It was becoming a pattern between them. Kevin's mood swings were certainly keeping Nina on her toes.

She rummaged through her closet and grabbed the first thing that jumped out at her and hurried back down the steps to find Greta was still standing at the stove with her concoction.

"I'm going out, okay?" Nina said, not considering asking for permission.

Greta glanced up from the stovetop. "You don't want dinner?"

Nina shook her head and started heading for the door, hurrying to her car. The Black Jewel was only a few minutes from her house. She made the turn onto his street and pulled in to his steep driveway and took a moment to take in the view of his home. The large, dark brick house looked old with ivy climbing the trellises on the sides of the carport and tiny cracks in the stone walkway leading to a large wooden door. It looked like a real home and not just a house like where she lived. Nina always hated that her father wanted new homes, constantly moving around Wexley into the newest neighborhood erected by the newest contractor. Her houses always seemed foreign to her, museum like and lacking character. Kevin's home was the type of place she dreamed about when she was a little girl.

She climbed out of her car and headed up the walkway. Before she was up to the first step, she saw Kevin sitting on the porch on a swinging bench. His porch was almost completely closed in and it was cozy with only a slight breeze traveling through the open sides and front where it faced the quiet street. Without a word, she made her way onto the porch and stood before him. She could see her bag propped up near the door. Letting her eyes wander, she noticed an amused grin on Kevin's face as he looked her up and down.

"What?" Nina asked.

"What's all this?" he chuckled, gesturing toward her outfit. She'd put on a dark gray hooded sweatshirt and sunglasses, trying to disguise herself since she was going to be at his home, a move she knew was inappropriate.

She sighed and rolled her eyes and removed the sunglasses. "This is a small town, okay? I know you haven't lived here long but I'm trying to be inconspicuous. You're new in town and my dad knows everyone so ..." Her voice grew faint until she gave up trying to make him understand.

"I think the neighbors would be more concerned about me meeting up with the Unabomber than one of my students."

A laugh escaped her lips. "What's a Unabomber?"

Kevin's face fell and he shook his head accompanied by a heavy sigh as she pulled the hood off of her head and took a seat next to him on the swing. For a moment they sat in the silence, just hearing the birds chirp and the wind blow through the porch.

"You know I didn't plan this," Kevin started.

Nina scoffed unexpectedly. "Right," she teased.

Kevin laughed and pushed his feet off of the wooden planks below them, setting the swing into motion again.

"This has been a really weird and really long week," Nina said.

They turned to each other, their eyes roaming over the others' face looking for some kind of sign. But it was no use.

"Do you ever feel like you're two different people?" Kevin asked, slowing the swing by dragging his shoe.

A gust of air puffed from Nina's lips. She didn't just feel like that. It was true. She was a liar with everyone but him and with him she was just confused. Silently, she nodded as the thought of how well he might really understand her sunk in.

"What do you think would've happened if we'd met at the beginning of the summer?" Nina asked, knowing the hypothetical thought was torturous for both of them.

Kevin shot her a look, the strong lines of his face bathed in the orange glow of the setting sun. "That depends. Would you have lied the whole time? The reality that we're in is bad enough. Don't go imagining that scenario," he said sternly.

Nina kept quiet. She thought about his rhetorical question, hoping it was rhetorical anyway. Truthfully she didn't know whether or not she would've been able to lie to him for very long. But to keep the fairy tale alive, she might have sold her soul. She saw Kevin run his hand through his hair and it made her instinctively smile. He was nervous and with her sitting so close to him, he was unable to hide it.

"I should get going, I guess," Nina said as she stood up. Kevin mimicked her motions and their eyes met for a moment and they smiled at one another. Though nothing could be done about the oddity of their relationship, they both seemed content to be near each other. Kevin bent over, picked up her bag and kindly handed it to her.

"I …" Kevin started, his voice cracking. Nina perked to him, waiting for him to gain the courage to continue. He dropped his head in shame and finished.

"I feel like I'm sinking. Drowning."

"What do you mean?" Nina asked.

His hand rose slowly and Nina felt electricity run through her as his fingers brushed her cheek in one gentle sweep.

"I don't know how I'm supposed to act around you. Sometimes I don't care but then other times I get so afraid that I'm doing something wrong I just want to run. I don't want to feel split in two. I don't want to feel broken over you. But I am."

His hand fell and Nina felt tears welling in her eyes. She nodded and forced a pained smile in an effort to let him know she understood. Then she made her way down the steps, turning her face from him as the tears began to fall.

Chapter Twenty-Two

It'd been close to an hour since she walked off of his front porch but he couldn't bring himself to move inside. The sun was finally below the horizon line when he finally pulled himself from the swing. He had to start looking over the senior's poem assignments.

Moving to the kitchen, he grabbed his black satchel and started digging for the assignments. He kept himself from flipping right to hers with every ounce of his being. Who knew what he'd be forced to read on her page. He couldn't start there. Besides, he wanted to be somewhat useful to the other students by being coherent when giving grades.

The work for the most part was decent. Creative Writing was considered an elective so he didn't have too many students who didn't want to be in the class. Mixed in with the good work were of course a few gems by the more lackadaisical students.

The car was blue
An airplane flew
On the green grass
There was dew

Fantastic, he thought sarcastically as he scratched the appropriate letter grade. Pushing the last paper aside, Kevin pulled the next page from the stack and stopped breathing when he read her name typed in the top left hand corner. He tried to prepare himself. What would Nina have written? Was there a chance it could be about him? He took a deep breath and started to read her work.

> *It was everything it should've been*
> *Everything it would've been*
> *Had we met another day*
> *You're so charming and amusing, see*
> *Blinding me with fantasy*
> *Now the cruelest joke's on me*
> *Can I wait*
> *Can I be strong*
> *Can I change your mind*
> *With a song*
> *Now it's nothing like it could've been*
> *We're nothing like we should've been*
> *But I'm glad we met that day*

The sound of his own breath being pulled from his lungs was the only noise in the room. It was beautiful. More than that, it was for him and he knew it. Any other teacher would write it off as teenage melodrama but Kevin knew Nina meant these words. If she was trying to get his attention, she had it. And with her forthcoming seriousness came Kevin's fear. Just when he thought he'd come to a clear decision about Nina, she turned his world on its head again.

CHAPTER TWENTY-THREE

OCTOBER

The weeks went by with no certain excitement. Kevin's morning class remained a source of awkwardness for the two of them and yet each tried to pretend it wasn't. They'd smile to each other, even talk for a few moments after class but neither made any effort to touch the other and they were careful to not stand too close.

Though nothing much transpired between them, it hadn't stopped Kevin from day dreaming of her. The text messages had stopped. Kevin had started writing to Nina a few times, but he always lost the courage to press send. He tried to tell her he no longer cared about what might happen until he realized how insane the notion was. He tried to tell her he was thinking about leaving the school to find another job to save them both from making a mistake. It didn't take long for him to delete those words either.

The first three weeks of school proved difficult but the weeks that followed were pure agony. Worst of all, their secret was still a secret, leaving them with no one but each other to share the situation with. The sleepless nights were beginning to wear on Kevin, keeping him sluggish and irritable all day.

It was nearing midnight when Kevin looked at the clock and decided to go to bed. He knew he wouldn't sleep but it was a pattern he'd grown accustomed to. As he walked through the kitchen to lock the back door after Sasha's last trip outside for the evening, he heard a noise from the living room. Ignoring it, he continued closing up the house for the night, shutting off the lights and closing an open window. He started up the steps but quickly turned on his heels remembering he'd left his cell on the coffee table. A flash of realization hit him and a small ache at the base of Kevin's neck forced him to look, to make sure.

He sat down on the sofa and with a quick tap the black screen lit up and showed he had a message. He jerked his arms up and away from the phone sitting on the oak table top and ran both hands over his face and through his hair as he sucked in a breath. His head tilted back, staring at the ceiling of the dim room. Fingers interlaced and cradling his head, he was blowing air out of his lungs rapidly. At last he let his eyes return to the screen. He blinked a few times, whipping his head back and forth in an effort to make sure he was awake enough to know what was really going on. His body became still and calm. His eyes were wide, his mouth twisted in discomfort. A shaking hand reached out and tapped once on the name he didn't think he would ever see on his phone again.

Tomorrow night. 8 o'clock. The Black Jewel. Conversation restarted.

Chapter Twenty-Four

"I wish I could see you tonight. My stupid group is made up of a bunch of assholes that had to pick tonight, the one night we don't have rehearsal, to get together and work on our song," James whined on the other end of the phone. Nina laughed, feeling only slightly sorry for him. His group was actually made up of a few nice guys.

"You'll survive. Plus, it's not like it's the last time I'll be singing there," Nina replied as she held the phone to her ear with one shoulder, looking through her closet in the section on the far left side where she kept all of her dresses. She flipped through them, examining each one for only a moment before mentally discarding it. Not the black one, not the blue one, not the floral. Finally she settled on red.

James was still chattering on the other end but Nina was ignoring him. Her thoughts were somewhere else. She'd been trembling since she'd hit *send* late last night. Her stubbornness willed her to do it. She wanted to force him to take another look at what they had. To take another look at her.

And what better place than The Black Jewel, the place where they first met. Nina's head told her what her heart refused to take note of. That carrying on with her teacher was wrong and could never end well.

She held the red dress up to her body and looked in the mirror. It would certainly force him to look at her. A smile spread wide on her face as she twisted and turned, watching herself in the mirror.

"Okay James, I've got to get ready," she said, cutting off his rambling as usual. They said their goodbyes and he wished her luck before hanging up. For the next hour Nina labored over getting ready. She took a long shower, shaved her legs and put on her best smelling lotion. While she put her makeup on, her hair was setting in rollers high on her head. Normally she didn't wear much make up on stage, but tonight she felt like playing the part of the vixen in hopes Kevin would show up. Her eyes were done subtly with just a bit of a smoky rimming and some thick mascara. Her lips were painted the same shade as her dress, cherry red.

There was a knock on her door and Greta entered just after, not waiting for Nina's permission. Nina whipped around to see her in the doorway as Greta let out a laugh.

"Well, don't you look like a little harlot?" she chided wickedly.

Nina rolled her eyes and turned back to the small mirror on her desk where her makeup was strewn about, turning her computer desk into a makeshift vanity.

"I'm staying over at Blake's tonight. Tell Dad and you're dead. You'll be okay by yourself, right?" Greta said. Her sharp voice nearly gave Nina an instant headache. Nina gave a quick affirmative and flitted her hand, shooing Greta out of her room.

Slowly, she pulled the curlers from her black hair and fluffed it with her fingers before spraying a sheen of hair spray over her completed look. For a moment she stared at herself in the full length mirror. The dress hugged her curves and stopped just below her knees. A waved line of red sequins traveled down one side of her, catching the light with each slight movement she made.

She grabbed her bag and her keys and was soon on her way to the restaurant. With her music turned up to drown out her nervous thoughts, the drive went quicker than usual. David met up with her just as she walked inside. She had a little less than a half hour before she was due on stage.

"Nina, wow," David gushed, giving her a quick look. Nina smiled shyly at him and waiting for him to continue.

"I wanted to talk to you actually. Louis told me today that he wants to cut his hours way back. Can I beg you to pick up a few more nights? Maybe even start singing with the jazz band on Saturdays?" David spilled his words out hurriedly. Nina was stunned. Beg her? It was an enormous opportunity. She couldn't turn it down.

"I'd love to David. You know, I've never really thanked you for taking such a leap of faith with me. I know you were nervous about letting a high school girl sing here but I've been having a blast and I hope you've been happy with me."

David smiled at her kindly. "You've been amazing, Nina. Some day you're going to be a bright star."

"Thank you," she sighed, holding back an excited squeal.

As David hurried off to tend to the restaurant, Nina scanned the room quickly with her gray eyes. She hoped Kevin would show up but he hadn't responded. One moment it felt right and easy and the next, her heart was jabbed by him shutting her out. Maybe it would be better if he didn't come to see her. But as she thought those words she said a silent prayer that he was walking down the street that very moment.

CHAPTER TWENTY-FIVE

He watched as she smiled and nodded at the man near the door then turned the corner to what he presumed was the backstage area. It was almost time for her to go on. Almost eight o'clock. He was thankful she hadn't seen him sitting alone at his table in the back. It was darkest near the bar and as such it was a little more difficult to see the stage but that's exactly where he wanted to be, closest to the bar.

Kevin was on his third drink by the time Nina walked in to The Black Jewel and his breath caught when he saw her. Dressed in red she was a flame in the corner of his eye. She disappeared into the shadows on the other side of the room and he took another drink. The scotch burned as he poured it down his throat but he didn't flinch.

He heard the light background music warming up for Nina. Kevin's eyes were heavy and his mind wandered until he saw her. The lights coming down on her caught the glittering design of her dress. The crowd gave her their attention and their applause. The lights went dark for a split second before lighting Nina up once again. Her back was turned to the audience and her lily white hand was out to one side snapping along with the horns that played.

Has there always been a band? He wondered. Kevin shook the question from his mind when he heard her smooth voice ring out the opening to "Hey, Big Spender."

Horns blew and the crowd went wild as Nina spun on her heels to face the room as she kept singing the sultry tune. All Kevin could do was stare. He squinted to see her on the stage and dammit if her face wasn't lit up with a grin.

She looked right at him and began her descent down the steps on the front of the stage, paralyzing Kevin in his chair. Her hips swayed and the words sparked out of her devilishly. He nearly choked on his scotch when she sang of popping her cork. The patrons at their tables watched as she walked by, further into the shaded back of the restaurant.

Watching her slink closer and closer to him, sitting motionless at his small table, Kevin was completely enraptured. His breath was pulled from him in a ragged draw as she spun around once before taking a bold seat on his lap. With one hand on the microphone and the other arm wrapped around his neck loosely, Nina sang the words directly to him, inching her face closer to his. Her final belt made him want to pull her to his lips when suddenly—he realized it had all been a waking dream.

"Another drink?" the waitress asked, staring him in the face. The room was dim again and about half of the people were missing from his sight. He shook his head trying to pull himself completely back to the present. Squinting at her, all Kevin could mutter was a weak, "What?"

"Can I get you another drink? Are … are you alright sir?"

His eyes cleared with a few more blinks and he saw the waitress gawking at him while he collected his thoughts. Nina hadn't even gone on stage yet. Once again his mind had wandered too far and this time the alcohol in his blood managed to trick him into thinking it was real. He nodded to the woman and she walked off, undoubtedly annoyed.

The thought occurred to him that it might be better for him to just go on home and spare himself another booze induced hallucination. But a glimpse at the real Nina was too tempting.

"Ladies and gentlemen, Miss Nina Jordan," Kevin muttered his own introduction under his breath. The minimal crowd clapped lightly, but Kevin gave her a true round of applause from his table in the back.

The lights shone down upon her and caught the sparkling sequins on her dress just as it had in his dream. A shy smile graced her face as she began playing the soft Norah Jones song she'd chosen for the night.

Kevin took a large gulp of his refilled drink, once again paying no mind to the fire it blazed in his chest. He listened in the dark as the sweet song came out of her and he tried hard to push the memory of her apparition out of his mind.

Chapter Twenty-Six

She heard the booming clap from the back of the restaurant as she ended her last song. It was the same thundering she heard when she walked out on stage. Her eyes strained to see the darkened bar area while she played but she couldn't see past Aaron, the bartender. She knew who it was though.

Glad her set was over, Nina hurried backstage and around the wings to the restaurant. A few patrons stopped her on her way through the tables to tell her they liked the performance. She smiled and pushed through to the bar, to the dark corner table where she'd heard the loudest clapping coming from. She saw his head hanging low and his fingers wrapped around a glass.

Nina pulled out the empty chair on the other side of his table and took a seat silently as he looked up and smiled at her.

"Nina," he said her name sweetly.

She grimaced, unsure of what to do with him in his drunken state.

"Hi Kevin," she said somberly. He reached out to her across the table clumsily, knocking over his half empty drink in the process. Ice and liquid spilled out and trickled down into Nina's lap. She jumped up, looking down at the mess while Kevin scrambled for a napkin and leaned toward her to help, soaking his own shirt in the remaining puddle that sat on the table. Nina sighed loudly and made her way over to the bar to grab a few rags from Aaron.

"Here," she said after drying herself as best she could, coming around to him and blotting his shirt. Kevin looked down at her crouched at his side, tending to him.

"I ruined your dress," he whispered.

Nina just shook her head and continued to clean him up. She stood and wiped off the table and returned the rags and the empty glass to the bar before going back to her place across from Kevin. His head was hung low again.

"Let's get you home," she said, grabbing his hand and helping to steady him as he stood up. He fumbled for his wallet and laid down more than enough money for his drinks. As they got outside she slung his arm over her shoulder, making herself a crutch for him. A breeze wafted over them as Nina helped Kevin into the passenger seat of her car. She smelled the pungent scotch they'd both been doused in and prayed she didn't get pulled over on the short two-block drive.

"Are we going to talk about this?" she asked cautiously.

"Talk about what?" Kevin slurred.

Nina craned her neck to look him in the face. His eyes were bloodshot and his breath stunk of booze.

"If I'd known you were going to come and drown your sorrows tonight, I wouldn't have invited you," she said pointedly.

"I'm sorry," he said, sounding pitiful.

They rode in silence for the rest of the journey. Nina helped him up the front steps to the porch and wordlessly coaxed his keys from him to open the front door, fear filling her up from the inside as she realized what a horrible decision she might be making. As she helped him, however, she made the internal choice to not let anything she might regret happen between them. She was only helping him.

"Oh God, you're in my house," Kevin said loudly, unable to mutter the phrase.

Nina laughed a little as she shut the door. Kevin plopped down on the bottom step of the staircase leaving Nina to stand awkwardly in the entryway.

Sasha, the large red setter, rounded the corner rather cautiously before walking briskly toward Nina. The dog immediately rubbed her face against Nina's legs and wagged her tail with excitement. Nina giggled and bent over to pat her on her head sweetly.

"That's Sasha, my dog," Kevin said, still slurring his speech.

"She's sweet," Nina replied.

"You're sweet," Kevin said with a goofy smile.

"And you're drunk," Nina said, rolling her eyes.

She came toward him and saw his red eyes widen. Kneeling in front of him, she slowly wrapped her hand around his ankle, pulling his leg up. Tugging at his shoelaces, Nina stayed quiet, careful not to encourage his loose lips. She could tell he was staring down at her as she slid one shoe off of his foot and set it to the side. He sighed.

"How can you be so wonderful and so gorgeous and only seventeen?" he breathed, the smell of whisky coming off him in waves.

Nina kept her head down as she slipped off his other shoe. She saw his hand reach out to her face and she pulled away and stood up.

"Come on, you need to sleep this off," she said, reaching for his hand to help him stand. He frowned at her and sighed in defeat, allowing her to steady his balance as they walked up the steps. Hopeful the amount of alcohol in Kevin's system was keeping him blissfully unaware of their surroundings, Nina felt a nervous twinge when they reached the doorway to his bedroom.

Nina uncomfortably stepped in with Kevin clinging to her shoulder. She felt her embarrassment creep up her neck in a hot, bright red splotch. Kevin stumbled forward and yanked the covers down before clumsily climbing into his bed. The silence that hung stagnant in the air between them was nothing short of pure torment.

"Okay, um … goodnight," Nina mumbled as she turned to leave.

Kevin's hand reached up and grasped her wrist delicately. A chill ran up her spine. Her head and her heart were playing a dangerous game with one another. She turned slowly, looking down at his pathetic frown, a wrinkle set in his brow.

"Stay," he said.

Nina shook her head back and forth slowly. She didn't have the will to say the word 'no'. She wanted to stay. Her dreams had brought her to his room many times and yet he was never drunk or sad with the guilt he undoubtedly felt about caring for her. This wasn't how she pictured it and she refused to let her weakness allow it.

"Not like that ... just for a little while," he said, still holding her hand.

Nina sat down on the edge of the bed as Kevin sat up, bringing their faces closer to one another. Kevin twisted onto his side and groaned before sitting up again. He tugged his shirt away from his skin and looked lazily down at it with a frown. The blue and white pinstriped material of his button down was soaking wet, covered in alcohol.

Swallowing thickly, Nina scooted closer to him. Her hands rose with what may have seemed like ease but she prayed he wouldn't notice—or wouldn't remember—the tremor in her fingertips as she placed her hands on the top button of his shirt and undid it. Her fingers carefully worked each button from its hole until she saw the material split.

Their eyes locked for an instant and she saw his mouth gaping as he shrugged out of his shirt, exposing his torso completely. She tried to keep her eyes from roaming his upper body but the sight was too wonderful to ignore. His skin was barely tanned and his frame was solid but not bulky. He had broad shoulders and slightly defined muscles. Nina felt her tongue slip out of her mouth to wet her lips and heard a noise come from Kevin as she did.

Slowly his hand reached out and though it wasn't the first time he'd been so bold with the gesture, she still shied away a bit. His fingers landed in her hair, toying with a single curl. His deep chocolate brown eyes grazed over her entirety. Nina shifted on the bed, unsettled by his lingering gaze. His fingers moved fluidly, tracing her jawbone.

Though she knew he was intoxicated, his eyes seemed so aware. He seemed in utter control as he let one tender fingertip drag a line down the bend of her neck. Nina shivered under his touch, shutting her eyes in ecstasy.

"You should sleep," she said, finding the will to shrug his hand from her shoulder. Kevin paused then nodded and leaned back, finally surrendering to his sleepiness. Nina forced herself to stand and walk out of his room, not knowing if she'd ever have another chance to be there. She flicked the light switch and headed back down the steps, her entire body trembling.

When she reached the main floor, her eyes scanned the space, this time a little more shamelessly. She didn't see the harm in having a quick look around before she left so she began in the living room. The décor was simple and classic, just like the house. She scanned the movies he had on display and approved of most of them. Next was his music collection. He had something from nearly every classic rock band from AC/DC to Zeppelin, with a large section in the middle which Nina figured had to be every single KISS album ever recorded. There was also an extensive list of 1980's hair bands in the mix of albums, something that gave her a little laugh. She dragged a lazy finger over the spines of the jewel cases that sat in the built-in shelves and then she stopped dead in her tracks.

She saw a collection of some of the greatest singers she'd ever heard sitting nice and tidy all in a row. Kevin's anthology could've been her own. With Dusty Springfield and Nina Simone, Julie London and Dinah Shore sitting on his shelves, it was as if he'd been eyeing her personal mp3 files. She smiled imagining him listening to the same songs she loved. The same artists she worshipped. Then she made a mental note to indulge in a little rock and roll in his honor.

Nina turned to head for the door, knowing it was late, when something on the coffee table caught her eye. A thick stack of white paper bound by brass fasteners sat looking untouched amidst books and graded school papers. Curiously she picked up the papers and read the cover page.

"The Long Road of The Father by Kevin Reed," she read aloud. It was Kevin's manuscript. Intrigued, Nina sat on the couch and opened to the first page. She just wanted to see what it was about. She tried pushing any guilt she felt for snooping out of her mind as she began to read.

It was two hours later when Nina looked at the clock after letting out a huge yawn. *I'll just shut my eyes for a minute and then I'll go home,* she thought.

CHAPTER TWENTY-SEVEN

Kevin sat up with a jolt. The sun was creeping in through the blinds and he felt his head pound as he glanced at the tiny amount of light. He looked around his bedroom not knowing how he'd ended up there. Suddenly his mind was flooded with flashes of memories from the night before. A day dream of Nina putting on a sexy production. Knocking over a glass of scotch onto the real Nina's dress. Nina driving him home. Nina in his bedroom undressing him.

His stomach flipped and he felt the stinging warmth in his chest before running into the bathroom and letting go of the contents of his stomach. He heaved once more and sighed at the feeling of the cool tile as his palms pressed against it. Raising his head, he took a few deep breaths, feeling better and better with each.

He continued to reclaim blurred memories as he became more awake, splashing water on his face and rinsing out his mouth. He shifted uncomfortably realizing he'd slept in his jeans. Tugging on a pair of sweatpants, he made his way slowly down the stairs, still feeling a little queasy.

Kevin wondered just how many drinks he'd consumed the night before. He hadn't drank heavily enough to vomit in years. Stepping off the bottom stair to the hardwood floor, he remembered the feeling of Nina slipping off his shoes as he sat in his drunken stupor.

He was headed to the kitchen to fix himself a hangover remedy when he saw something out of place in the living room from the corner of his eye. He backed up and peered suspiciously and then he saw her. Nina lay on his couch, still in her red booze-stained dress with his manuscript tented over her chest. A smiled grew on his lips instantly as he watched her sleep peacefully. He tip-toed to her and carefully picked up the manuscript. Silently he hoped she hadn't read as far as the page was turned. Though he was proud of his work, he wasn't ready for anyone but a potential publisher to read it. Certainly not Nina.

Nina didn't budge. He debated whether or not to wake her. Yes it was inappropriate having her in his home and no she probably didn't mean to fall asleep but he secretly liked the idea of her being so comfortable in his house. But as they often did on the subject of Nina, his thoughts suddenly turned pessimistic. He wondered who might've seen them going inside together. Which nosy neighbor had been waiting on Nina to leave the next morning in the same clothes she'd been wearing last night?

As Kevin crept quietly away from the couch and to the kitchen, he continued to let his mind run through horrible scenarios of ways he might get caught with her. He shook away the thoughts. He couldn't get caught do anything with her because nothing happened. She was just a nice girl who helped a drunk man back to his home then accidentally fell asleep on his couch. Kevin rationalized it over and over as he pulled ingredients down from his cabinets. Then he remembered more about the night.

He wondered if it had been a dream, his hand touching her hair, her face, and then her neck after she'd tentatively helped him undress. A sigh escaped his lips as he scooped the first cup of baking mix into the glass bowl in front of him. His stomach churned, less from his hangover and more from the nervous acid building inside of him.

"Hi," he heard her say as she slowly entered the kitchen. He looked up from the batter he was mixing and smiled at her. Her hair was a mess, flat in the places she'd been laying on it and wild everywhere else. She had black smudges around her eyes from her makeup, but Kevin still couldn't believe how beautiful she was.

"Good morning," he said. "You like pancakes?"

Nina bit her lip and smiled through it, nodding as she took a seat on a barstool next to the island in his large kitchen. They were silent together for a while, Kevin making breakfast and Nina anxiously picking at her fingers.

"I'm so sorry about last night. I'm really embarrassed but you were incredibly kind to drive me home," Kevin said, handing her a plate of warm pancakes, leaving out everything else about the evening.

"It's no big deal," she replied.

Kevin nodded, watching her carefully. The moment felt so surreal he couldn't name any of his feelings. He saw Nina shift and glance around the room.

"This is too weird, isn't it?" he asked dimly. Nina laughed unexpectedly and looked up at him, her smile not fading.

"No. Well, kind of. This is just …" she trailed off, trying to find the right words.

"I know," he replied easily as he sat next to her.

"Yeah." She let out another nervous laugh. "I … uh, I didn't mean to fall asleep."

Kevin grinned at her wickedly. "Right." He was teasing her the same way she'd teased him after ending up at home with her book bag.

Nina smirked back at him and went to tuck her hair behind her ear when she must have realized what a tangled mess it was. Her eyes widened and her mouth dropped as she scrambled to smooth her hair with her hands, clearly embarrassed. Kevin wordlessly reached out and stopped her frantic hand, shaking his head.

They ate in silence, only making passing glances at each other as Kevin thought about the things he said to her the night before. He wondered if she remembered, too. His mind held on tight to the memory of him calling her gorgeous. His skin tried hard to remember the feeling of his fingers tracing her jaw.

Kevin stood and gathered the empty plates and put them in the sink while he stared at her for a moment, not really sure what he was waiting for, but enjoying the sight of her face.

"I'd better go," Nina said in a near whisper. Kevin nodded and walked behind her as she headed toward the front door. They passed the living room and Nina glanced in, seeing his manuscript on the table.

"It's good. I know I overstepped by reading it but it's really good," she said, nodding her head in the direction of the papers.

Kevin smiled gently, embarrassed at the thought. They reached the door and without warning or thought, Kevin's arms wrapped around her in a hug.

"Thanks again," he whispered into her hair.

He pulled away and saw the look of bewilderment in Nina's eyes. Instantly he regretted the embrace. He scolded himself in his mind, calling himself everything from an idiot to an asshole.

Nina forced a smile. "Well this has been sufficiently awkward, huh? I'll see you Monday," she said before stepping out onto the porch.

Kevin closed the door and leaned his back against it, exhaling. *What the hell am I doing*, he thought.

CHAPTER TWENTY-EIGHT

The bell rang as Nina raced from her locker to Kevin's classroom. The halls were clearing out as she scurried around the corner and into his room, which was already full of students. She halted just inside the door and her eyes locked on Kevin at the front of the class. He held back a grin but she could see him smiling with his eyes.

"Consider this your lucky day," he said, gesturing towards her desk and she smiled shyly as she took her seat. The class faced forward as he turned to them to begin his lesson.

Nina diligently took notes on his lecture about fiction writing and continued to be surprised by how at ease she felt in his class. Neither had made mention of what happened between them over the previous weekend. In fact, the entire week had been tame for the two of them.

Nina was still wrestling with how that evening made her feel. Each day had been a little less awkward and by this point, she was wondering if she should bring it up. Kevin gave the homework assignment and listened as the majority of the class grumbled at the notion of having homework over homecoming weekend. The bell rang and students raced out of the room more swiftly than usual due to the change in the schedule. Nina had never been a fan of spirit week, especially this year due to the fact that second period was when the pep rally would be which only meant a longer rehearsal for her that evening.

"You're not rushing off to the gym for the assembly? Where's your Wexley spirit, Nina?" Kevin kidded before he swiped the eraser over the white board. Nina rolled her eyes and walked to the front of the room, picking up a second eraser to help him clean.

"You try living in this town full of assholes your entire life then tell me if you have Wexley spirit," she retorted with a laugh.

"Late for class *and* swearing? Do you expect special treatment?" he asked teasingly.

"That depends, have all of your students carried you home and poured you into bed?" she snapped playfully as she watched Kevin's face fall.

"I'm sorry. I shouldn't have ..." she started.

Kevin forced a smile and shook his head. "No, you're right. I've been avoiding the topic."

"I already told you it wasn't a big deal," Nina said.

Kevin took a set on the edge of his desk and folded his hands in front of him somberly before he started to speak.

"I'm sorry you had to see me like that and I'm sorry for what I said ... and did," he said precisely. He remembered? Her stomach tied into knots. She was sure he had no idea they'd had any kind of exchange in his bedroom but clearly he had the same memories she did. Nina's face contorted as she thought of what she should say back to him.

"That's only somewhat insulting. You should never apologize for calling a girl gorgeous," she replied, taking a seat on top of one of the desks near him.

He sighed. "Look, you know what I mean. I can't take back what I said and I'm not saying I didn't mean it but ... I'm your teacher and what happened shouldn't have happened," he said, trying to sound convincing.

Nina scoffed at him. "We both know you're not *just* my teacher."

Kevin ran a hand through his dark hair and sighed again, glancing back at her.

"Okay, maybe I'm not but there are rules." His voice faded out as Nina stood up and came toward him, her eyes fixed solidly on him. *It's now or never*, she thought. She'd had a lot of time to think about how she really felt and now was the time to tell him.

"Screw the rules," Nina said, coming dangerously close to Kevin, her hands almost touching him as he sat paralyzed on his desk.

"Come on," he whispered a plea.

"I'm serious," she replied in the same hushed tone.

Kevin drew in a ragged breath as her hands moved forward and slid over his knees slowly. She saw him shift uneasily though he didn't stop her. His eyes flashed to the door. The hallway was empty. The bell had blared a while ago and they were missing the assembly.

"Haven't we been through enough? We've tried fighting it, but what's the point? Sometimes rules need to be broken. I think it's time we say screw the rules and do whatever we want," she said, reaching up to run her fingers through his hair.

Nina was nervous being so forward with him but she'd already decided he was what she wanted, no matter the cost. The only thing she knew might be difficult would be pulling the truth from him as to whether he wanted her, too. The lines in his forehead softened as he searched her face with his chocolate eyes. She could see him giving in.

He began nodding before he let his hand reach out to cup her cheek, his thumb sweeping over her lips, parting them.

"Whatever we want," he repeated in a whisper. Her lips curled into a smile under his thumb.

CHAPTER TWENTY-NINE

"Catherine, Hannah. You two move down one row. Okay, now. Everyone stop fidgeting and face forward so I can see if this is right," Mrs. Benson hollered out to the students on the stage. It was the worst part about a show, blocking the stage and giving everyone their places on the risers. Mrs. Benson was incredibly obsessive in her staging, making it a miserable night of standing on stage and constantly being moved from place to place.

Lucky for Nina she wasn't participating in act two of the senior concert as anything more than a pianist. As a result, she was sitting in one of the red upholstered theater seats in the front row, finishing up her Physics homework. Her mind started to wander and she imagined Kevin's trembling hands reaching out to her again.

The three little words ran through her mind a hundred times. *Whatever we want.* When had she gotten so bold? Where had she learned to play the role of the seductress? She didn't know where it had come from. The only thing she knew was her feelings for Kevin were blinding her to everything else in her life, including the evening's rehearsal.

Feeling fidgety, Nina left her things on the floor below the cushy seat and headed out into the halls in search of the soda machine. She took her time, not anxious to get back to watching the misery in her fellow students' eyes as they stood under the hot lights and were barked at by the meticulous Mrs. Benson. Before long, Nina found herself wondering what Mr. Benson was like.

Nina wondered if he looked at all like Kevin or if they sounded similar or had the same mannerisms. Maybe they were nothing alike. Nina and her sister were nothing alike. At least to her they weren't.

The main hallway was still bright from the descending sun coming through the high windows of the two story ceiling. The bright red soda machine was in the distance but she had no desire to quicken her pace to get there. Rounding the corner just beside the machine was a tall figure and when she recognized him, she nearly burst out laughing.

Of course, she thought, *why would it be anyone else?*

She kept walking as she watched him feed the machine a dollar bill, punch his selection and bend to retrieve the bottle. Nina tried to hold in an audible sigh of bliss as she took in the sight of his strong back rounding and his perfect rear end as he bent at the waist.

Kevin straightened and turned toward her unknowingly. Their eyes met as they had so many times before and Kevin shook his head laughing as she approached.

"Fancy meeting you here," he said when she finally reached him.

Nina grinned back at him. "What are you doing here so late?" she asked.

Kevin cleared his throat before he spoke. "Figured I'd do some grading before heading home."

She eyed him carefully, hearing a fib in his voice but not minding. Seeing him was always a pleasant surprise. Breezing past him, she popped four quarters into the machine and chose a diet drink for herself.

"Want a little company?" she asked. A grin grew on his face and they made their way to B100 in comfortable silence.

Nina's second clue that he hadn't stayed at school to grade papers was the fact his classroom was dark. She felt him step into the room behind her, his breath the only sound she could hear. With the lights still off and Kevin close at her back, Nina felt a shudder roll through her as he placed a familiar hand on her hip gingerly. His fingertips slid lower, grazing the top of her thigh and all she could do was lean back into his body in consent.

A second hand landed on the other side of her waist, as he now had more of a grip on her than a loose touch. She turned instinctively in his grasp to look up at him. Nina heard him sigh as he stared down at her.

With their eyes locked she felt the weight of the moment. A change had been made and this was the first time the temptation was a different shade of gray. She saw the clear intensity coming through Kevin's eyes. Had he completely given in? Through the shadows of the room she saw him tighten his gaze on her, squinting in either desire or hesitation. She couldn't decipher the look.

Just as he had earlier in the day, he let one hand move from her waist to the apple of her cheek, smoothing his knuckles against her blushed face. Nina's lips were parted in awe. Mimicking him, her hand raised to his face, sliding through his hair and landing on the back of his neck.

It was all she could do not to yank him down and kiss him hard on the mouth. It had been so long since their kiss she'd nearly forgotten the feel of his lips. But looking at him like this, in the dark with their hands on each other just like in the handful of dreams she'd had, there was one thing she wasn't counting on.

An irrational notion crept into her head just as he started to read her body language and dip his head low to kiss her. It was something she'd never really counted on feeling. Of course every seventeen year old girl wishes but not like this. She didn't want the thought now, not when she had Kevin right where she thought she wanted him. Coaxing him to give into the physical had been her intention, not the new and insane feeling building within her now.

Nina didn't want to believe her mind. She just wanted to kiss him, climb all over him and do whatever she wanted. But one powerful word stood out in her mind. A simple sentence of three words changed it all.

She pulled back from him and saw him accept the rejection as a flicker of pain in his eyes.

"Sorry," he said, dropping his hands from her.

"It's okay. I just … need to get back," she lied.

Kevin gave her a wounded smile and nodded before walking out into the florescent lights of the hallway. She glanced up at him hoping it was a trick of the darkness, maybe the thought was fleeting. But as they walked to the auditorium in dead silence, she kept her eye on him stealthily. It didn't matter the lighting, it didn't matter how close or far away they were. The three little words that popped into her head were true.

CHAPTER THIRTY

Nina saw James spot her walking toward him. Rehearsal was over and the dreaded stage blocking accomplished. James caught up with Nina and gave Kevin an obvious look, half in suspicion and half in lust.

"We going?" James asked.

Nina glanced at Kevin, her heart still pounding.

"Goodnight, Mr. Reed. Thanks," she said, stumbling over the proper name she wasn't used to calling him. Kevin nodded and flashed her his charming smile before leaving in the opposite direction.

"You're not going to believe this. Let's just say I have more proof," James said shrewdly. They made it to James' car, hopped in and just as the engine clicked on, James turned to face Nina.

"Did he come and find you?" James asked.

Nina made a face at him. "I was getting a drink. He was getting a drink. So I guess if that's what you mean …" Her voice trailed off. She was trying so hard to sound convincing.

"Yeah right! He is *so* in love with you!" James exclaimed, jumping up and down in his seat.

"Are you going to drive me home or not?" she said angrily, annoyed by his consistent assumption about Kevin. It made her nervous that James could be so in tune to what was building between them. She was still wrestling with the idea of coming clean with her best friend, the lies that kept coming out of her seeming more and more normal. She had no idea how much further it might escalate. The thought scared her more than being found out.

"I'll drive in a minute, just listen to me," he begged.

Nina sighed. "Fine."

"So we were doing the stage blocking thing, right? And, by the way, Mrs. Benson is the devil for making us do that. I think I got sunburned from being under the lights so long. Anyway, I see super hot English teacher come rolling in to the auditorium just after you bounced. He stands in the back for half a second looking all around. Then he gets this grumpy look on his face and leaves through the side doors. He's totally stalking you," James finally finished, taking in a gulp of air. A proud and mischievous smile graced his face.

Nina took a moment to pull the useful parts of the story out in her mind. She sat staring blankly, thinking of a response. James' grin was lingering as he waited for her to comment on the hilarity of it all.

"Well, that's interesting and all but we just saw each other at the vending machine and he walked me back because I was asking him about an assignment. If he has some sort of scandalous feelings for me, he's doing a good job of hiding it," Nina said, wanting to smile herself.

James' face fell and he started to drive out of the parking lot.

"What a waste. If he were gay I'd be having the time of my life sneaking around with him," James said defeated.

Nina laughed. "I'm sure if someone were to have the kind of torrid affair you're dreaming up, it wouldn't be all fun and games. I imagine it would be really hard to …" she felt her throat getting tight with each potentially incriminating word but she couldn't stop. "Lie to everyone. It would be hard to lie," she finished and stifled her remaining confession.

James shrugged, apparently bored by the conversation already. He clicked on the radio and they listened to a sugary pop song as he drove to Nina's house.

"Can't you just let me dream a little?" he asked with puppy dog eyes.

"Sure, pumpkin. I just don't know why *your* dreaming has to involve me and my English teacher hooking up?"

James huffed playfully then grinned at her. She swatted his arm before climbing out of the car and heading inside.

Nina wasn't surprised by the sight of a sticky note on the mirror in the entryway. This time Greta scratched something about having dinner with girlfriends. Strolling into the kitchen, Nina poured herself a glass of water and sat down at the kitchen counter to skim through the mail that had piled up.

A few coupon flyers were the only things that interested Nina until she saw a big envelope on the very bottom. She barely glanced at it, sure it would be some sort of business package for her father. Pulling it to the top of the stack, she looked at it and did a double-take.

With her lips pressed against the cool glass poised to take a sip, she stopped and stared at the white envelope and its return address. While she tried to remain calm and move slowly, she ripped the package open like a child on Christmas, shredding paper as she went.

Her breath heaved as she read the first line. Then she read it again. *The Caldwell Conservatory of Music at Caldwell-Hampton College of the Arts is pleased to tell you of your acceptance for the fall semester.* Nina flew off the barstool and leapt into the air in private celebration, squealing.

She continued to stare at the words on the page, beaming. After a moment, her face fell and she looked around the empty kitchen. She hadn't spoken to her father in days and technically then it had only been an email exchange. She barely ever saw her sister. James was so preoccupied with his group performance and seeking out evidence of Kevin's supposed love she'd spent little time with him outside of rehearsals and school. An unexpected tear rolled down her cheek. She had no one she wanted to share her good news with.

That was a lie. There was one person. Nina wiped the tear from her face and sniffed, ordering the rest of the moisture to stay away as she slumped back onto the wooden stool. Along with ripped up bits of paper and sorted mail, the table had one object on it Nina couldn't help but stare at.

Her eyes grazed over her black cell phone for a moment before she snatched it off the table. She let out a sigh and felt her stomach twist as she quickly pulled up his number and hit 'call' then waited for the first ring. Shutting her eyes for a moment as she listened, she thought about hanging up. But she didn't.

"Hello?"

Nina gasped, her voice trapped in her throat for a second. "Hi," she said dumbly.

"Nina?" Kevin asked.

"Yeah, hi," her voice was the size of a mouse's. She was thankful he couldn't see her face twisting in agony as her brain reprimanded her for her actions.

Stupid, stupid, stupid, she thought.

"Um, what's ... h-how are you?" he stuttered.

"I'm fantastic," she said, feeling almost like she was talking to herself.

She heard him laugh a little—the laugh she adored—and hearing that put her at ease.

"What makes tonight so fantastic?"

"I got in to Caldwell."

The other end was silent, stagnant.

"I ... wow! I didn't even know you applied there. That's great, Nina. I'm really happy for you. I'm ... proud of you." She heard the stiffness in his voice.

"You're the only person I wanted to tell," she sighed.

"Why?" he asked.

The three little words almost spilled out of her mouth but she didn't dare say them.

"I'm not sure," she replied.

"Well, you've got to celebrate, right?"

Nina's face lit up. "Sure! What should we do?" she asked.

Silence.

Stupid, stupid, stupid, she chided herself again.

"Sorry, I know that's not what you meant," she said through her teeth.

"No. Of course we should celebrate," he said.

Nina was speechless.

"Give me an hour. Be here in an hour," Kevin said firmly.

"Okay," Nina choked out, stunned at what transpired from a phone call she hadn't fully thought through making in the first place. She hung up and looked around the kitchen in disbelief. A moment of silence passed and she glanced down at herself. She needed to change.

Chapter Thirty-One

Kevin glanced at the clock on the oven then hurried across the kitchen to the table where he set two places as he paced back and forth thinking of what he needed to do. It'd been a non-stop rush since he got off the phone with Nina. Scurrying back to the stovetop, he stirred the pot of sauce and he checked the steaming vegetables.

Sasha peered up at him, her doe eyes blinking lazily as he jumped from place to place throughout the kitchen. The door let in a cool gust of air as he opened it, letting himself out to the back porch where the grill was running. The pieces were falling into place. The steaks were done and he brought them inside, plating them with the red wine reduction he poured over the top. He added the vegetables to the plates and set everything on the table, including a basket of bread, his salt and pepper shakers and the vase of flowers he had found for her. Kevin took a moment to breathe and looked at the clock impatiently at the same time he heard a knock at the door.

Sasha swished her tail back and forth as she got to the door first, pressing her nose to the window that ran along the hand carved wood. Nina bent down and scratched her fingertip over the glass where Sasha was, smiling at her sweetly. When she saw Kevin, he watched as she straightened back up.

"Hi," he said, welcoming her in, holding the door wide open. A shy smile crept onto Nina's face as she walked into the house.

"That would be dinner."

"You did all of this in an hour? F—for me?" Nina stood staring at all of the work Kevin had put in to their impromptu party. She looked around again at the spread then Kevin heard the beep on the oven timer.

"Damn! I knew I wouldn't have time for all of it," he said, grabbing a green potholder off the counter before reaching into the oven and pulling out a dozen cupcakes, piping hot.

Nina gasped dramatically. "Yum."

"Maybe we could ice them together after dinner?"

Nina nodded excitedly as she took a seat with him at the table, each of them taking in the sight of the spread, not quite knowing what to say to the other as they began eating.

"I knew you were a pancake master but this is rather impressive," she said, taking a sip of water between bites.

"Just one of those hidden talents I suppose," he grinned at her.

"You got me flowers," she stated quietly, her bashful smile returning.

"Well, yeah. You deserve flowers." Kevin raised his glass to her for a toast and she mimicked him.

"To Caldwell," Kevin said, clinking his glass against hers.

When they finished, Kevin cleared the plates from the table and knocked a few scraps into Sasha's bowl as a treat. Nina stood and he watched as she started fidgeting, picking at her fingernails.

He tried to avoid gazing at her like he truly wanted to because he didn't want to make her uncomfortable. He'd been too bold earlier and he knew it. Though he was starting to wrap his brain around the idea of going with whatever *this* was, he still felt completely lost on how to act.

"Where's the frosting?" Nina said, breaking the silence. Kevin snapped out of his trance and pulled a can of vanilla whipped icing from the cabinet nearest the refrigerator, taking it, two knives and the cooled cupcakes to the table.

"Is this too much?" he asked quietly.

Nina was standing beside him about to take a seat when she stopped and put her hand on his forearm gently and he met her eyes. They were serious, heartbreakingly beautiful pools of steel.

"It's perfect," she replied.

"I'm sorry about earlier," Kevin whispered.

He saw her cringe and then relax her face into an embarrassed smile. "Don't be. I …"

Kevin cut her off, trying to save her from explaining herself. "It's alright. You don't have to say anything."

She shrugged a bit, her lips twisting with nervous energy as her eyes roamed his face. He didn't want her to speak for fear she'd change her mind and take back her daring insinuation and run for the door. He didn't need a kiss or the feel of her skin against his. He'd take anything. He'd take dinner and decorating cupcakes, her eyes on him the whole time, anything.

He swiped his finger over the top of the last cupcake he covered and licked the sugary goop from his index finger watching as her grin grew.

She did the same, gathering a dollop of icing on her finger but she reached over and dotted it on Kevin's nose with a burst of beautiful laughter.

His mouth gaped comically. "Oh, so that's how we're gonna play?" he asked, wiping the tip of his nose then going for his second fingertip of icing. He dove for her and she squealed, backing away from him, putting her hands on his chest, slinking back into her chair. They were laughing like fools, play fighting, Kevin still trying to smear her with sugar when their eyes met and Kevin felt his face soften. He couldn't help but look at her with warmth and affection.

His eyes narrowing, he examined her face. He was hovering over her, her hands pressed lightly against his chest, his finger pointed at her

116

face. A sigh rolled out of him as the words just slipped out without thought.

"You're so beautiful."

It came out in a whisper and with it her eyes softened as did her smile. Her head cocked to one side and she bit her bottom lip. He tried to think of why they shouldn't be in this position but he had nothing. It felt too right, too wonderful, to be bad. Besides, they hadn't done anything wrong. What exactly was the problem?

Nina inched forward and unflinchingly let her lips close around his fingertip, licking the icing from his skin. His brow lifted in awe and his jaw went slack as he quivered through an exhale.

Chapter Thirty-Two

"Stop cheating!" Nina squealed, throwing down her hand of cards on the table angrily. Kevin busted out laughing, throwing his head back. Nina was fuming as she glared at him.

"You can't cheat at *Uno*," Kevin said through his laughter.

"Apparently *you* can, 'cause *you* are," Nina growled.

"I can't help it that I got all of the blue fives. You dealt the hand, remember?" Kevin chided her. She rolled her eyes and then a smile began brimming on her face as she peered at him through squinted eyes. But just as Nina's face eased, her eyes darted to the clock and she realized how much time had passed.

"It's late," she sighed.

They stood in unison, leaving the mess of multi-colored cards strewn about the coffee table. Although the door was just a few feet away, they were taking their time with slow, deliberate steps that direction and it was almost as if a magnet was pulling them back, deeper into the house. Nina picked up her purse and slung it over her shoulder.

"Thank you for all of this," Nina reached up boldly and put a hand on Kevin's face. His eyes widened, shocked at the feeling of her skin against his. She took her hand and slid it around the back of his neck just as she had hours earlier. But this time fear and that other foolish word were out of her head. Nina pulled him down slowly and pushed herself up until they'd almost met at the lips. She could feel his breath on her mouth and she felt him moving closer when they were stunned apart by the loud ringing of Nina's cell phone.

They stared at each other in bewilderment for an instant, the phone still buzzing and screeching. Nina heaved a sigh and rolled her eyes before digging the phone out of her bag. James. She looked at Kevin and frowned.

"Goodnight, Nina." His voice was hushed as he opened the door for her.

Her mouth twisted awkwardly. "Night."

"Hi, James." She went down the steps and got into her car as she answered.

"God, what took you so long to answer?" James was barking at her but all Nina saw was Kevin still standing in the doorway.

"Uh, couldn't find my phone," she lied with ease. She pulled out of Kevin's driveway wishing she could stay. Wishing she would've thrown the phone on the floor and kissed him. Wishing they could make Wexley Falls disappear around them.

"Are we going to the game tomorrow night?"

"The football game? Why? We hate football," Nina scoffed.

"But it's our senior year and it's Homecoming," James pleaded.

Nina agreed to go without any more convincing when the thought popped into her head that Kevin might be going. That was motivation enough. She listened to James ramble on about how high school was going to end up being the best days of their lives and they should have the ultimate experience. She held back a laugh as she wondered what she would think of her senior year and everything that came along with it when it was time for her ten year reunion. Sadness stuck in her gut for an instant as she thought about how absurd it was to imagine her and Kevin still together then.

They agreed James would pick her up at four the next afternoon and Nina hung up just as she pulled into her driveway. Greta's car was still gone and Nina was thankful she wouldn't have to talk to her. Walking upstairs, Nina decided upon a bath before bed.

The tub was filled and brimming with steaming bubbles when Nina shed her clothes and dipped one toe in to test the temperature. It was hot but perfect. She slid herself carefully into the water until she was resting comfortably with her head against the tile wall. Her body pulsed in the sweltering water but it felt good. Sweat was beading up on her forehead as she lay in the bathtub letting the vapors rise around her. She shut her eyes and let her mind wind down. The day had felt like a lifetime. From her forward assertion with Kevin that morning to their rendezvous in his darkened classroom to the Caldwell acceptance and another evening spent in Kevin's home. Her life was turning into a ride that left her spinning. She thought the three words in her head just once then she shut them out.

Nina was getting sleepier by the second. The heat brought with it deep, sighing breaths and her mind was taking a turn. As usual, Kevin's face appeared. She remembered the vision and the sensation of her lips enveloping his tender fingertip, the way his chest felt sturdy under her hands as he took subtle control of her in that moment. She imagined what it might have been like if she hadn't stopped with the enticing taste of him. What if he'd pulled himself nearer to her and placed his lips against her collarbone? What if he went further down to kiss her high on her thigh where a tingle burned for him.

Nina heard her heart beating in her ears. The thoughts wouldn't stop. Then those pesky three little words crept in again. She tried to focus on the lust she was feeling but it was tangled in a web of that *other* emotion. She envisioned it clearly as Kevin towered over her in his kitchen. As he drew her nearer, sliding his hands under the back of her shirt lifting the material higher, he said the words into her ear ever so softly. Nina's hand slipped below the surface of the water and she succumbed to her thoughts of Kevin.

CHAPTER THIRTY-THREE

It seemed as though the entire town of Wexley Falls had turned out for the high school homecoming game. Cool October air rushed through Nina's hair and she instantly regretted coming to the game, being stuck in the stands filled with screaming students and parents. She was trying to keep warm in her sweatshirt and jeans but each time the wind blew, she cursed herself for not bringing gloves or a scarf. The stadium was a sea of black and yellow, Wexley colors. James and Nina sat near the bottom of the bleachers where most of the other seniors were stationed watching the game. But James and Nina could've cared less about football.

"Don't look now but here comes Laura Correll. What a bitch," James whispered into Nina's ear. She almost didn't hear his comment as she was preoccupied with the feeling of warmth on her ear from his breath.

"You just hate her because she dates Chris Cumberland," Nina said, taking another scan of the crowd as they all went wild, most likely from a touchdown.

"He'll figure it out in college and then I'll have my chance," James muttered as he took in the sight of the boy they spoke of on the football field. The air brought smells of hot dogs and pretzels causing Nina's stomach to growl loudly.

"You gonna answer that?" James teased, poking his index finger into her side. Nina scooted away from him and yelped playfully as he kept jabbing at her as the fans went on again with hoots and hollers for another point scored.

"What do you want? I'll go get it before the lines get crazy at half-time," James said, standing up. Nina smiled at him and dug in her pocket for a few dollars.

"Nachos and a diet something," she said, handing him the money. He nodded and hopped down the metal steps, headed for the concession stand. Nina breathed in the fall air once more. Even though she despised the cold, she couldn't deny that she loved the different smells of each season as it rolled in to Wexley Falls.

"Go Eagles." A voice came from behind her almost as close to her ear as James had been earlier, sending a chill up her spine. Nina whipped her head around to see him behind her but he was already claiming James' empty seat next to her. Kevin was decked out in black and yellow just like the rest of the fans. A black knit hat was pulled down to cover his ears and his cheeks and nose were rosy from the chill in the air. Nina felt herself going red as she locked eyes with him and suddenly remembered her fantasies the night before.

"You're not here by yourself, are you?" he asked. Nina shook her head keeping her lips tightly closed in a thin line. Kevin stared at her for a moment and she avoided his eyes. His brow furrowed and he started to grin as she sat silently looking forward at the field.

"What are you doing?" she mumbled as the people around them cheered loudly.

He leaned closer to her. "I'm enjoying a football game."

Nina peered at him out of the corner of one eye as she puffed out a breath. He scooted just slightly closer and whispered in her ear as the stands grew louder.

"You could say I'm doing *whatever I want.*"

"Mr. Reed, when did you get here?" James asked as he made his way up the steps and scooted back in close to Nina on her other side. He handed her the nachos and drink and she felt him elbow her hard in the side. She shot him a look before flipping her head back to Kevin.

Kevin smiled at James. "I was just saying hello to Nina. I'll let you guys get back to the game," his voice trailed off as he stood up and looked down at Nina. She glanced up at him, letting bliss fill her as she enjoyed his handsome face just as she had in her fantasy.

"No. Stay," James interjected. Kevin and Nina shared another look, each of them testing the other. Kevin reclaimed his seat next to Nina, a tight squeeze at best. The three of them were huddled together staring onto the field in silence for more minutes until James began his interrogation.

"So Mr. Reed, where did you move here from?" he asked, leaning over Nina.

"Michigan."

"And what made you move to Wexley?" James continued. Nina looked at James and opened her mouth as if to speak when she realized how she'd be giving herself away if she stopped James from asking his questions. She glanced back to Kevin.

"I have family here," he replied easily.

"Ooh, it's a small town. Anyone I know?"

"Actually, Mrs. Benson is married to my cousin, Jeff."

James laughed and slapped Kevin on the back, reaching around Nina to do so. "Man. Sucks to be you," he said.

Nina's eyes went fiery. She couldn't believe James would be so obnoxious. What kind of game was he trying to play? Kevin burst out laughing and James followed and then they were both cracking up. Nina wrung her hands tightly as they continued.

"I know, right?" Kevin said through fits of laughter.

"I'm going to see if there are gloves in the car," Nina muttered as she got up and started her descent on the stairs, pushing past Kevin to get out.

"Lock it when you're done," James said, handing her the keys, watching as she walked away.

She was nearly to James' car when she heard footsteps behind her. She didn't dare turn around. Pressing the unlock button on the rectangle key fob, she heard the beep and put her fingers on the handle when she saw him in her periphery.

"You got out of there fast," Kevin said, leaning against the car alongside her.

"Someone will see you," she said, her voice quiet and soft.

"What is this? What's the matter?" he asked, reaching over slowly linking a few of her fingers with his. Nina shut her eyes at the feeling. His touch was something she was sure she'd never grow tired of. She shook her head back and forth, unable to think of a response. She had none. If she told him she was scared, he'd ask why. And she wasn't ready to tell him why. She saw him pulling something from his jacket pocket then he held the object out for her. She looked over and smiled when she saw the pair of black gloves. Nina took the gloves and slid them on her hands, staring back at the ground.

"You're worrying me," he said.

"It's nothing, just paranoia. You know, so much has happened in just a few days. I wouldn't want anyone to catch on." It wasn't quite a lie but it wasn't the truth either. She did worry about someone noticing them but her hesitation wasn't driven by that. She just needed more time to get used to the words in her mind. Those three little words she wanted to shout every time she saw his darling smile.

"We'll talk later, okay?" she said, putting a gentle hand on his chest just wanting to feel him again, to fuel her dreams some more.

"Sure. Later."

"See you Monday," she said before heading back to James without looking back.

CHAPTER THIRTY-FOUR

Monday came and went, as did the next few weeks. Each morning in class Kevin and Nina shared something. A glance, a smile, a brush of the hand. One day Nina ran her hand through Kevin's hair and he'd been dreaming of it ever since. But Kevin was waiting for her to bring up whatever it was she'd been so preoccupied with. He tried not to worry himself about it. When she wanted to talk, she'd talk.

Halloween fell on a Saturday and Kevin was reluctantly following his cousin and his wife for a night out. Jeff told Kevin that a band he loved was playing the Halloween show at The Black Jewel just like last year. When they entered the restaurant, Kevin looked around at the transformation. Halloween decorations were everywhere. Fake cobwebs and skeletons graced the walls and hung from the ceiling. The eerie purple glow of black light bathed the bar in the back, a spot Kevin was quite familiar with.

The place was more crowded than Kevin had ever seen it with people dressed in costumes dancing to the blaring music. It was a fluke they'd found an empty table given it appeared to be a standing room only crowd. But Jennifer snagged the small round table at the very back of the sunken area near the stage. Kevin left to get drinks absentmindedly bobbing his head to a song he recognized and loved. He didn't remember Jeff mentioning anything about the band having a female lead singer.

Kevin made it back to their table through the swarm of people, creatures really. They were ghosts, goblins and even a few dead presidents. He doled out the beverages and took his seat next to Jeff.

"This sucks, Where are The Basement Snakes?" Jeff asked, staring at the stage.

"Oh shut up about that stupid band, this is way more exciting!" Jennifer squealed to which Jeff just rolled his eyes.

"What's going on? This isn't the band that was supposed to be here?" Kevin looked at Jeff rather than at the stage.

Jeff leaned in closer to Kevin, trying to avoid having to scream over the noise.

"I guess they got replaced. Jen's freaking out though 'cause that chick up there is her student," Jeff said.

Kevin's heart stopped. How could he have missed it? Why didn't she mention it? Her voice was different. Nina sang with a ferociousness he would've never recognized. He looked at Jennifer staring wide-eyed with a beaming smile as she watched the stage closely. Then he saw her. The regular Black Jewel stage had traded in the piano for guitar, bass and drums.

She gripped the long-corded microphone and writhed on the stage as she sang out rock lyrics. Her hair was messy and wild with artificial pieces of blue streaked throughout. She wore a tight fitting black corset top with thin black straps, electric blue slim fitting pants and stiletto black patent leather heels. Her wrists were stacked high with black and silver bangles that slid up and down each time she shot her arm into the air, letting out another forceful belt. He watched carefully as her hips swayed to the pounding beat. Even after months of the strange relationship they shared, she was still such a mystery to him. A constant surprise.

"She's so talented. What a force. Hard to believe she's only seventeen, right?" Jennifer said, still watching her student in awe to which Kevin thought to himself, *yes, incredibly hard to believe*. He downed his drink quickly, trying to calm his nerves. As soon as he felt the burn trickle down his chest, he reminded himself to take his time. He didn't want a repeat of the last time he heard her perform. He wondered if that was the reason she hadn't told him she'd be singing tonight.

He glanced back up at Nina and realized she'd spotted him, too. The audience clapped before the drums hit quickly, then the guitar and finally her voice ripped into her singing "I Want You To Want Me."

She sang out, looking right at him, before bouncing around the stage. Her eyes kept coming back to him, even as she went back to back with the guitarist as he shredded through the classic beat. Kevin's heart filled with a sense of pride for her and he felt a surge of happiness that she was standing singing, out from behind the piano, where the world could really take note of her.

Kevin looked over to Jennifer who gave Nina a booming applause when the song ended. His head was reeling at the oddity of the situation. If only Jeff and Jennifer knew Nina was the singer he'd been out on a date with after their failed attempt at setting him up. Kevin shook the thought away and stood up to get another drink. He pushed his way through the mob of people to get to the swarming bar.

He let his eyes drift back to Nina and he clumsily bumped into the back of the person in front of him. The man turned around and Kevin saw it was not a man at all, but a boy. James. He grinned ear to ear looking at Kevin.

"Mr. Reed. Happy Halloween," James said gleefully.

Kevin nodded and absentmindedly glanced back at Nina and the band as they started the next song. His curiosity peaked as he saw her pick up a guitar, strapping it to her before starting to play.

"Isn't she fabulous? She never ceases to amaze me. She hasn't played guitar in years but she was determined to play one tonight. Been practicing for weeks," Kevin heard James' voice but it sounded a million miles away.

He saw Nina searching the crowd as she started playing the electric guitar. Was she searching for him? As she caught a glimpse of him, the male guitarist on stage with her took over lead vocals for a fitting song, a cover of Winger's "Seventeen." His heart stopped at the song he knew so well. He had the album sitting on his shelf at home. Finally Nina's voice came in to mix for the chorus. The drums hit and the smile on Nina's face grew, her lips stretching across her white teeth.

"Yeah. She's fabulous alright," Kevin said with a chuckle before clapping James on the shoulder and breezing past him to the bar. He ordered his drink and watched Nina as she let out her inner rocker, making him grin. A constant surprise.

CHAPTER THIRTY-FIVE

Kevin watched intensely as Nina's mouth moved but her microphone pointed out at the crowd, letting the masses sing for her. She pushed the microphone back into the grip on the stand grinning wickedly as she played the last rift on her guitar. The crowd went wild for her at the song's ending.

The band played on, with the lead guitarist taking over vocals. Nina jumped off the front of the stage and her excitement shone as she took a moment to dance with strangers in the crowd. Her smile was infectious. She spun, her arms reaching to the sky, her hips hitting the beat of the drums rhythmically. She only danced for a moment then she was heading right for him.

"Hey, Mrs. Benson ... Mr. Reed," she said, her breath heaving, her voice hoarse.

"Nina, you're amazing! Why did it take four years for you to sing for me? I can't believe you never told me you play guitar," Jennifer gushed, pulling out a chair for Nina, gesturing for her to sit and join them.

Nina took a seat and bit her lip, smiling through it shyly.

"Just one of those hidden talents I suppose," Nina joked.

She looked at Kevin and smiled innocently. His heart was swelling, his stomach jumping. Sitting so close to her with his family completely oblivious to the tension thick between them made his palms sweat.

"What about The Basement Snakes?" Jeff asked dimly.

"Excuse my husband. He means to say you were great," Jennifer chided.

Nina shrugged. "They bailed. That's actually the Saturday night Jazz band. I've only performed with them a few times and they asked me for tonight. It's definitely different from my usual set," she said with a laugh.

"Who knew you had rock and roll in you," Kevin said, catching her eye for just a moment too long. Nina smirked and tucked a few strands of hair behind her ear. He hoped she was just as nervous as he was given the peculiar circumstances. He saw her eyes flit around the table looking at everyone's drink.

"Do you want a drink?" Kevin asked.

"Kevin!" Jennifer snipped.

He rolled his eyes at her. "I'm not going to buy her alcohol, Jennifer. I'm not an idiot," he said.

Kevin stood up and looked at Nina. "You want water or a soda or something?"

Nina's eyes widened and she stood up, too. "I'll go with you. I'll get you my discount," her voice trailed off.

Kevin nodded before they walked off to the bar together. Kevin felt Nina's hand slip into his and she was dragging him through the swarm of people. They passed the bar and before he could object, Nina was glancing around suspiciously and opening a door he'd never noticed. She pulled him inside and Kevin looked at their surroundings.

The walls were grey stone and the stairs led to some sort of basement. There was a dark hall that led in the direction of where the stage was on the other side of the door that now separated them from the crowd.

"That hall leads backstage but everyone always uses the other side. I thought we could be alone for a minute," Nina said, her voice low.

Kevin's back was to the door they'd come in through leaving Nina in front of him. His hand came toward her, picking out a tendril of the bright blue that was somehow hooked in her hair, examining it with a grin.

"What are you supposed to be?" he asked.

"I'm a rock star," she said plainly.

"You certainly are." He let his fingertips brush her cheek lightly. "I didn't know you were singing tonight. You didn't tell me. You've been so … quiet lately."

"I guess I just needed some time," she replied, nuzzling her face closer to his hand.

He squinted at her. "Okay."

Nina pursed her lips before letting them curl into a sweet smile. Her face all of a sudden fell and her tone became serious and bold.

"You realize every time I'm up there I'm signing to you, right?"

A moan seized from Kevin's throat and he nodded to her, unable to speak.

Nina let her fingertips press lightly against his chest. She felt the heat from him even through her clothes. Kevin's head dipped down and she could feel his hot breath on her face.

"You can tell me to stop," Kevin whispered, taking her face in his hands. Nina's breath caught. She knew what was coming. It was the moment she'd been waiting for.

"Don't," she croaked.

His mouth grazed her cheek, first just below her eyes then at the corner of her mouth, teasing her with the anticipation of it. Her breath was ragged as she waited what seemed like a lifetime for the kiss she'd been dreaming of. His lips pressed against hers slow and tender at first. As the sensuous feeling took them over, the sweet kiss quickly turned into a something neither of them had felt so intensely before. Nina's hands slid into Kevin's thick hair and gripped him tightly. His hands found her waist, cinched small by the corset, and her pulled her as close as he could, their mouths never unlocking from the kiss.

The warmth of their tongues dancing upon one another sent Kevin into a frenzy. He held onto Nina tightly and pushed himself off of the wall and turned her against the door. They finally separated and stared into each other's eyes eagerly. Nina took her hands from Kevin's hair and let them fall to her sides, leaving her open to him, vulnerable.

He let a finger trace her jawbone and slide down the curve of her neck ever so slowly. Nina flashed back to every moment between them before this. The sweet kiss of their first date, his intoxicated hands touching her in his bed, the shadows of room B100.

She heard his uneven breaths and it only thrilled her more. Again his head bent low, only this time he turned her head to the side with a lightly dominating hand and let his lips and tongue pursue the white skin of her throat. She sighed at the feeling and he continued down her neck to her collarbone. When neither could take any more, he came quickly back up to her craving lips.

Though they were lost in the moment, it was Nina who broke their lips apart when she heard the band playing the song she knew was her cue. She was panting, staring up at his brown eyes that begged for more. Her lips were full and had exchanged their natural subtle pink for a feverish red.

"I have to get back on stage," she exhaled. Kevin's brows shot up worriedly as he thought about how long they must have been missing from Jeff and Jennifer's table. He nodded vehemently, straightening out his slightly rumpled clothes.

"What about me? Do I look … disheveled?" she asked naively.

Kevin smiled at her and smoothed a hand over her hair.

"You look beautiful."

Her body eased even more than it had in his embrace. She wanted to say the words.

"Kevin … I-I want to tell you something," her words were choppy and she berated herself for the faintest tremble in her voice.

"My place later?"

She nodded and awkwardly waited, for what she didn't know. He smiled at her and this time she beamed back at him, enjoying his handsome face for a moment before making her way down the backstage hallway alone.

Chapter Thirty-Six

"Welcome back to the stage, Nina Jordan!" the guitarist yelled out at the crowd, moving back to his spot on the side. The thunderous applause coaxed Nina to the microphone, her lips still cherry red. Kevin was almost back to the table when he heard her voice from the stage singing "I Put A Spell On You." He grabbed his seat next to Jeff with a beer in his hand watching with a silly grin on his face as he and Nina shared a knowing glance from across the room. His heart was getting the better of him now and each time his thoughts turned condemnatory, he squashed them with another sip of beer and a glance at Nina.

"That took a while," Jeff hollered at Kevin over the music.

Kevin leaned in towards Jeff's ear. "The bar was packed. She's really good, huh?" he asked. Jeff nodded and glanced back at the stage where Nina was back into her roaring performance.

"She's hot," Jeff said to Kevin. Kevin pulled back from Jeff and shot him a look. Jeff shrugged innocently and they turned their attention back to Nina and the band.

The night wore on with Nina continuing her blazing show and Kevin, Jeff and Jennifer taking in more and more drinks. Jennifer was ready to leave, feeling a bit sleepy after all of the amaretto sours. Kevin wanted to say goodbye to Nina but he had no idea how to be secretive about it. Instead, he waved goodbye to her on the stage as he got up to which Nina tilted up her chin.

She couldn't leave fast enough. Her car didn't start fast enough, didn't drive fast enough. It felt like it had taken an hour to get to Kevin's house.

Nina waited, letting her thoughts continue to race as her heart started to pound. How would she tell him? Would she blurt the three little words or would she try to prepare him in some way? She wanted to write it across the sky in stars and simply point up. She worried she wouldn't have the courage when the time came. She glanced back at the house then back at the steering wheel, contemplating going home and avoiding the conversation all together.

She looked up once more and saw Kevin's silhouette standing in the window next to the door. He moved when she looked at him and he opened the door. When the noise from her cell phone vibrating in her purse nearly scared her to death, she realized how ridiculous she must look.

You gonna sit out there all night?

Nina smirked, shaking her head as she stepped out of the car and stared at his shadowy figure before making her way up to the door.

"Hey," he said, opening the door for her when she reached the porch.

Nina drew in a sharp breath as she walked through the threshold. Each time she'd been in his home their relationship escalated and she wondered if she'd have the courage this time to tell him exactly how she felt.

They walked in to the living room together, Kevin leading the way to where Nina sat on the couch and curled her legs underneath her with ease. Her head leaned against the back of the couch as Kevin sat down next to her. He was close, his face turned to her.

Nina was quiet, breathing in the scent of him. His deep brown eyes were captivating her, keeping her speechless. He seemed to be just as lost in her eyes. Nina felt his hand lay gently against her leg and she couldn't move.

"Didn't you want to talk about something?" he asked, his voice barely flowing out in a raspy whisper.

She didn't say a word. It wasn't time. She could feel it. Moving slow and cat-like, she slid closer to him and unfolded her legs from underneath her. One leg swung over his lap gracefully and then she was sitting on top of him, facing him closer than before. She saw the look of panic in his eyes as she let her hands hold his face. Kevin shifted underneath her causing Nina to inch closer to his chest, her wide-spread legs hiking higher on his lap. He grabbed her arms and she feared he would push her away. Instead, his grip tightened and he pulled her closer to him, pressing his lips against hers forcefully. Nina melted in his arms as they left her biceps and wrapped around her completely.

A moan growled deep in Kevin's chest as Nina began to grind against him while their mouths meshed. Kevin's hands roamed upwards and made their way into Nina's hair. His hands didn't stop moving, feeling each inch of her; the small of her back still bound in the corset, the nape of her neck, her spindly arms and her strong thighs that were squeezing him around the waist. Nina was growing wilder with each new place his hands traveled. When he gripped her waist, their lips separated.

Nina stared at him, mouth open, breathing heaving. He looked at her closely and she saw his face soften into a tender smile. She wanted to ask him what was wrong but she was too busy thinking about how badly she wanted him to kiss her again.

Kevin's head tilted slightly to one side as he took in her features with a dreamy look in his eyes.

She was at peace not telling him. Just having him in her arms was enough. After everything it had taken to get them to this point, she was happy just being with him. There was no reason to make it more complicated. She could keep the rest to herself for a little while longer.

Nina's open mouth curled into a huge grin. His mouth copied hers and they shared beaming smiles. Her hands clasped behind his neck as she giggled and pulled herself back to him, joining her lips to his once more.

CHAPTER THIRTY-SEVEN

NOVEMBER

Looking up from her notes, she caught his eye and was unable to hide her delight. The rest of the class that Monday morning was either taking notes or pretending to as Kevin lectured. He stood at the front of the class, perched on an empty desk, looking over the room full of students but his eyes kept coming back to Nina. They'd been locking eyes and sharing smiles the entire morning. Nina even winked at him once.

"The test will be …" Kevin's voice trailed off as he caught another quick glimpse of Nina with her head down and her pencil absentmindedly placed between her lips. He let out a tiny puff of a laugh. "What was I saying?"

A boy in the front row gave Kevin a look and grumbled. "The test."

Kevin's hand reached up and ran through his dark hair as he beamed when Nina looked up to see him staring at her again, the rest of the class oblivious.

"Right, the test is, uh, next week."

The bell rang at his very last word and his students shot up and to the door. All but one.

Once again Nina and Kevin were alone in his classroom. Nina stood up from her seat and made her way to him at the front of the room. She thought of saying something but all that came out was a goofy grin. Kevin smiled back like a giddy boy. She couldn't help but pull her bottom lip between her teeth. He reached out his hand and let it slip into hers. They watched as their fingers interlaced. It was a feeling neither of them expected would be so gratifying. Their thumbs danced with one another for a moment until Nina pulled away giving Kevin a look. Her head was dipped down and she stared up at him through black lashes.

She had to go to class. The bell was about to ring. Students would be coming in to Kevin's room any minute. Their moment was lost. As Nina bent down to pick up her bag, the first of Kevin's second period students walked in. She turned to breeze past the student, unable to give Kevin the goodbye she wished and she locked eyes with the boy in the doorway.

"Nina …"

The boy's voice was deeper than she remembered and he'd grown a few inches but his hair was still the same sandy blonde and his eyes were the same emerald green. His skin had taken nicely to a tan. The kind of tan someone gets in Arizona but never in Wexley Falls.

He was staring at her with a sparkle in his eyes and she watched as he came toward her and put his arms out for an embrace. Nina tensed, feeling Kevin's eyes on her back as the boy put his arms around her. She kept her distance in the awkward hug and shrugged out of it quickly.

"Todd. What are you doing here?" she managed to speak finally.

He grinned at her. "I'm back."

Most of Kevin's second period class had come in to the room and were taking their seats as Nina stood stunned between Kevin and Todd Dawson, waiting to wake up. She looked back at Kevin then to Todd. Her head shook back and forth in disbelief and then avoidance as she refused to accept this strange reality. She pushed passed Todd and headed toward her second period class.

"I have class," she muttered to herself.

Nina stormed into the auditorium where Mrs. Benson was watching one of the group performances rehearse on stage while the rest of the class sat in the audience. Her eyes scanned the large space until she saw James talking to his group mate, Nick Fields. Her feet pounded against the burgundy carpeting until she was standing next to him, waiting for him to look up.

"Hey honey, what's up?" he asked, both he and Nick staring up at her.

She felt her face growing hot as she let the vision of Todd Dawson staring at her in that classroom fill her mind. Her breath shot out of her nostrils in quick, forceful spurts and her hands balled into fists.

"Nick, could you give us a minute?" James said in a sugary sweet voice.

Nick took the cue and moved to another row of seats, giving Nina a worried look before heading on his way.

She sat and stared forward, her anger still seething.

"What happened? Is this about Halloween? I'm sorry I left you but this guy was super hot and we ended up making out behind the restaurant and …" She cut him off in the middle of his rant with a growl.

"Todd. Dawson."

"Uh, what about him?" James whispered his question in fear.

"He's back."

James's mouth gaped as he searched her profile with his eyes. Her mouth twisted and her jaw clicked. Mrs. Benson shouted from the front of the stage for the next group to come up and do their blocking and a run through of their song. It was James' group. Nina caught Mrs. Benson's eye wondering if she needed to be at the piano. She waved her off and Nina was relived.

Nina shooed James with her hand, knowing he had to perform. She'd be okay by herself for a few minutes.

Nina's mind was reeling. Todd coming back was going to be one more obstacle for she and Kevin to navigate. Things had just started getting easier with Kevin. They'd crossed a line and changed the game. She was in such a giddy, honeymoon state with him and now Todd was back to ruin it all.

"Hey babe," the voice behind her sent a chill up her spine. She whipped her head around to see Todd sitting in the row behind her with his arms outstretched as if he had supermodels sitting on both sides. She was beginning to remember everything about him that ever made her cringe. Like the fact he treated every chair like a throne.

"Are you cutting class on your first day back?" she asked, letting her eyes squint at him viciously.

"Just a quick bathroom break. Thought I'd come see if we could talk some more," his smile was charming but Nina knew better.

"What happened to Arizona?" she asked, figuring if he wanted to talk he'd have to answer some questions.

"I didn't like living with my mom as much as I thought I would," he leaned forward, letting his elbows rest on his knees and his hands fold. "Plus, I missed you."

Nina laughed so loud most of the students in the auditorium turned and shot her a look.

"That's really something, Todd. You missed me. I'll bet you did. In fact, I bet you wrote me a letter every day and they all got lost in the mail. Or did you have my phone number stored in your cell wrong? What's your excuse going to be?" she spat.

He sat straight up in his seat and pointed a finger in her face. "You didn't call me either, Nina. It goes both ways."

"And that should speak volumes to you," she said before turning back to the stage taking in a deep breath. She stayed still, feeling sick as his hand pulled back her dark hair away from her face and he leaned in to her ear.

"Well, I'm back Nina. You might just grow accustomed to me again."

CHAPTER THIRTY-EIGHT

Nina felt her cell phone vibrating in her pocket as she stopped at her locker before lunch. She pulled it out and secretly took at peek at the text message. A smile stretched across her lips when she saw who it was from.

Know any top secret hiding places in this school? I want to have lunch with you.

Nina pondered the question and thought of the perfect place. She sent him the directions quickly before giving herself a look in the mirror. Nina saw James walking toward her from the corner of her eye. She needed an excuse fast. He reached her and slumped against the locker next to her looking pitiful.

"I have *three* classes with Todd frickin' Dawson. Three!" he griped.

Nina let out a stifled laugh and smoothed some cherry gloss over her lips.

"I have to do this thing during lunch. You can sit with Nick, yeah?" she asked.

James eyed her. "What kind of *thing*?"

With one hand fluffing her hair and the other shutting her locker, she shrugged at him before scooting past him.

"A thing for English." *Shit*, she thought, *way to be obvious.*

James' ears had perked up at that. "With Mr. Sexy?"

Nina rolled her eyes and tried to will the redness from her cheeks. Nick came running up behind James and slowed right before he reached them. He stood behind James and very precisely flicked James' ear. James turned around in one quick spin and the two carried on with a play fight.

"Okay Nina, have fun with your boring English thing. See you in seventh period," James said before strolling off to the lunch room with Nick.

Nina nearly laughed out loud. *That was rather easy,* she thought. She took off in the opposite direction toward the performing arts hallway, careful not to run or seem as though she was going somewhere she wasn't allowed. The door was open when she got there and she glanced around before entering. Kevin's head popped out from behind a corner when she stepped all the way into the room.

It was a small room hidden in the corner of the music hallway. The walls were papered with a yellow-stained floral print that looked like it might have pre-dated the rest of the school. There were two vanities, complete with cushioned benches and huge, light bulb outlined mirrors. At one time it had been where the girls got ready for the musicals and school plays. With the senior choir alone now topping out at roughly fifty girls and the school productions getting bigger each year, Mrs. Benson put the room out of use a few years ago.

Kevin stood looking around curiously as Nina snuck in and shut the door behind her with a Cheshire grin.

"I don't have much to offer you …" he said, his words trailing as he held out the contents of a packed lunch.

Nina giggled. "What, no four course meal?"

Kevin stood awkwardly for a moment, looking around the room. Nina happily took a seat on the floor but tried not to think about the last time it had been cleaned.

"Is this a good idea?" Nina asked as Kevin took a seat on the floor across from her, his legs folding under him. He started dividing his sack lunch between the two of them.

"Terrible idea," he teased. "But what the hell?"

Nina found it somewhat amusing that she wasn't worried. It was funny to her that having a meal with Kevin had become more normal than a meal with her family. She started in on half a turkey sandwich thinking to herself how good it was.

"So who's that guy?" Kevin asked to which Nina looked at him blankly. She knew the question would come sooner or later, she just didn't think it would be this soon.

Nina cleared her throat. "What guy?"

"Todd. The new kid," he spoke in a quiet voice in between bites.

Nina avoided his eyes since she couldn't avoid the topic at hand.

"He's not new. He used to live here and he just moved back. We used to be ... friends."

"Friends." His face looked paler than normal as he repeated her words softly.

"Our dads are old friends so ..." she replied, tucking one side of her hair behind her ear. She caught a glimpse of Kevin nodding as he finished his half of the sandwich.

"You know the senior concert is next week. The one where I close the first act," she said, changing the subject. Kevin let a sweet smile grace his face.

"Is that an invitation?"

"Yeah, I guess it is," she said, watching as his fingertips smoothed over the back of her hand sweetly before linking his fingers with hers.

Chapter Thirty-Nine

A few days later Kevin sipped the last of his beer at The Black Jewel. He put a twenty on the table to cover his meal and a tip. He noticed the crowd was made up of only a handful of people and most were people he'd started to recognize as regulars. He supposed he fit into that category as well.

Nina was sitting at the piano playing some of the standards, singing about every third song. He was so happy when he heard her sing. He knew she was aware he was in the audience so when she let a sweet note hang in the air and lifted her eyes to the crowd, he knew it was for him. Though their routine seemed like it was developing into a sort of normalcy, he was still unsure what they had. It felt big. It felt right. He was finally starting to feel at peace, a feeling he hadn't had in a very long time.

It had been years since his chest didn't ache with tension waiting for the next big blow. His own senior year of high school had probably been the last time he felt completely at ease. His father, not yet ill, surprised him with a trip in the middle of the school year for no reason. They went camping along the Appalachian Trail. It wasn't the beauty of the land or the serenity that gave Kevin the calm feeling. It was his father. Sitting in silence with him. While it might seem like torture to anyone else, Nina specifically, to Kevin it had been wonderful.

His dad told him story after story about his time spent traveling the globe and all of the adventures he'd enjoyed on that trip. It was the first time Kevin thought about writing it all down, writing an account of his father's amazing life.

Kevin headed for the door as Nina finished her set. Pulling out his cell phone, he typed a quick message as he picked up the pace toward his home.

You were great tonight. Meet me at my place?

Sasha was waiting by the door with a swinging tail when Kevin walked into his house. Not since the first day he moved in had he looked around the house only to be flooded with memories of growing up there. He tried to change the look of the house enough to keep him from being reminded of the time he'd lived there as a kid. But now it was different. With his father having been on his mind all day, suddenly Kevin was overcome with grief. Thinking about that trip and the rest of the year before he left for college was painful. Thinking about how much he wanted his father back, how he craved that time, was nearly unbearable. He wondered if his dad would've liked Nina. Would he have approved? Kevin wondered if his father were alive would he have told him already.

Staggering through the kitchen, he opened the back door to let Sasha outside. When the cold air wafted over him, he couldn't keep from crying.

Nina parked in Kevin's driveway and headed to the front door with a spring in her step. She'd read his text before changing back into her school clothes and she was giddy with the thought of seeing him.

The door opened and she called out his name in a song.

She didn't see him or the dog anywhere so she headed back to the kitchen. And that's when she saw him. He was standing with his hands pressed against the kitchen table and his back turned to her but she could see a slight tremble roll through his body.

"Hey," he said with a crack in his voice.

Nina rushed to him without thinking and tried to look at him but he avoided her stare.

"What's wrong?" she asked.

Kevin scrubbed at his eyes and sighed heavily. "It's nothing. It's stupid."

He moved past her and leaned against the island for a moment, his breath still quaking, slowing down. Nina followed him and hopped up on the island putting herself in front of him, their eyes at the same level. She put her hands on his face tenderly and looked into his deep chocolate eyes. They were glassy and bloodshot. Clearly he'd been crying.

"What is it? You're scaring me," she said.

He cocked his head to one side and stared at her forlornly, his brow tense, his red eyes heavy.

"It's my dad's birthday today," he said quietly.

A sad sigh came from Nina's lips before she could stifle it. She had no idea what to say. Kevin had only mentioned his father a handful of times and she still knew little about the circumstances. She saw the light in Kevin's eyes every time he mentioned the elder Mr. Reed.

Never having lost someone, she didn't know the right thing to say.

"It's stupid. It's just a day," he mumbled, rubbing gruffly at his face again before pushing his hand through his hair.

"No. No it isn't," she said clearly.

He moved in between her legs and they instinctively wrapped around his waist. His silence was killing her. She wanted him to be able to tell her anything. She wanted to help him when he was sad or hurting. That was what having someone to hold was all about, right? Unexpectedly he pulled her close to his chest and smoothed his hands down her back, the feeling wonderful. It was a simple hug but the comfort it gave Nina was indescribable. She only hoped

Kevin felt the same.

"Do you want to talk about it?" she whispered into his chest.

He started to speak without pulling away from her. "I just miss him," he choked.

Nina tightened her arms around his back, squeezing him before pulling back and meeting his eyes. She saw him chewing on the inside of his cheek, struggling to keep from crying.

"I just want to know if he would've been proud of me. If he would've thought ... I was a good person," he stammered and averted his eyes.

She felt the wind knocked out of her for an instant. Was he saying what she thought? Was he worried about whether his father would've damned him for their relationship? Her stomach twisted into knots. There was no way she could say anything to him about how he felt. She had no idea what he was going through. She had no idea how she would feel if she lost her father.

Her fingertips rose again and she barely touched his jaw line. His mouth relaxed and his lips parted as he looked back at her.

"You *are* a good person. You're a good man," she said firmly.

Kevin nodded absently and leaned forward, kissing her gently before wrapping his arms around her again. Nina nuzzled back into the warmth of his chest, her arms around his back and her legs around his waist as she sat on the edge on the cool countertop. She breathed in the subtle scent of his cologne and wished for things to stay the way they were forever. She couldn't put her finger on what the moment should be labeled. It was different from any other exchange they'd had. Nina felt Kevin kiss the top of her head.

"I'm really glad you're here," he said in a trembling tone. He grew heavier in her embrace and she heard him quietly crying against her.

She felt his sadness ripple through her and she ached for him. There was far more than lust between them. It was a closeness Nina had never felt with anyone. *Intimate.* That's what the moment was. It only made it clearer to her that the words she'd been thinking were true. She wanted so badly to say it to comfort him but a quiver in her stomach kept her from doing so. Nina imagined he would know soon enough and deep down, she believed he felt the same way.

CHAPTER FORTY

Nina dragged the soft bristled brush over her cheek and saw the pale pink shade liven up her skin. Her worries made her even paler than she normally was. The blood seemed drained from her. For a moment she stared blankly into the mirror, letting the bright vanity bulbs the size of softballs wash her in sparkling light. Her lips were painted soft pink, her eyes rimmed in black, the false eyelashes already beginning to feel uncomfortably stiff against her eyelids.

James appeared in the mirror behind her, popping his head around the door she'd made sure to pull shut earlier. He smiled at her at warmly. He was clad in a black suit and tie and his hair was slicked back and parted on the right. A giggle escaped Nina's lips at the sight of him. The perfectly tailored suit showed just how skinny he was. He rolled his eyes at her, shutting the door behind him.

"I've been looking everywhere for you. Why are you getting ready in here instead of in the band room with the rest of the girls? No one ever uses this tiny dressing room. I can understand why, too. It smells like 1982 in here," James' made a face as he looked around the small room. It was true. A musty smell had absorbed into the walls. Nina felt like being alone as she prepared for her performance. Plus, she wanted the comfort of being in the room where she'd spent time with Kevin. Maybe it would somehow give her the assurance she needed to sing her song in front of everyone. She glanced at herself in the mirror again and smiled brightly.

"This room makes me feel like a star," she teased.

The truth was Nina was more nervous about this show than she let on. She'd been singing in front of audiences for months now but tonight was different. It was special.

"I think Nick is going to come out to me tonight," James blurted, causing Nina to turn to him with wide, inquisitive eyes.

"It's kind of obvious but he's shy. Something's been going on between us since we started working together in our group."

"What kind of something, James?" Nina pressed.

James ran a soft hand over his gelled hair as he stared at himself in the lit mirror. "I think we almost kissed last night when we walked out to our cars."

Nina's mouth dropped over-dramatically as she imagined James would have done had it been her scandalous confession.

"Well, go get 'em tiger," she kidded him.

As their laughter subsided, Nina took notice of the clock. It was almost show time. She had to suffer through playing the piano for all of the other performances before she got to go on. Last.

Someone rapped on the door and it opened before James or Nina could grant the stranger entry. Nick. His head poked in and the moment he saw James, he rolled his eyes and sighed relief.

"Thank God you're in here. I've been looking all over for you," Nick huffed, stepping in just enough to grab James' hand and pull him out the door. James turned before being yanked completely into the hall and smiled knowingly at Nina and blew her a kiss for good luck.

Nina's last quiet moments were spent fixing her hair a few more times, smoothing out the silver dress she wore and layering on another coat of lip gloss. Then she was off to the pit to take her seat at the piano, still unable to name the tremble in her gut. Her mind was elsewhere as she played through each song easily. She was in a trance when Mrs. Benson tapped her on the shoulder to take over. That meant one more song and Nina would be up.

"You're gonna nail it," Mrs. Benson whispered, giving Nina a sweet, encouraging smile.

The audience whopped and hollered for James, Nick and the other boys as Mrs. Benson played out the end of their song. James beamed at the microphone, eating up the crowd's reaction. Nina caught the subtle glance James and Nick shared as they made their way into the wings when the curtain came down. James looked as though he was going to jump out of his skin as he twirled around and grabbed Nina's shoulders, spinning her as well.

"I love you, break a leg," he whispered in her ear before kissing her cheek.

He turned on his heels and headed down the back hall where Nick was waiting for him when he turned back to Nina and whispered.

"Professor Hot is dead center. Can't miss him. He's right in front of Todd Dawson."

The news put a pin-prick in her head and butterflies in her stomach. The orchestra boomed down in the pit signaling Nina to take her place on the stage before the curtain rose. Her steps were careful as she moved, her head reeling. The microphone was at her rosy lips when the red velvet curtain rose swiftly, revealing a spotlight and a packed house.

Her stomach continued to flutter as her eyes adjusted to the glowing light and then she saw him. Kevin's lips stretched wide across his face as his eyes locked with hers. She took a breath and sang out the song she'd written for him.

"It was everything it should've been, everything it would've been, had we met another day. You're so charming and amusing, see. Blinding me with fantasy, but the cruelest joke's on me."

Nina's eyes never left Kevin's and she sang only to him. And just as it happened in the halls and in the classroom so many times before, every other person in the room faded away. Only Kevin remained. The music built and the look on Kevin's face made it clear he knew she was only looking at him and that he recognized the words as her poem. But he'd yet to hear the rest. The part she wrote hoping it would be true. Now that it was she could sing it with pride and power.

"When it's meant to be, it's meant to be. It feels right and easy. Don't let me go, just say you'll stay, all I need is one more day."

Her hands gripped the microphone and she noticed she was no longer shaking. Her voice ripped out of her as she continued and the music hit its crescendo.

"Can I wait, can I be strong, can I change your mind with a song? I know you're scared, but you've got to choose. Baby we've got nothing left to lose."

Her hand reached out to him in her passion-fueled performance. Through the blinding spotlight, all she could see was him.

"Let's be everything we could've been, everything we should've been, had we met another day."

CHAPTER FORTY-ONE

The curtain fell hiding her from him in a moment when he wanted nothing more than to see her face. She'd singled him out of the crowd and told him with her eyes that he was the one. Every moment they'd shared so far had brought them here. A certain excitement filled him knowing even with her direct gesture toward him, it was still their secret. As far as the rest of the audience knew, even Jeff who sat right next to him, she was just a great performer. But Kevin knew better. She'd been lost in that song and he'd been lost in her eyes.

The first act was finished and the lights in the auditorium came up to a dim glow. He leaned to Jeff and mumbled something about getting some air before scooting his way out of the row of seats and to the back of the theater. The lobby was swarming with people talking and buying concessions and flowers. Kevin swooped in to the shortest line and bought the largest bouquet. They were ridiculously over-priced but it was worth it to him.

With roses in hand, Kevin trekked back to the bustling music hallway where students were running from room to room, some changing their hair, some slipping into different shoes. He tried to blend in, to go unnoticed. Then he saw her as she walked with the grace of a ballerina through the mess of teenagers to the door at the far end of the hall. He watched as she looked left and right before entering then shut the door behind her. She hadn't seen him down the hall from her. He followed quickly behind her and soon he was standing at the door, holding the flowers at his side when he knocked. The students were all filing back into the classrooms and into the stage wings ready for the next half of the show.

His heart jumped when the door opened a crack and then wider, the weight of the door opening it rather than Nina's hand. Kevin peered in more boldly then stepped in and shut the heavy door of the room he had only been in once before. He gasped unexpectedly when he saw her.

She sat on the pillow-topped stool in front of an old style vanity. She was leaning forward, close to the mirror, as she smoothed a tissue over her cheeks, fixing her makeup. However, the most shocking sight was the amount of skin he could see. She'd changed out of her dress and into a black pencil skirt but she hadn't yet put on a blouse. He stood with his back against the door staring dumbly at Nina in her bra and skirt as she pulled on her eyelashes. He'd dreamt of seeing her like this but he never imagined she'd be able to take his breath away.

Nina whipped around when she noticed him in the mirror, the spidery false eyelash left hanging, obstructing her view of him. She folded her arms across her nearly bare chest and stared at him in disbelief. Embarrassment washed over him immediately and he looked away, turning his back to her awkwardly.

"Oh God. I thought you were James. No one knows I'm in here but him. I'm not supposed to be changing in here," Nina laughed the words as she searched the surrounding area for her top.

"I … I saw you come in here. I'm sorry. I can leave," his voice quaked.

He felt her touch him, taking the flowers from his hand that hung limp at his side. He turned to see she'd given up the search for her shirt. She was still half dressed but now she stood before him unabashedly. Kevin tried to keep his breath shallow, to not give away how she was making him pant.

He watched as she brought the flowers up to her face and breathed in the scent of them while staring up at him through her black lashes. Nina pursed her lips and their eyes met as she continued to smell the roses. He felt his brow furrow as he gazed upon her.

"What's wrong?" she asked him.

"You're beautiful," he said with a sigh.

"Why does that make you sad?" she asked, this time her voice fading into a whisper.

"I'm not sad," he said, letting his hand come up and cup her cheek, his thumb running smoothly near her lips. "I'm terrified." Nina instantly dropped the roses to the hard vinyl floor and reached up to take Kevin's face in her hands. His hand fell from her cheek and he hesitantly grasped her waist, his fingers resting on her bare flesh. Both of their heads whipped towards the door as they heard booming applause and the start of a song. The second act had begun.

Nina knew no one was in the hall outside the door and now that Mrs. Benson had started the show without her, no one would be coming by until the end of the show. This was her chance. From the moment Kevin had first Nina kissed her, she'd wanted nothing more than to be with him. Before she could push herself up on her toes to make her lips meet his, Kevin stepped into her causing her to walk backward a few steps until she was pressed up against the vanity counter. The sweet scent of his hot breath near her face made her weak. She looked up at him, waiting for his next move. She thought she would have to be the one making advances, pushing him to break the rules with her. She was wrong.

Kevin snaked one arm around her bare waist and pulled her to him roughly. She instinctively leaned back against the cool mirror and wrapped her legs around his hips, causing her skirt to hike up on her thighs. He leaned in closely, her heart pounded in her ears, every part of her feeling a different emotion.

Their mouths met, fueling the forbidden fire that had burned since that first warm August night. Kevin's hands twisted in her hair and then roamed down the length of her. He caressed her bare back and her neck while their lips moved in harmony. Nina's warm tongue slipped into his mouth and he crushed her lips with the fervor of a man on the brink.

Her hands gripped his solid arms, pulling him closer each time he even slightly pulled away. The tips of her fingers drew lines down his torso until she reached the hem of his shirt. She tugged it over his head and then stared in awe of his physique before pulling him close again. The amazing feeling of skin on skin, being chest to chest made them both stop for a moment.

Nina wanted him to take her, to undress her and give into temptation. She could feel he wanted it too and with one hand, she reached between them and began tugging at the button on his jeans. The zipper slid down with ease and upon hearing the sound, she felt Kevin's hands slid up her thighs and under her skirt. His thumbs hooked around her panties and Nina let a moan fall from her lips, begging for him to tug them down. Kevin heard the tiny noise and stopped quickly, his hands still up her skirt, his breath coming out in huffs.

"What are we doing?" Kevin asked, knowing very well what they were doing.

She smiled dreamily and smoothed her hand over the fabric of his exposed boxers. "Whatever we want."

She felt him pull away and he ran a hand through his mahogany hair, picking up sweat from his brow and dragging it through the strands. His head bent down as he huffed.

"No, not like this. This isn't …" he trailed off, unable to make a point more eloquent than that. Whatever he thought, it didn't matter to

Nina. She wanted him for all the right reasons and nothing should stop them.

"It's okay Kevin. I … I love you." The words finally slipped out. Before she had time to process it, she saw Kevin staring at her blankly.

"What?" his lips stayed parted as he waited for her to respond but Nina dared not repeat herself. She was at her most vulnerable and she knew instantly after she made such a heartfelt confession, he wouldn't be saying them back. She felt sick at her stomach thinking about all the time she'd waited to tell him.

Nina shook her head and let her legs loosen around his hips, sliding limply to either side of him. Her slender hands pushed at his chest and he backed off with the slightest shove from her.

Kevin stood speechless and shirtless in the small dressing area watching as Nina slid off the vanity and scrambled to find her top once more, this time determined. The audience applauded loudly making Nina stop for a moment to look at the door. She yanked her shirt over her head and smoothed it down the front of her. He was still staring at her in disbelief. She went for the door and he stopped her, placing his body in front of her as a block.

"Move please, I—I have to go," the words stumbled through her.

"We have to talk about this," he breathed.

"There's nothing to say, Kevin. Just let me go," she yelled, tears threatening behind her eyes. She pushed passed him and put her hand on the door and he pulled her back around by her shoulders, forcing her to look at him. Her eyes were brimming with tears as she stared up at his confused face.

"You can't …" he started.

Nina shrugged her way out of his grasp and paced back into the small room.

"You have to understand …" he tried again and she cut him off.

"No, *you* understand. We stopped fighting it, we gave in. I gave in and I fell. This is bigger than both of us. It's bigger than this school and this stupid town. I won't apologize and I won't take it back," Nina shouted at him.

His hand reached out to wipe the tears from her face when she slapped his hand away angrily then wiped her tears herself. Kevin stared at her in silence. He stepped to her and Nina recognized the look in his eyes. It was the look he gave her before each time he'd kissed her since that first kiss. It was a look of pain and regret, as if he were telling himself 'no' a thousand times as he bent down to reach her lips.

Nina held up her hand to him and turned her face.

"No. Figure it out, Kevin."

She forced her words, proving to him she was serious. She pushed passed him and flew out the door, leaving him staring at the floor, shattered roses lying beneath his feet.

CHAPTER FORTY-TWO

Nina waited in the wings watching as the finale of her senior concert went on without her. It was fitting, she figured, her life had been going on without her for a while now. She knew enough time had passed for Kevin to have left the dressing room so she headed back that way to gather her things.

She opened the door and was shocked to see Todd standing there waiting patiently for her. He turned at the noise of the door and grinned widely at her. He was the last person she wanted to see. Her makeup was smudged from crying, her clothes were rumpled from her encounter with Kevin and she clearly hadn't made it to the pit for the second act.

"What are you doing here?" she asked as she starting putting her makeup into her bag.

"Don't play coy, Nina," he smirked. "I heard you loud and clear. That's why I'm here," he said, leaning against the vanity she'd just leaned against with Kevin over her.

She continued packing up her things as she tried to figure out what Todd was talking about. *Of course*, she thought. Blinded by not only the spotlight, but her feelings for Kevin, she'd sung out her solo directly to Kevin and even reached for him in the crowd. But who'd been sitting just behind Kevin? Todd Dawson. He must have thought she was singing to him.

"Come on, Todd. It was just a song," she laughed nervously as she put her first act dress on a hanger, avoiding his eyes at all costs.

She felt his hand brush her hair behind one ear and she faced him in amazement. Her eyes fixed on him and she felt anger seething just below the surface. After dealing with Kevin and his boyish flaws, she wasn't in the mood to deal with Todd's lothario act.

"Get out, I have to change," she said sternly.

An even wider, devilishly smile fixed itself on his lips.

"I could stay. It's nothing I haven't seen before," he said.

She glared at him, sadness filling her unexpectedly as she thought about what a shame is was that she wasted her body on Todd when she could have waited for someone she truly loved. She wouldn't think his name though. If she started regretting everything she could've saved for Kevin, she'd drive herself mad. Her head turned slowly and she grabbed the first thing she saw, a can of hairspray. She reared back and chucked it hard at Todd and watched as he ducked just in time. The can hit the floor with a hard smack and Nina noticed the roses Kevin had brought her still laying where they had fallen.

Her voice became a growl. "Get. Out."

Todd's eyes widened, astonished at her behavior. He stood up and walked out muttering under his breath.

"Crazy bitch."

Her hands were shaking as she picked up her bag and began walking to her car without looking back and without waiting on James. The air was cold against her face as she shoved the door open with one push. She heard the howl of the wind and the click of her heels against the snow-cleared pavement and that was all. Though her mind was swimming, her thoughts were unrecognizable. They were screams in her head, not words or feelings, just shouts and flashes.

She climbed into the driver's seat and gripped the steering wheel for a minute, staring forward, letting a calm wash over her. It was more like numbness. Nina drew in a deep breath and blew it out, shutting her eyes. She tried to tell herself everything was going to be all right. When her bag began to vibrate, she looked and saw several missed calls then read the text message Kevin had just sent her.

Please talk to me.

A raging scream came tearing out of Nina's lungs as she let the scene in the dressing room creep back into her mind. Her hand strangled the cell phone tightly before she tossed it out the window, hearing it smack against the pavement. She threw the car into drive and sped home. Pulling into her driveway, a sinking feeling overtook her as she recognized parked next to her house. She shook her head in disbelief as she walked up to the front door. She almost felt like laughing but the threat of tears was still close by.

"Nina? Is that you?" a voice called out to her as she let herself inside. The tall man came toward her and Nina felt stomach acid tickling the back of her throat. She let her eyes examine the man as he came nearer, his faint smile, his tailored suit and the sprinkling of gray hairs at his temples.

"Hi, dad."

Her father pulled her in for a hug and the bile jumped again.

"I'm back just in time for your show tomorrow, isn't that great?" her father said, clearly pleased with himself.

Nina followed him to the kitchen feeling her anger bubbling up inside once again.

"It was tonight. You missed it," Nina spoke without so much as a quiver in her voice.

Her father turned around and cocked his head to one side, grimacing.

"Oh Nina, I got the date wrong. I'll be here for the next one."

His forged regret was easy for Nina to detect. She'd been listening to such let-down speeches her entire life, although they'd become significantly shorter as she grew older. Nina felt her numbness turning into insanity and she stifled a laugh.

He can't even say he's sorry, she thought.

"I'm a senior. There won't be another one. When's your next trip?" she asked.

"Two weeks. I guess I'll miss Thanksgiving with you girls. But then it'll be time for Christmas in Florida with the Dalton's. And then back to the grind, probably London again. Maybe another month or two," he said trying to sound cheery.

Thank God, she thought. Nina had become so accustomed to her father not being around she wasn't sure how the rest of her year might go if she had to learn to live with him again. Especially now that she knew the rest of her year was going to be pretty horrible. Nina tried to keep Kevin's face out of her head but his image was burned into her memory.

"I talked to Jim Dawson on my drive home from the airport," her father started. Nina stared at him blankly, resisting the urge to roll her eyes and vomit.

"Yeah. Todd's back from Arizona. We're not getting back together. Don't even start," Nina spat.

He shrugged silently before Nina turned and walked out of the kitchen without another word, heading up to her bedroom. She heard her father call out a goodnight from somewhere behind her.

Opening the door to her bedroom, she stared at her bed. That was all she wanted, to sleep it all away. She wanted to sleep to forget August, their date and the first day of school. Dream through September and October, forgetting how she'd fallen in love with him and how she foolishly started to believe he was falling in love with her, too. She wanted to let the blinds stay closed and keep the covers pulled high over her head and block out the images of him standing with flowers in his hand. His chiseled face dipping down to kiss her lips. She wanted the scent of him off of her and the sound of his voice to be stripped from her mind. As she climbed into her soft bed, she let the comforter wrap her up tight and as she drifted off to sleep, she saw his bewildered face, having just heard her say the three words. *I love you.*

Chapter Forty-Three

A churning, bubbling in her middle woke Nina with a start. Her stomach growled and she felt a wretched empty feeling inside. She pushed herself up on her elbows and looked around her room. It was dark outside. Nina had awakened a handful of times. Her father had been in her room asking if she was all right at least once and she remembered telling him she was sick. It was a lie but Nina had no intention of going to school when Monday rolled around. The darkness of her room and the comfort of her bed were all she wanted.

Her legs felt wobbly as she set her feet on the floor. Her hand reached over and flicked on the light and her eyes burned and squinted, not prepared for the brightness.

Nina ran a hand through her hair and felt the ratted mess but didn't care what she looked like as she walked out into the hall and headed down to the kitchen. The house was mostly dark but a light was on in the living room. She paid it no mind. All she wanted was something to eat and the kitchen was getting closer and closer.

The lights inside the refrigerator were shockingly bright against her eyes but she managed to rummage around and find a few things she wanted. She piled the mismatch of ingredients onto a plate and headed back towards the stairs.

"Hey," she heard from behind her.

Nina turned and saw James looking at her with a fear in his eyes she'd never seen. She raised her chin at him and put a piece of cheese into her mouth before turning back toward the steps.

"Nina, wait," he called out, hopping forward to get to her.

She looked at him vacantly as he searched her face with worried green eyes. He grabbed her hand before she could turn away and led her into the living room, Nina's brow furrowed in weak protest as she followed him.

"How do you feel?" he asked, coxing her to sit on the couch.

Nina did so and continued to eat, shrugging and bobbing her head only to please him.

"Well, how do you feel bad?" he pressed.

Nina stared at him, blankly.

"Just tired," she croaked.

"Just tired? Tired. Not your head or your stomach or your throat? Just tired?"

Nina looked at him square in the eye for a split second then bit off the end of a strawberry that had been on her plate, tempting her stomach.

"Is this about Todd?" a whisper came out of James.

"Why would this be about Todd?" Nina's voice rose.

"Well when you missed the whole week he ..."

Nina cut him off. "A week?"

James stared at her cautiously, "Yeah, sweetie. You missed this week of school. Tomorrow is Saturday. I've come by every day but you haven't come out of your room."

Nina remembered her father coming in her room a few times but it didn't seem like it had been that long.

"I'm fine. I'm awake and I'm eating so I'm fine," she said, convincing herself more than James.

"Good, I'm glad you're up. You had us all worried."

"Including Todd?" she asked.

"Yeah, he told me you freaked out on him at the concert. I just thought maybe you were having a hard time dealing with him being back. If that's the case, it's nothing to be ashamed of," James' mouth twisted into a sympathetic grin.

"It's not about him. It's not about anyone … anything. I guess my body just needed the rest." Her eyes avoided him and she stood cueing James to leave.

He stood with a stretch and patted her arm sweetly. "You've been hitting it pretty hard these past few weeks. I picked up your homework and put it on your desk. It's quite a pile."

Nina smiled. "That should make for an awesome weekend."

James was standing in the doorway, ready to leave yet still eyeing Nina carefully. She knew her grey eyes were puffy with the remnants of sleep. Nina silently prayed he wouldn't ask her if she'd been crying. Her eyes burned bad enough from the amount of tears she'd shed into her pillows. James gave her another weak attempt at a smile and walked out into the night.

Nina went back up to her room, having her fill of human contact. Her mind was still grasping at the concept she'd been in her dark cave for an entire week when the thought crept in. An entire week of Kevin's class, missed. What had he thought? She damned herself as soon as she pondered it but she did nonetheless. She'd been trying so hard to keep his name, image, and voice, among other things, out of her head while she hid under her blankets. But now as her mind began to work normally, he was starting to pop up everywhere.

The computer desk at the far end of her room had, as James said, a high stack of papers and her school books on it. She took a seat at the desk, not interested in sleep at the moment but needing another way to distract her mind from the thoughts of self-loathing. She began looking through her assignments. None of them seemed too challenging but the quantity sure scared her.

She was shuffling through papers, worksheets and notes from

different teachers when his handwriting caught her eye.

Nina covered her mouth to stifle her sobs. There was no doubt in her mind this particular note, in a closed envelope with her name scrawled on the front, was personal. It had nothing to do with missed work from his class. She quickly tore the envelope in half and then in half again before running for the bathroom. With her back against the closed door, she breathed in deep. The urge to vomit had gone as quickly as it came and now she stood in the bathroom with tears rolling down her face. She moved to the shower, starting a steady stream of water from the head and as soon as the temperature was right, she peeled off her pajamas and climbed in.

The water roared in her ears and was lukewarm against her body. Her eyes stayed slammed shut as she continued to let tears fall. Her body convulsed, her breaths chokes and gasps as she stood unmoving under the raining shower head. With her hair plastered to the sides of her face, her mouth gaping and her limps overcome by trembles, Nina hugged her arms tight around herself and slid down the tile wall before finally taking a seat in the tub. She pulled her knees to her chest, let out a few more sobs and waited for the water to wash away her pain.

She only had two days until she would see him again.

Chapter Forty-Four

Kevin's mind was filled with the chatters and whispers of the students coming through his door, the noise of them slumping down in their seats and unzipping their backpacks thunderous in his ears. He welcomed the random sounds rather than his own sullen thoughts. He was beginning to feel like there was no hope for him. Maybe Nina would transfer to a different school and he would be left wondering would could've happened if he'd only been honest and brave and said the words back.

With his back to his class, writing on the board what they'd be discussing, he heard the shrill sound of the bell and turned quickly. His eyes instinctively darted to the back row. Nina's seat. He drew in a sharp breath at the sight of her. Blinking to make sure she wasn't a hallucination, he stared at her. She however had her head turned toward the door and her eyes wandered every which way but toward him.

He took a moment to collect his thoughts before he started the lesson. Trying to be casual, he went to his desk to be closer to her, to view her better. She looked tired and angry. A sort of scowl was etched on her face as she kept her eyes moving anyway but toward him. The class was waiting for him to start and he finally forced himself to begin where he managed to get through his lecture and leave plenty of time for the class to work on their assignments, giving him quiet time. Time to think. And time to stare at her.

He caught her eye just once when she let her guard down and just as suddenly as they were locked, her jaw clenched and she whipped her head the other way. After that, he watched the clock, the wait excruciating. He thought of the way he'd felt on the first day of school when his anger kept him hot the entire hour of class, waiting for the moment when she'd be out of his sight. Oh how the tables had turned.

The bell rang and Kevin exhaled loudly before saying goodbye to the mass of students. Nina shot up out of her seat and headed for the door as well. He was so used to her waiting around for him, watching her change the rules flustered him.

"Nina? Can I talk to you?"

She turned to him with a tight jaw and a wrinkle in her forehead.

"About your absences?" he pressed.

"Right." He finally heard her voice, weak and pained. She was shaking her head and digging through her bag before shoving a stack of papers at him.

"That should cover it," she whispered.

They were alone in the room, as usual. Kevin took her assignments and set them on his desk with a sigh. Of course she'd done the makeup work. But he knew she wouldn't be talking to him today. He'd have to give her more time. Maybe he'd never bring it up again. He nodded absently and opened his desk drawer, grabbing something for her.

"Here," he said, handing her the object slowly.

Nina reached out, her face twisted in confusion as she took her scarred cell phone from Kevin's grasp.

"I found it in the parking lot."

"When?" she asked.

Kevin's heart leapt at the sound the crack in her voice made.

"When I came looking for you."

Nina scoffed. "Well thanks."

She started toward the door and Kevin's mind was paralyzed.

"Did you get my note?" he whispered.

She turned back suddenly.

"I burned it," she spat.

He watched her grit her teeth at him again and his insides ached. His eyes lowered and he nodded in shame then saw her leave. His hand reached up and stroked at his brow while he closed his eyes in pain.

Chapter Forty-Five

December

Nina forced herself to wake up as she done for the past few weeks. She dragged herself out of bed and into the shower, to her closet, to the car. She did the same thing each day like a zombie, exactly the same way. Kevin managed to take the hint a few weeks prior and he hadn't tried talking to her since.

Though time had passed, her wounds still felt fresh every time she saw his face. She noticed his eyes were growing steadily darker, with deeper bags underneath them. They probably shared a common theme at night. Stare at the ceiling for a few hours, roll over and stare at the wall for another hour then fall asleep only to be rudely awakened by the alarm just an hour, sometimes minutes, later.

She looked at herself in the mirror and sighed before heading downstairs to leave for school. It was the last day of school before Winter break. She had two finals to take then she'd be done with school for two weeks. After school she'd be packing her things to accompany James on their family's annual Christmas getaway to Florida. Nina always hated missing the Christmas Day snow in Wexley Falls but this year she was glad to be getting away.

Nina took a deep breath before walking into room B100. Sometimes it seemed like she never left. Each time she sat down, all of the memories from before came flooding back to her. From the first day of school to the countless days she and Kevin eyed each other secretly. Even the time they stood wordlessly feeling each other in the dark. Now all of that seemed so long ago.

Kevin handed out the final not looking at Nina as he did so. For the first time since their fight, Nina felt sorry for him. It came on suddenly, just a slight pinch in her stomach. She'd been having long conversations with herself, trying to think of what she should say to him. At other times she thought she never wanted to talk to him again. But each time she remembered their encounter in the dressing room she couldn't help but let her mind stay fixed on what she'd told him. *Figure it out.* And then she thought maybe he had figured it out and she should let him plead his case.

When the bell rang the students leapt from their seats with more enthusiasm than normal. Only a few more hours until break, then only one more semester until freedom. Nina waited, putting her books in her bag slowly, something she hadn't done in so long it felt strange.

Glancing to her side, Nina saw Kevin at his desk with his head down. He was staring intently at the stack of tests in front of him. Nina also saw his hands were balled into fists, his knuckles growing white.

She wanted to talk but when she opened her mouth, nothing came out. She didn't know what to say to even break the silence. Maybe she should just leave. Then Kevin looked up at her, his eyes piercing right through her.

"Hi," she squeaked.

His face softened. "Hello."

Nina let out a heavy sigh. She was still so angry and yet his face warmed her heart unintentionally.

"I was just wondering if you felt like talking."

His brow lifted and he blew out a gust of air from his lips. She watched as he instinctively glanced at the door before his hands relaxed and one moved up to grip the back of his neck as he looked in thought.

"Nina, I've thought a lot about us. I feel like that's all I've been doing lately but I still don't know what the right thing is to say."

She walked to him slowly and leaned against his desk casually.

"Say how you really feel," she said trying to coax it from him gently.

Nina saw him open his mouth with the threat of words approaching but nothing came. His eyes lowered, avoiding her before he actually worked up the courage to speak.

"It's not right. I know it's more complicated than that but there's only one realistic option. To end it."

Her heart felt strangled and her mouth went dry. It wasn't that she expected him to propose marriage or even to profess love but she didn't think he'd make it sound so final. So matter of fact. There were plenty of other options but he was too much of a coward to even think of them.

"That's bullshit," she snarled.

"Nina, come on …"

"No! You're just saying that because it's what you think your friends and Mr. and Mrs. Benson and … your father would say," though her voice was hushed, the iciness of her tone was clear.

"You didn't know my father, Nina. Watch what you say next," he warned.

"I know enough. About twenty pages short of what you'd have the world know."

Her body became ridged against the side of his desk, no longer leaning but steadying herself, careful not to be knocked over by her own rage.

Kevin's eyes lit up with fury, nearly matching Nina's. She instantly regretted her cruel words and the low she had stooped to. But she wasn't satisfied with his answer and she wanted another one.

Kevin stared at her shaking his head. "Jesus, you're seventeen. Never mind the fact that I'd lose my job. It's a felony."

His words kicked her in the stomach. She clutched her abdomen and lowered her head as the wind was expelled from her lungs in one breathy gust. Her eyes started to sting, a warning tears were on the way. The inner battle began with her mind screaming at her eyes not to cry, not until she was out of his sight. She refused to let him see her cry again.

Her head whipped to him and her eyes squinted, locking on him viciously.

"Sex? Right. Because *that's* was this is about," she picked up her bag and started for the door, tears fast on their way. But she turned back to him, to his stunned face. His handsome, magnificent face.

"You're an idiot," she choked before hurrying to the hall and letting the tears flow.

CHAPTER FORTY-SIX

Her gray eyes drifted in and out watching the tide rolling toward her then away from her as she squished her red lacquered toes deeper into the white sand and let out a sigh. It was morning, the day before Christmas, and she was sitting on the beach while her family and James and his family slept in the multiple villas they'd rented for two weeks of winter vacation. Nina didn't know what time it was but she knew she was waiting to watch the sun rise. It was early.

The trip had been uneventful thus far, mostly consisting of James and Nina taking off by themselves making sure to stay far away from their parents and Greta and her boyfriend, Blake. On the first day Nina made a point to complain as much as possible about Greta being allowed to bring Blake along until James reminded her that the year before she'd brought Todd, a memory she had succeeded at forgetting.

Even with all of the books and gossip magazines she had to read and the soothing sounds of the ocean, there was one thing Nina couldn't stop thinking about. She'd tried so hard to leave her thoughts in Wexley Falls but they'd followed her without her permission. She brought a hand up to wipe the few silent tears that were sliding down her cheek as she mindlessly watched the morning tide. With each crashing wave, she got a flash of him. A moment they'd shared or his voice in her head saying something sweet or silly.

Each time the water moved away from her, she was hit with a memory of Kevin pulling away, telling her no. She looked out onto the horizon and saw the slight changes in the sky. Deep blue was suddenly flecked with purples and pinks. It wouldn't be long before orange and red bled in and the yolk orb of the sun would begin its ascent.

With the crashing waves and her own tormenting thoughts flooding her mind, she didn't hear James coming up behind her where he took a seat next to her on the sand, pajama clad with pillow lines marking his face. James was silent for a moment, taking in the beauty of the sea alongside her.

Then he nudged her. "Merry Christmas Eve," he croaked his first words of the day.

Nina smiled but didn't look at him. Another wave crashed and the tide swept out and she burst into tears.

His arms instantly wrapped around her and squeezed her tight. He waited, letting her cry out as hard as she needed to, as she convulsed against his body. Nina continued to hear the sea mock her but the warmth of James' hand sweeping over her back tenderly was bringing her out of it. She pulled back from him slowly as her sobs lessened. Staring into his green eyes, filled with worry, she knew she could tell him.

"I should have told you a long time ago," she whispered.

"What is it?"

Nina wiped her face with the backs of her hands and drew in a deep breath in preparation. She realized she'd never said any of it out loud aside from with Kevin. "That guy from this summer. I kept seeing him, sort of. Secretly. But things are really screwed up right now and I … I," she shook her head trying not to believe what had really happened.

"Not that I don't think you can be sneaky but when exactly are you seeing this guy? I think I would have noticed," he mused timidly.

Her eyes went blank as she looked James in the face. "You did."

James was silent. He searched her face for some hint of a joke, some clue she was just honing in on her inner actress and not being serious. But there was no sign of trickery.

"Oh my God. Mr. Reed."

Her chin quivered again and James pulled her back into his arms. She told him everything.

The sun was glowing just above the surf by the time the entire truth was out. James listened quietly, nodding his head and rubbing Nina's back as she spilled her secrets. Her tears subsided but the quake in her voice was still ever present, her nerves getting the better of her as she told him the baffling story. When she finished, her eyes met James' waiting for his response.

"Say something," she pleaded quietly.

James let out a sigh and stared out into the water for a moment. "I'm sorry you've been dealing with this alone."

"I wouldn't say I've been *dealing* with it at all."

He glanced back at her, noticing they were in the same position, knees pulled up, bare feet in the sand.

"I know I'm not always serious and I know I made jokes but if I would have known …" his voice trailed off with another heavy sigh.

Nina's lips pressed together tightly, the sun now bathing her skin in delicate orange.

"Nina, you know I'm not the one who'll tell you who to be with. But I think maybe you should follow his lead and take a step back from this. It's a serious situation and it has the potential to go very badly for the both of you. Maybe ending it isn't such a bad thing," James said, his voice wavering as he spoke.

She knew he had a point. It was something she'd been thinking about since the beginning. But there was one thing that kept her from holding onto that rationality.

"I know," she said, turning to him letting another slow tear fall absently. "But I love him."

CHAPTER FORTY-SEVEN

Holiday music rang throughout the Benson's home, bells and violins along with the wholesome voices of the nineteen fifties. Kevin sat on the window seat in the living room staring dully into the Christmas tree, watching the rotation of the twinkle patterns the lights went through. He was in no mood for a party, no mood for Jennifer and her high intensity smile and holiday cheer. Kevin could only imagine the look of disdain on his face as he avoided his own gaze reflecting in the colorful Christmas bulbs.

Jeff came toward him, through the crowd of people Kevin didn't know, with two drinks in his hands and no quicker than he offered it to Kevin, it was gone.

"Whoa, drink much?" Jeff teased.

Kevin glared at him and before he could reply, a squeal came out of the other room.

"Oh my God Lynn! I'm so happy for you!" Jennifer screeched. Jeff and Kevin shared a look then listened as Jennifer addressed the entire party.

"Everyone, my good friend Lynn just got engaged! Let's have a toast to Lynn and Tom." Jennifer raised her glass and Lynn raised her left hand, showing off a glittering new diamond. The party guests toasted and clapped, sickening Kevin's stomach.

"Well that was fast. She and I went on a date like four months ago," Kevin muttered under his breath. Jeff chuckled and took a drink after raising his glass only because Jennifer's eyes were fixed on him.

Kevin stared at Lynn and whoever this Tom person was as they held onto each other lovingly, smiling and flashing the ring. She looked happy and Kevin was jealous of the feeling.

"What's your problem?" Jeff asked, giving Kevin a nudge.

Kevin stood up and grimaced at his cousin. "Guess I just don't have the holiday spirit."

He made his way to the back door, grabbing his coat and stepping out onto the deck. No one was outside, though remnant smoke hung in the air as if someone had just been there. It had snowed all week and close to a foot was left stacked on the wooden planks of the deck. Kevin didn't mind the cold. He barely felt it through his wool coat.

His breath showed in the air and he suddenly imagined himself on the beach with Nina.

Shaking his head, he immediately damned himself for the thought but they just kept coming. He thought about how nice it might be to be able to enjoy a party with Nina, to introduce her to the people he knew. To exchange gifts with her on Christmas Eve, hold her in his arms in bed on Christmas morning.

Kevin hadn't been able to stop thinking of her. Maybe it was because of their last conversation. Maybe it was because this time of year always made him feel romantic. But Kevin was kidding himself thinking any of these were a real reason. He hadn't been able to stop thinking of Nina since the first time he'd laid eyes on her.

His heart was in a vice each time her face popped into his mind. His breath caught and his face grew hot when he imagined hearing her voice again. And now his stomach twisted when he remembered the last time they'd spoken. When he thought back to the horrible way he'd handle things in the dressing room. The anger in her voice when he asked her about his stupid note. Then, the courage he lacked to be honest with her when she asked him to be. Instead of telling her what he knew was true, he hurt her for what he thought was her own good.

A part of him was unsure what he felt. He remembered the only other time he thought he'd been in love. Melissa Green, a girl he met at a basketball game his freshman year of college. She was a pretty girl and she was sweet. He dated her for a year or so. He told her he loved her but he always questioned whether or not he truly knew what that meant.

Did love mean having a good laugh every now and then? Did love mean good sex? Was love something he felt or something he knew or something he forced? Melissa and Kevin broke up badly to say the least. While he'd taken care of his father in his last few years, there'd been no one, just a sprinkling of random dates and shameful one night stands until Nina.

With Nina it was different. When they laughed together his heart swelled like it never had before. He was comfortable enough to be himself around her, to be honest and vulnerable. And every time he looked at her beautiful gray eyes, her porcelain skin, her tender pink lips, he felt it. When he heard her quick breaths, her thudding heart, her vivacious laugh, her silky voice … he felt it. Kevin had known the feeling all along but was too scared to admit it even to himself for all the more fear the truth would instill in him. No matter how complicated it felt, how scary the idea, how wrong it seemed, he loved her.

CHAPTER FORTY-EIGHT

Nina held up the new pair of jeans to her body and forced a smile for her father. Soon the presents were opened and all that was left to do was gather the copious amounts of red and green paper and ribbons. Nina quickly snuck off back to the room she was staying in and found her phone, glancing at it seeing a text.

Merry Christmas, Nina

Instead of crying, instead of throwing herself on the floor ridden with anguish, she smiled. She just smiled, thinking of Kevin sitting with his family, Mrs. Benson and her husband most likely, on Christmas morning knowing he'd been thinking of her. Clearing the message from her screen, she saw another alert message. *New voicemail.* Nina's heart jumped. Maybe he'd called her, too. The thought of hearing his voice, no matter how angry she may have been, warmed her.

She tapped play and held her breath for an instant as she anticipated hearing Kevin's deep voice. She was denied.

"Hey Nina, it's Todd. Uh—Merry Christmas, I hope you're having a good time in Florida. Anyway, I just wanted to tell you I'm sorry. I haven't gotten a chance to talk to you since the concert and … well, I was an asshole. I'm really sorry. I hope you forgive me. Give me another chance. See you when you get back. Bye."

There was a click and Todd's voice was gone. She looked at the phone and saw two options. Call back or delete. *Good question,* she thought.

Todd, as usual, had been far in the back of her mind. Nina thought it was unfortunate he'd witnessed her breakdown but that didn't change the fact that he was just as rude as ever. She remembered last year when things had been pretty great between the two of them and even James had been getting along with Todd for the most part. Nina didn't love Todd but she cared about him which is why she felt like taking the next step was the right thing to do.

It came up in conversation just about every time they were together. Inevitably they would wind up on a couch or a bed making out like the wild teenagers they were and Todd would push the boundaries a little further each time. Nina felt beautiful when she was with Todd. Like any high school boy, he worshiped the ground she walked on due to the fact she continued to let him see her topless.

But soon there was only one more step to take, one more base to cover. Todd would whisper sweet things in her ear like how he wanted to be with her forever. How he could imagine spending every moment with her from there on out. Though a tentative fear in Nina held her back from labeling what they had as love, the thought of being with her father's best friend's son forever seemed kind of fitting. Maybe not so fitting for her as for her family.

At one point it just seemed right and finally Nina didn't feel like she had to cling to the idea of holding her virginity any longer. The American flag waved smoothly through the tepid May air in front of Nina's house and the yard was buzzing with the annual block party that kicked off the summer. Todd and Nina snuck off down the street to the park, the most cliché place for them to conduct the majority of their sexual experimentation Nina thought but nevertheless, she continued to go.

They ducked through the trees and Todd grabbed her, kissing her hard. They spent the next hour running through the set list of things they'd already done. Then the time came and instead of grimacing at

Todd, shrugging back into her clothes, she simply nodded.

Nina was lying on a bed of grass with her clothes on top of her like tiny blankets, Todd at her side propped up on one elbow. She was lost in her own mind, having a conversation with herself. *That was it*, she thought. From now on, nothing would ever be a first. Except maybe first love. She sighed, not regretting what she'd done, just confused as to why she thought Todd was the right choice. *Too late now.*

"Are you okay?" Todd asked. Nina looked over at him and gave him a weak smile and another nod. She hadn't said a word.

"I have something to tell you," he started. Nina sat up and pulled her tank top over her head. She stared at him, waiting as a pinprick of worry hit her.

Todd sighed and sat up to meet her eyes. The woods had grown dark and the party in the distance was getting louder.

"I've decided I should live with my mom for a little while … in Arizona. She and I don't know each other that well and I think I should make an effort. I—I'm going in two weeks."

There was a loud boom and Nina looked up through the trees as glittering blue sparks started to fall. Glancing over at Todd, he was staring up, too, the colors of the sky bathing his face as he looked in awe. He didn't look at her. Did he not care about the severity of what he'd just told her? Her eyes moved back to the fireworks that crackled through the night sky, the reds and golds that shimmered out of their different shapes then dissolved falling to the earth. What was once a tight cannon with no certain extraordinary look soon became a magnificent flash and just as fast, its brilliance faded with no avail. A tear slid down her cheek as Nina realized she'd just had a first. Her first one night stand.

She was standing in her room, the sounds of the ocean just outside the window, when she snapped out of her trance. Just when she thought no memory could haunt her the way Kevin did, she was proven wrong. It was hard to believe that happened just a few months before she met

Kevin. She sighed and looked down at the black phone in her hand and hit the red button. Delete.

CHAPTER FORTY-NINE

JANUARY

Her stomach was doing flips, a feeling she'd grown accustomed to, as Nina pulled her bag from the passenger seat and headed toward the school. She pulled the zipper of her coat as high as it could go for the short walk through the flurrying snow. The bottom of her jeans would surely be soaked by the time she got to her first period class. Nina sighed, first period used to be a class she couldn't wait for. Kevin's class. Her second semester schedule arrived in the mail while she was on vacation and when she returned home, it was the first thing she ripped open.

She didn't care about what lunch she had or even what classes she shared with James. She just scanned the paper for the name Reed, room B100. *Nothing.* She knew there was no chance of it happening. Creative writing was a one semester elective and his only other class was freshman English. James, however, would be in his fourth period class. Nina made her way into school and thought about making a stop at his room, just popping her head inside for a moment or even just walking by without looking in but she didn't.

Nina went to her first class and started the semester fresh, with a clear head. No Kevin as her teacher to distract her from getting good grades. *Yeah right,* she thought. More than four hours in and she had yet to see him. Yet to pass him in the hall or even hear his voice somewhere in the distance. It was the end of fourth period and Nina shot to B100 like a mad woman. She was going to meet James so they could go to lunch together.

Slowing herself to a near halt as she approached, she took a deep breath and peered into the room. James and the other students were shuffling their papers together and leaving. Kevin was at the front of the room wiping off the board. Then he turned, almost like he knew.

Nina's heart thudded seeing his face. His hair had been cut since the last time she saw him. His eyes were soft and sweet as he looked to her. She didn't want to smile. She wasn't sure how she felt. But she knew it was time to see him. Kevin smiled.

"Come on. Nina. Let's go," James said breezing past her, linking her arm.

Nina turned with him but whipped her head around to look back at Kevin. His smile faded and his lips went thin. He nodded and lifted his hand giving a small wave her direction. James pulled Nina away into the hallway and before she knew it, before she had a moment to think clearly about seeing Kevin, he was out of sight.

"What's your problem?" Nina barked at James.

"I'm not going to enable your self-destructive behavior. He broke your heart, leave it alone," he whispered back.

"James, I'm not being self-destructive. I just wanted to see him. Plus, I was coming to get you for lunch."

Nina saw him roll his eyes out of her periphery and her stomach flipped again. The words James used stuck out in her mind. Had he broken her heart? It was as if seeing his text message on Christmas morning had thrown a switch that told her something still existed between them. Then seeing his face, that half smile, warmed her from the inside so much that she cursed herself for falling for him all over again. She couldn't stop wanting him. As they found their table and sat to eat, Nina looked up through the glass windows that gave a view into the hallway and saw him.

Walking by the cafeteria casting a casual glance inside, Kevin locked eyes with Nina for a moment. His faint smile showed as he strolled on and Nina knew. It was still there.

CHAPTER FIFTY

FEBRUARY

James was sick and out of school with the strep throat that had been making the rounds in Wexley Falls. Nina made sure to stay clear of him but she did take it upon herself to collect his assignments that week, returning the favor from her lost week before the holiday. It was the end of the day and Nina was traveling around the school with James' schedule in hand. Her arms were full of papers and packets, her bag overfilled with double the books.

Nina entered B100 with an ease that left her slightly unsettled. Though she'd stopped meeting James in his classroom to walk to lunch, going into Kevin's room still seemed so normal to her. They hadn't spoken in weeks, only sly glances across the parking lot, brushing past one another in the halls just like before. Nina put on a brave face as she knocked on his door and watched him look up from his desk full of papers.

"Oh, hello," he said faintly. Nina smiled and entered the classroom sitting her overweight bag on the floor.

"Hi. I need James Dalton's homework."

Nina felt stupid. She practiced what she'd say to him a thousand times during the day but what came out still made her feel like an idiot.

Kevin mussed with folders and gathered up a stack for her then hesitantly reached out to her with the assignments. She reached for them slowly. She wanted to brush his hand, to barely touch his fingertip, but she couldn't. Nina felt her guard slipping as she got near him so she grabbed the papers, said thank you and turned to leave.

"Nina?"

Her feet stopped and planted hard into the floor when she heard him say her name. She solidified her walls of security before turning back to him. At least she thought she had.

"I feel like we have things to talk about," he said.

She almost felt a laugh coming on. *No shit*, she thought. Her lips pursed and she didn't respond to his ridiculous observation.

"Do you *want* to talk to me?" he asked.

Yes, she thought. *I want to scream at you until you understand what a fool you are for what you've done. I know you love me, Kevin.*

Her eyes lowered to the floor. "What do you want me to say, Kevin?" she asked quietly. They stood frozen, their story hanging in the air between them, keeping them apart.

"Just tell me you don't hate me."

"You know I don't," she replied, the words forced.

He nodded absently. "Right."

She could tell he couldn't reach deep enough for the words or the courage. He was holding back.

Nina pulled her bottom lip into her mouth and turned to leave, having nothing else to say. Reaching the door, she heard a noise behind hermit felt like she'd been hit with a live wire, her skin burned as he placed a hand on her shoulder and twirled her back around to face him, a little too close.

His deep voice crept out in a whisper. "I got scared. Firsts are … a big deal."

She sighed loudly. How was it possible for him to be so clueless? Just like before, it was obvious he was stuck on sex. Nina wanted to scream. He was stuck on the fact he might have taken her innocence.

Nothing would've made her happier but instead she would have two memories forever. Losing her virginity to Todd before he skipped town without so much as a phone call afterward and feeling ready for Kevin, the man she loved only to have him deny her.

"It wouldn't have been," she sighed. Nina's heart was heavy and she barricaded herself in silence, building the walls back up. She turned on her heels one last time and walked out into the hall, leaving Kevin alone in B100 just like old times.

CHAPTER FIFTY-ONE

Nina dropped off James's homework but neglected to tell him about the conversation she had with Kevin. She didn't need James treating her like a child. Her plans for the evening were rather lackluster; homework, a little TV then sleep. Anything to keep her mind from wandering.

Walking up the stairs, Nina saw a light coming from her room. She figured Greta left the light on after stealing an outfit. As she moved closer slowly, she convinced herself that was all it was. Then she saw a figure move through her room, putting a shadow on the hallway wall. Nina stormed in the room with her calculus book raised high above her head, ready to smash the intruder in the face. Then she recognized him.

"Honestly Nina, a math book?" Todd said with a laugh. Her arms lowered as she rolled her eyes.

"What are you doing in here?" she asked.

His turned from her and back to the mirror on the closet door. He was thumbing at one of the photographs Nina had stuck in the mirror's frame. An absent smile formed on his face as he looked at it for a silent moment then glanced back at Nina.

"You remember this? Prom last year? I like that you have this up," his voice had a dreaminess to it Nina hadn't heard in a long time.

"Yeah, it's a great picture of me," she sneered. "What are you doing here?"

Todd laughed and waltzed further into her room as if he were welcome. "Greta let me in. I thought maybe we could hang out. It's been awhile."

Indeed it had been awhile. Nina had been successfully avoiding Todd since he'd arrived back in Wexley Falls. A few conversations, a few lunches together at school but that was all. They hadn't even talked about the message he left her on Christmas, the one Nina hadn't only deleted but hadn't replied to. She knew what Todd would try to do. She knew if she gave him an inch, he would take a mile. Nina saw Todd flirting with other girls around school and wasn't surprised he was making moves while still trying to get back on her good side. Todd always believed he could get whatever he wanted.

"I have things to do. I'm not in the mood for company," she huffed, putting her bag down on the bed.

Brazenly, Todd took a seat on the edge of Nina's bed.

"You seem different this year. Sad."

"How would you know?" she snapped.

"Come on Nina, I know you. I know when there's something wrong."

"Correction, Todd. You *knew* me. And probably not as well as you think."

His mouth turned up on one side, a remorseful smile. Nina immediately felt bad for snapping at him, seeing his eyes lower to the floor. Her heart tightened. Was he playing her? She'd been fooled by him before and yet a twinge of guilt pooled within her as she looked at his sad eyes. Nina sighed and took a seat next to him on the bed staying quiet for a moment.

"I'm in a lot of those pictures. I guess we had some good times. How come we don't talk anymore?" he whispered, looking over at Nina.

"Because you hurt me. You left and I grew up."

Todd's hand moved and Nina felt her stomach twist, hoping he wouldn't do anything she didn't want him to.

"I was a fool for leaving you."

He leaned in close and Nina saw him shut his eyes. She drew in a sharp breath and pulled back before Todd could press his lips to hers. He must have sensed her draw back because Todd's eyes flashed open and looked at the bewilderment on Nina's face.

"Todd, I … I think we should go downstairs." Nina offered.

He smiled, visibly embarrassed and nodded quickly. "Sounds like a plan."

They stood up and Nina's stomach twisted in knots, the thought of Todd trying to kiss her lingering. What surprised Nina most of all was how it made her long for Kevin. A kiss with anyone else, especially Todd, would never be the same after kissing Kevin. Her mind was swimming too fast. Just when she thought she'd be able to keep her thoughts clear of Kevin, he'd crept back in to ruin another night.

Chapter Fifty-Two

He tried to keep her from his mind. He tried to keep reminding himself of the way he wanted to think. A relationship with Nina was wrong and too complicated to ever work out in the best interest for either of them. He forced himself to repeat it over and over in his head like some sort of self-deprecating mantra. *It's wrong. It's dangerous. You'll break her heart.* That last bit always made him cringe for he feared he already had.

But Kevin's mind, no matter how hard he tried to train it, had plans of its own. He dreamed of her regularly and in those dreams he knew the perfect thing to say to make it all better.

When Kevin thought of her, even for an instant, the L word burned in big, glowing red block letters behind his eyelids. He'd try to shake the words out of his head and repeat his mantra again with no luck. Nina was a part of him and he couldn't get rid of her.

There was another reason he couldn't stop thinking of Nina. She was everywhere. If she wasn't in the hallway, her hips swaying as she walked to class, she was by her locker, primping in the mirror or staring off into space. She was in the lunchroom, at the same table every day. She was in the parking lot singing to herself as she opened the passenger door to throw her bag carelessly inside.

The bell rang and he looked around his classroom suddenly realizing the boys significantly outnumbered the girls in his second period class. *Weird*, he thought. Then, his thoughts took a turn. As he handed out the test he remembered what Nina said the last time they talked and he started scanning over each boy in his class. If he could've he would have lined up each boy at Wexley Falls High School, but for now his classes would do. None of them particularly stood out to him. He ruled out a handful of them quickly due to their severe awkwardness, a dead giveaway they were still virgins. Watching from his desk as they filled out their answers, Kevin made mental case files for the few candidates he'd picked.

Ryan Palmer, tall, dark hair, baseball player. The baseball team had taken the state championship last year making him pretty popular. Ryan dated Lucy French now but Kevin wasn't sure how long they'd been together, not that it mattered. High school boys were notorious for being unfaithful.

Next was Mike Christensen, sandy brown hair, kind of short, horrible grades, drummer for the school's most popular garage band. Nina liked music, maybe she liked musicians, too. Mike had a way about him that let everyone know he was a hot shot. He had the 'gotta-get-out-of-this-town' attitude, a sentiment Nina shared.

Nick Fields, choir boy. Kevin had seen Nina and Nick walking together in the halls, eating lunch together and of course they were both involved in the infamous Senior Concert. Kevin thought Nick was a good kid, not one to take a girl for granted, maybe even be a good boyfriend. He didn't like thinking about it.

Kevin sat up straight when the bell rang and students were suddenly handing in their tests. *So much for cracking the case*, he thought. Kevin hopped out to the hallway to the drinking fountain and felt a shiver up his spine when he heard her laugh. He whipped his head around to see her, swallowing the cool water slowly.

Nina was in a yellow cardigan sweater and dark blue jeans with gold threading on the back pockets. Her hair was hanging down straight but it swayed as she giggled. He slid past her, back through his classroom door and turned to glance at her again. She saw him and her eyes went panicky. Then the boy in front of her, the one she'd been walking with, the one she was laughing with, took her hand for a moment. Kevin's breath caught as he watched the exchange and Nina looked over the boy's shoulder at him.

The boy dropped her hand and she smiled before walking away, giving a meaningful glance at Kevin when she did. Sitting down at his desk, getting ready for the next class to take the test, he waited for the boy to sit down then he looked at him.

He was retaking the one semester class due to his late admittance last semester.

Todd Dawson; tall, tan, blonde, no sports, no clubs, no activities, moderate grades. He was a good friend of her family and clearly, Nina's first.

CHAPTER FIFTY-THREE

MARCH

"Tell me again why we're going to this?" Nina asked as she secured the clasp of her necklace and fixed her hair around it. James was smoothing the front of his navy blue button down shirt and picking the tiniest bits of lint off of his jeans.

"Just like what I said about the football games. You and I are going to have the ultimate senior year experience. Even if I have to force you."

Nina let out a huff of a laugh and shook her head. She didn't need to be forced. High school parties weren't necessarily her thing but she wasn't opposed to it tonight for some reason. It was time she started acting like a seventeen year old. *Live a little*, she thought.

"Plus, it will only help us in the popularity department and I'd like to be a little higher on the list by prom," James said, eyeing her.

"Please, we are by far the coolest people in our class and you know it," Nina teased. She slicked on some lip gloss and sprayed herself with perfume.

"Well of course *I* know it, darling, but we've just got to show the others," James said in his best, overly dramatic stage voice. He was sharing the mirror with her now, grinning at her. They primped a little longer and finally they were ready.

"You look … fantastic," James said, looking his friend up and down. Nina was in black leggings and a dark gray sweater that came down off both her shoulders. The slinky fabric hugged her curves and her bare shoulders showed only the perfect amount of skin.

"I'll drive. You look like you could use a drink," James said, only half kidding. They got in James' car and headed to the party.

Hannah Bruckheimer was one of the most popular girls in school. She was gorgeous and funny and involved in just about every school activity from cheerleading to choir to student council. She was the real All-American girl. Nina always had the sense Hannah didn't like her but it wasn't stopping her tonight. Everyone knew Hannah's parties were open invitation. Nina was never quite sure how she managed to get her parents out of the house so often to have her bashes but she always did and they never got busted.

It was the first time Nina would be going to an infamous Hannah Bruckheimer party but James had been once last year when he was hanging around a senior named Andrew Furman. It was a mess Nina was sad to see James get mixed up in. Andrew wasn't out but he still wanted James around. They'd have their fun in secret but when Andrew's soccer buddies were around, James was the butt of every joke. Nina sometimes forgot James had had some rough times in school, too. She supposed everyone they knew had.

"Is Nick coming to the party?" Nina asked.

"How should I know?" he retorted.

She smirked to herself. James loved to pretend as though Nina couldn't see right through him. She didn't press him further. Letting him have a few secrets was one way to keep from feeling guilty about her own.

James turned onto Fourteenth Street and Nina felt a jump in her stomach. When The Black Jewel was in sight, she suddenly remembered where Hannah Bruckheimer lived. She whipped her head to the side to look down the street, his house just barely out of view. Then James turned just one street past The Black Jewel. Hannah's house was about two blocks down on the right.

Holy shit, Nina thought. They practically shared a back yard. Her palms started to sweat as she thought of how close she was to Kevin at that moment. Of course James had no idea and Nina wasn't about to fill him in. He'd been keeping too close of an eye on her as it was.

Hannah's front yard was already swarming with teenagers. The music was loud but nothing Nina imagined would get the police called. Anxiety started to set in. She wondered if she'd have the will power to keep from heading to Kevin's house. James put the car in park a few houses down.

"I see that look in your eye," he said pointedly.

Nina tensed and gave him a worried sidelong glance from the passenger seat.

"It's just a party. We aren't going to get *busted* and you don't have to do anything you don't wanna do. If it sucks, we leave. Now get the wrinkle out of your forehead or you're going to need Botox," James teased.

Nina tried not to smile, pursing her lips until the grin couldn't be avoided. Glad he hadn't figured her out, she breathed out what remained of her anxiety and they climbed out of the car and headed toward Hannah's house.

It was like all the other houses in that part of Wexley Falls, a medium sized Victorian that sat back off the street with a big, rounded front lawn. Sometimes a few steps took you from the sidewalk to a pathway to the front door, as it was in Hannah's case. Her house was a deep green with cream trim and a large dark oak door.

There was no need to knock or ring the bell. The door was standing wide open with a portion of the party happening on the front porch. Nina recognized most of the faces she saw but couldn't consider any of them friends. James and Nina headed inside with the masses and James immediately took Nina's hand, leading her to the kitchen.

Hip hop music was pounding through the house as Nina took in the sights of her fellow students dancing, or rather grinding on each other in the spacious living room. The kitchen was crowded but they managed to work their way in. The island was covered in various alcoholic drinks and mixers as well as soda and chips, snacks for everyone's taste. James filled a cup with soda for himself and looked at Nina for her choice. The bottles were too overwhelming and she really wasn't in the mood to drink.

"I don't think I want to booze it up. I'll just have some of that punch," she yelled over the music.

James grinned and seemed to chuckle to himself as he ladled the orange punch and its various bits of fresh fruit from the bowl into a red plastic cup before handing it to Nina.

She took a sip and tasted orange and pineapple juice with maybe a bit of cranberry splashed in. It would be the sugar rush she needed.

"Let's find a spot," James shouted near her ear.

She nodded and they snaked through the kitchen saying 'hi' to a few of their classmates along the way to the screened in porch where more people were hanging out.

"Just the girl I wanted to see!" A voice rang out from behind Nina and she turned to see Todd with a beer in his hand. He threw his arm over her shoulder and tried to pull her close.

Nina glared at James with daggers in her eyes. She had no idea Todd would be there and to say he was the last person she wanted to see was an understatement. She shrugged out of

Todd's hold and took a seat on the wicker loveseat James had claimed leaving Todd forced to sit across from her in a matching chair.

"Doing a little drinking, Todd?" James asked sipping his soda, hiding a smirk.

Nina elbowed him in the rib evoking a huff.

"Just loosening up a bit. Having fun. Nina, you used to have fun.

What happened?" Todd's words were one long, slurred sentence she barely understood. She gulped the punch instead of answering.

"Look at that, need a refill already," she said hurriedly as she stood quickstepping toward the kitchen again.

Nina sighed when she was far enough away. Why did he have to be there? She could hardly stand seeing him in the halls, let alone want to socialize with him on a night when she was supposed to be having a good time. And what did he mean, she *used* to be fun? Nina filled her cup up to the brim with the citrus punch and took a few more gulps before topping it off again.

Nina was bobbing her head to the music as she walked back to the screened in patio. She searched with her eyes for James but she didn't see him anywhere.

"Nick stole him away," Todd slurred from the floor.

Nina looked down and saw him sitting cross-legged still nursing his beer. A heavy sigh rolled out of her as she plopped down on the floor next to him. She took the bottle from his hand and he let out a tiny groan of protest.

"Nope, you're done dude," she said firmly.

"Sorry about the other night." His voice was quiet and she glanced at him to see his head hanging low. She knew he was drunk but she felt bad for him. He looked pitiful sitting there like a kindergartener with a frown and his eyes lazily staring at the floor. She remembered the visceral response she'd had when he tried to kiss her the other night. Maybe Todd wasn't so bad. They'd had some fun together. He was good looking … for a guy her own age. It was hard to look past the summer and how he'd left her and never called. But she wondered if she had it in her to take him back. Maybe she'd be better off with him.

"Don't worry about it. I … I'm sorry too," she said.

Todd's eyes rose to meet hers and he cocked his head to the side, "Why?"

She sipped the juice and felt words churning from within her. She tried hard to hold them back but they rolled out anyway.

"I haven't been very nice lately. You're not a bad guy. But sometimes people aren't meant to be. Sometimes even though you really care about someone you have to do the right thing and stay away from them. Stop fighting for it. There's a point where it's just too hard and too miserable and …" Her voice trailed off and suddenly she was stuck in her own mind. She wasn't talking about Todd at all. It was Kevin. Maybe it was time she let go. But Nina wasn't that easily convinced by her own words.

Nina patted Todd on the forearm as she stood up. "I need some fresh air."

She walked across the room to the screen door that led to the back yard. No one was outside but her. She heard the music fade the further she walked into the grass. It was black outside, the stars shining overhead, the distant glow of street lamps giving the houses halos.

Her eyes were roaming the row of houses in front of her. Her head felt funny. Suddenly Nina realized she'd walked a diagonal line through Hannah's back yard. She stopped and a giggle escaped her lips as she tried to center herself and get a better sense of direction. Which way was *his* house? Steadying her toes in the ground she turned her head and saw it.

Nina's breath caught in her throat for an instant. His back porch light was on and he was standing just below it. She knew his silhouette even from the distance, even in the dark, even as her head spun.

Fear flew away, doubt was crushed and she marched toward him through their adjoining lawns. It was closer than she thought but by the time she was just feet from his deck, she could just barely make out the thumping dance music from Hannah's house.

He hadn't budged. As she boldly walked up the steps of his wooden deck, his face became clearer, his expression stone-like. Sasha, his Irish

Setter, came to Nina immediately, her tail swishing. Bending down to pet her, another giggle came out of her and she internally chided herself for sounding dumb. Her lips were loose and she knew it. She warned herself to stay quiet.

"Hello," he finally said, breaking the stagnant air.

"You look like a creep hanging out here alone," she blurted. *Dammit,* she thought.

A dizzy feeling rolled through her and she felt herself trying hard to concentrate as she straightened from petting the dog.

Kevin laughed, nodding his head. "Fair. I'm just trying to keep an eye on the party. As a concerned citizen of Wexley."

Nina scoffed, "No need. Nobody's drinking the hard stuff you like. It's all wine coolers and cheap beer."

His brows lifted in amusement and he nodded toward the red cup she still held in her hand. "And that?"

Yet another giggle rolled out of her mouth. "It's just punch, nothing to worry about here, *concerned citizen.*"

Kevin reached for the cup and took a quick whiff before sipping some. He chuckled and coughed a bit. "Yeah. That's rum."

Nina was laughing with him for a second then her face fell. "Wait. What?"

"How much of that have you had?" he asked, still chuckling a bit.

Nina tried to remember how many times she'd filled her cup. James did it once and then she went back for more, then … "It's really good," she uttered exasperatedly. Kevin went on laughing at her before ducking into his house.

He came back in a flash with a bag of pretzels.

"Here, eat something," he said, offering her the bag.

Nina plopped down in one of his Adirondack chairs and started munching on the pretzels. Though fuzzy, her mind wandered. She felt pathetic sitting there drunk. She berated herself in silence. She couldn't even pick a decent beverage at a party. How could she possible be trusted to choose someone decent to be with?

If she had to choose someone though, wasn't Kevin the best choice? Sure he had flaws but she'd never known a sweeter man. Anger bubbled inside of her thinking about every day since the senior concert. She missed him. She missed everything they had. She'd take any small part of it over this painful silence.

"I don't like this," she exclaimed.

Kevin looked up. "You want me to get you something else to eat?"

Her face scrunched in annoyance. "No. *This.* I don't like *this*," she said, gesturing back and forth between their two bodies.

"I hate that we're just sitting here. We can't even talk anymore."

"What am I supposed to do?" He ran a hand through his dark brown hair and sighed.

"You know exactly what I want." Nina stood as she said the words pressingly. It was easy. She couldn't understand why he didn't see it. They cared about each other. What they had was real.

"Nina …" he objected, his brows knit together in unease.

"No. Forget it. I know you … I know there's *something* here. I just can't take the rejection again." She handed him the bag of pretzels and turned to leave with a heavy heart.

"Do you have someone to drive you home?" His words rushed out and she could feel him close behind her near the edge of the deck.

She glanced at him. "Of course I do. Why does it matter to you anyway?"

His eyes narrowed and she felt him taking in her face. Her heart started to flutter with his eyes so tight on her. She willed him to kiss her with her mind. *Just say the words and kiss me,* she thought.

"You know why," he whispered.

"Say it," Nina pleaded.

His eyes left her face and looked at the ground gravely. "Go back to your party Nina."

She took off with a swift stride before she had time to think, to say something else. How could he lie like that? What was so bad about going back to the way it was before? She flung open the screen door to Hannah's house and nearly slammed into James.

"I wanna go," she said.

He put his hands on her shoulders lightly. "You okay? Where were you?" he asked, looking past her to the back yard. He squinted and she was sure he saw the same silhouette when he glared back at her.

"What the hell, Nina?"

She shook her head and pushed out of his grip, charging through the house to get out front to James' car. He was chasing after her, Nick following close behind him. She made it to the passenger side as she felt the tears start to well up.

"What do you think is gonna happen?" he asked.

"I love him," she growled.

"And?"

Nina stared angrily at him. He couldn't possibly understand. She'd never given him enough information for him to get it. It was too precious to talk about.

"He loves me, too," she answered.

James rolled his eyes and moved closer to the car, waving Nick to come with them.

"Did he tell you that?" he whispered before Nick was in earshot. The three of them climbed in the car and once Nina was buckled in the passenger seat, she peered out the window despondently.

"He didn't have to," she said in barely audibly cry.

Chapter Fifty-Four

For the first time in months Nina woke up with a smile on her face. The weather was getting better; birds were chirping outside her window and it was a very special day.

"Happy Birthday!" James yelled as he and Nick popped into Nina's bedroom, flinging the door open unexpectedly. Nina jumped then the flash of a camera went off in her face. James' annual surprise birthday photo, a tradition Nina had many times tried to outlaw. She laughed as she flopped back down against her pillow, covering her eyes.

"Thank you," she grumbled, a chuckle in her voice.

"So it's up to you whether or not we skip school today. The day is yours my dear," James said, opening up her closet to pick something fabulous for her to wear. Nina sat up and wiped the sleep out of her eyes.

"We should *probably* go to school."

"Okay, get ready. Breakfast will be waiting downstairs," James ordered, throwing two hangers of clothes onto the bed before he and Nick bounced out as cheerfully as they'd come in.

Nina ate the breakfast James and Nick prepared with love as quickly as she could choke it down. There were pancakes that were a little runny in the middle and eggs that were dark brown on one side as well as an assortment of cereals Nina had always loved. She liked the clothes James picked and was thankful the weather was nice enough to wear a dress. She had to throw on a white button-up sweater over her shoulders but the look was still cute.

Spooning a mass of marshmallow bits and honey grain stars into her mouth, Nina remembered the last time she'd worn the dress. It was an emerald green linen dress that fit her tightly in the bodice, with thin straps and a bell skirt that came above her knee. It was the dress she'd worn on her first date with Kevin. She lowered her eyes as she finished up her bowl of cereal, thinking about the breakfast she'd had with Kevin once.

"Ready to go?" Nick asked sweetly. Nina smiled at him and nodded, swallowing the lump in her throat.

When they arrived at school, Nina saw her locker had been decorated with balloons and glitter-covered construction paper cut-outs of birthday cupcakes complete with candles. James and Nick smiled at each other, proud that their two days of scheming had paid off. Nina hugged both of them and kissed them each on the cheek. Opening her locker took some maneuvering. Moving the balloons that were taped to the metal door, she finally reached the combination wheel and got it open.

"Gosh, you guys really went all out, didn't you?" she exclaimed, reaching inside pulling out a large white box. It was wrapped with a big red bow. Nina looked at James with a wide grin as she started pulling the ribbon loose. James, however, had a very confused look on his face.

"That's not from me, Nina," he said.

She made a face at him as if she didn't believe him. Setting the big, rectangular box on the floor, she shimmied off the top and looked down into red tissue paper. A small note had been folded and placed on top which Nina grabbed and read to herself.

For the one I ruined. Happy Birthday, Nina.

Her heart leapt inside her chest and she felt her skin growing red. She took a deep breath and pulled the red tissue paper back to reveal a stunning black dress. Nina made an audible sigh as she lifted the dress out of the box and took in how beautiful it was. Holding it up to her body, her smile was beaming uncontrollably until she glanced up at James. His lips were tight and his eyes were empty as he watched her nearly twirl around the hallway like Cinderella.

"Who's it from?" Nick asked innocently as Nina shot James a warning look.

"My dad," she lied easily.

James and Nina parted ways to get to their classes. Nina tucked the dress back into its box and back into her locker carefully and soon she had only one mission for the day. Find Kevin.

She was heading toward his classroom, not caring about the fact she might be late for her own class when Todd stopped her in the hall just outside Kevin's door. *Damn*, she thought. Nina had forgotten Todd had Kevin's class third period. She flinched when he touched her arm.

"Hey gorgeous! Happy birthday," Todd said smoothly. He dug in his pocket and pulled out a small box wrapped in pink paper. Nina stared at the box nervously. Small boxes from boys were generally a big deal.

"Aren't you going to open it?" he asked.

Nina met his eyes and forced a smile as she awkwardly took the gift from his hands. She pulled at the paper and revealed the small black box underneath. She lifted the top and nearly dropped it. The usual noise of the busy hallway grew louder in her ears as she stared down at the pair of square cut diamond earrings. She knew they were real. The way the sparkled even in the crude florescent light of the school was brilliant. At first she simply shook her head, mouth gaping. Then Nina looked up at Todd to see him grinning from ear to ear.

Then her eyes focused past Todd for an instant and she saw Kevin standing behind him taking in the scene. She locked eyes with Kevin before he turned into his classroom, his jaw tense, his eyes harsh.

"Do you like them? You should put them on," Todd offered in a quaking voice. Nina looked Todd square in the eye and jutted the box forward. "I can't accept these Todd."

"Of course you can, they're a gift. Eighteen is a special birthday and I wanted you to have a special gift," Todd replied. He wouldn't take the box from her. Nina pushed the box into his chest and let her frustration get the better of her. Her head was reeling, only imagining what Kevin might be thinking watching this play out from just a few feet away.

"We're not getting back together. Thanks but no thanks," she said angrily as she took one look into Kevin's room and stormed off.

Chapter Fifty-Five

Kevin watched the clock waiting for the obligatory bell to ring and prayed Todd Dawson would be late though he was just outside the door. Todd managed to sneak in in the nick of time and Kevin grit his teeth as he watched him walk to his desk. He'd noticed Todd the minute he saw Nina's reaction to him the first day he showed up at school. Ever since he'd made his assumption about Todd's relationship with Nina, each time he saw the boy his skin crawled. Seeing Todd with his devil-may-care attitude and his wannabe haircut made Kevin want to scream or laugh or punch him in the face.

He cleared his throat before standing to start his class. "Alright, pass in your homework and turn your books to the start of chapter twelve."

A shudder ran through Kevin as he heard a voice from the back of the room.

"Uh, Mr. Reed? I forgot my paper in my locker, can I go get it?" Todd asked.

Kevin's eyes zeroed in on Todd and a pulse of excitement went through him when he realized this was his chance.

"Did you mean '*May* I go get it'?" Kevin retorted.

A wrinkle set between Todd's eyes and he blinked for a moment, confused.

"*May* I go get my paper, Mr. Reed?"

Kevin turned to the board to write his notes for the day, turning his back on Todd as he spoke.

"No, Todd. You may not. You had time to visit in the hallway before my class which means you had time to get to your locker and get your homework."

"But Mr. Reed," Todd pleaded.

Kevin whipped around to see the look on Todd's face. "Maybe you'll learn to be more careful with your time."

Todd shut up fast and the rest of the class stared in awe of their teacher's surprising bravado. When Kevin finally broke the gaze he'd fixed on Todd, he went on teaching with a sense of satisfaction he hadn't felt in some time.

When the bell rang and the students started to leave, Kevin took a seat at his desk. Todd walked by glaring as he did, his ego bruised twice that day. Kevin smirked when the last student cleared the room and he began grading papers, thankful he had a free period. A whole hour to himself to gloat.

There was a tiny knock on the door and his brown eyes lifted lazily to see a figure in the doorway. His heart clenched when he focused on Nina standing before him, her head cocked to one side, a half smile on her pink lips.

"Hi," he breathed.

"How did you manage to get into my locker?" she asked with a skeptical look.

"I have my ways."

"Well thank you. The dress is beautiful," Nina said coming further into the room.

"Yeah, it'll look great with those earrings."

Nina pulled her head back and made a face. He saw her eyes squint at him and he regretted his words instantly.

"What the hell does that mean?" she asked, coming closer, keeping her voice in an angry hush.

His hand ran through his hair as he grasped for words. An apology?

A comeback? He didn't know whether or not he should fight her. Was he even angry at her or just that scumbag Todd?

"I ..."

"Not that it's any of your business, but I gave those earrings back because I didn't like what they implied. Todd thinks he's someone he's not and he doesn't know I have feelings for someone else," Nina said, turning her eyes away from him in shame as she finished.

Kevin sighed and looked her over slowly as she dug her foot into the cheap blue carpet. She was wearing the green dress she'd worn on their first date. All he had to do was say it back. Tell her the truth and all of the pain in her eyes would go away and the clench he felt in his chest each time he saw her would stop as well.

"Nina ..."

"Thanks for the dress. I have class," she said, cutting him off.

"Why won't you let me talk?" he blurted.

A waning smile graced her delicate face and she breathed deep before she answered him.

"Because you've made it clear you have nothing to say."

CHAPTER FIFTY-SIX

Nina walked out to meet James at his car, slightly annoyed she hadn't driven herself. Nick and James were standing together, James leaning against the car, chatting Nick up about something, playfully touching his arm every few minutes. It made Nina smile to know James had found a boy. Though Nick still hadn't been able to tell James he liked him in return, it was easy to see he did. Just then Nina heard feet pounding on the asphalt behind her and Todd rushed to her side.

"Hey," he said out of breath. "I've been calling your name. Why didn't you stop?"

"I didn't hear you. Sorry," she said quietly, still keeping a brisk pace toward James. She wasn't interested in having another awkward conversation with Todd about those stupid, albeit gorgeous, earrings.

"It hurts my feelings that you won't take my gift. It's not some ploy to try and get you back, I picked them out for you and I want you to have them," he started.

Nina held back the urge to roll her eyes then she saw someone doing it for her. Kevin brushed past them on the narrow sidewalk heading over to the teacher's lot. He caught Nina's eye for a moment, looked down at Todd holding the earrings once again and rolled his eyes before walking off. She watched him carefully as Todd continued to try and convince her of his innocent intentions but Nina wasn't listening. Kevin was shaking his head as he nearly stomped his way to his vehicle. It looked like he was talking to himself.

"Can you give me a second?" she stammered. She didn't wait for him to reply before she walked over to Kevin swiftly.

"Hey!" she called out, close enough for Kevin to hear but far enough from her friends to be heard distinctly. Kevin turned and saw Nina trying to keep herself in check as she approached.

"Do you have something to say now? Whatever you're mumbling to yourself you ought to have the guts to say to me," she said, her eyes piercing him.

Kevin gave her a look of disbelief and opened his mouth to speak when Nina cut him off.

"You can't keep rolling your eyes at me and giving me the cold shoulder all passive aggressive every time you see me with Todd. He's my friend," she snapped.

Kevin laughed unexpectedly. "Yeah, I remember you told me you two used to be *friends*. He's the guy, isn't he?"

Her face fell. She searched his wild eyes for something more than his jealousy-induced quest to figure out who she'd slept with. She knew what he was doing. He was scared and she could see it.

"God, Kevin," her words were breaths coated in exasperation. "Does it matter?"

With softer eyes he lowered his head shamefully but Nina wasn't done. Her irritation with him was pushing her far enough over the edge to make her use anything she had against him. All she wanted was to pull him out of himself and help him realize the truth.

"You know it's too bad Todd sucked at being my boyfriend because at least he's fighting for me. He's doing everything he can think of, good, bad or crazy, to try and show me he cares."

Kevin looked as though he'd been stabbed in the chest as he shut his eyes in a wince. Nina tried not to look at him, knowing what she said had hurt him. But what would it take?

She knew James was watching her, she could feel eyes on her back.

"But Todd's the only guy who ever hurt me so badly he could never make up for it. He's the *only* guy who could never win me back," she whispered. She turned from him and started walking back to James's car, holding in threatening tears.

"Let's go home," she said to James, opening the passenger side door.

Todd looked at her closely. "I guess we can talk later?"

She nodded and closed herself in the car while James sat silent for a moment. Nick leaned forward from the backseat.

"Did you have a good birthday?" he asked.

Nina forced a smile and nodded. He was a sweet guy and as a new friend, he'd done a lot for her to make her birthday special. Nick smiled at her and she sensed he knew she was lying.

"Are you trying to start rumors?" James whispered.

"James!"

His hands flew off the wheel for a moment in defense. "Just saying."

"Well I don't need you to *just say* anything else, okay?" she growled quietly.

Although she woke with a smile to a day she'd been waiting for to change something within her, she cried herself to sleep that night. Eighteen had done nothing for her. Same life, same loneliness and as far as she could tell, same Kevin. She wondered what else he could be waiting for.

CHAPTER FIFTY-SEVEN

"This place is pretty nice. You say she's been singing here for a while?" Todd asked, glancing at James as he took a sip of his soda. James resisted making a rude face at Todd. He'd been trying to be nicer lately, a feat that proved to be challenging when it came to Todd. But nevertheless, the night was about supporting Nina. James' feelings about Todd or Kevin weren't going to keep him from being there for her while she did something she really loved. The Black Jewel was busy, only a few tables were empty and chatter filled the restaurant as the crowd waited for Nina and the Saturday night Jazz band to begin.

"Yeah, she started singing here over the summer," James replied, wondering if he'd been around late last summer if maybe Nina wouldn't have gotten involved with *that older guy*. Todd nodded and let his eyes scan the room, taking in the atmosphere.

"Is that Mr. Reed?" Todd asked, signaling to a table near the back bar, shrouded in near pitch black. James' eyes darted over to see him. Sure enough it was. He was sipping a beer and flipping through a stack of papers, sitting alone.

"He—uh, he comes here sometimes. I saw him at the Halloween show," James said. Suddenly he remembered that night. The way Mr. Reed let his eyes sit on Nina a little too long. James had met up with a good looking guy who graduated two years before for an impromptu make-out session and he hadn't seen Nina after her set was over. He wondered what happened between them that night.

"He's a real dick," Todd laughed.

"What?" James and Nick asked in unison before glancing at each other sweetly.

"He totally freaked out on me in class for forgetting a paper in my locker the other day. I used to think he was this quiet, regular guy, maybe even cool, but then he got all weird about this stupid assignment, almost like he was mad at me personally."

James took another glimpse of Mr. Reed in the dark corner on the other side of the large space and fought to keep Nina's secret inside. Then the lights dimmed on stage and the five members of the band took their places. Nina stepped out into the spotlight, a place she certainly belonged. Her raven hair was set in loose waves flowing around her perfectly porcelain face.

James looked at her dress and shook his head slightly, a reaction he didn't want Todd or Nick to notice but one he couldn't resist. It was the same dress she'd pulled out of the white box that had been left in her locker on her birthday. And her secret admirer was there to view her in the gift he'd given her.

The instruments began to play a soft tune and soon Nina let out the first sweet lyric. Todd sighed audibly hearing her sing the love song from the stage. Nick and James both looked over at Todd, seeing the dreamy look in his eye.

"Um—Todd?" Nick started, holding in a laugh.

"What?" he replied softly, his eyes not leaving the stage. A smile was lingering on Nina's face but James knew it just the performance. He hoped she hadn't seen Kevin in the back.

"You know, I keep carrying these around hoping one day she'll want to put them on," Todd said, pulling the black box out of his pocket and sitting it on the table. The earrings. Nick and James exchanged another look.

"I thought she said she didn't want those?" James asked.

"She did. But I'm still holding out hope."

"That she'll want the earrings or you?" James joked.

Todd let out a soft, thoughtful laugh, smiling at Nina still singing her song. "I guess love just makes me crazy, huh?"

"Love?" Nick nearly shouted.

He finally let his eyes break away from Nina to look into two shocked faces. "I don't know why I couldn't realize it when I had her but that's it guys. I think I love her."

Nina finished and the room clapped for her until she started another song. The boys clapped for her the loudest, with whistles and hoots causing Nina to shoot them a look.

"Todd, I think you should be careful about how you approach Nina with the earrings," James warned.

"Why? It's not like there's some other guy. It's just a matter of time before she realizes what's right in front of her," he said with a smile. His delusional confidence made James want to vomit. If he only knew what he was up against.

Nina finished her set a half hour later and headed over to their table. She took a seat with them and saw something brewing in the looks between Nick and James.

"What? Was I awful or something?" she asked.

"No sweetie, you were great! We were just having a moment," Nick said.

"Really Nina, you were amazing. And you look ravishing," Todd said with his voice smooth and cool.

"Ravishing?! Have you been drinking?" she asked, having a laugh at him, stealing a sip of his drink teasingly.

James stood and Nick followed and they waited, staring at Todd for a moment.

"We should head home, don't you think Todd?" James asked forcibly.

He didn't want Todd making more of an ass out of himself than he already had. And James didn't want anyone mentioning the fact they'd seen Mr. Reed sitting in the back. Better Nina didn't know.

"Thanks for coming, you guys. It means a lot. I've got to get my check and pull my stuff together. I'll see you later, okay?" she said, watching as Todd reluctantly stood.

James pulled on Todd's arm. "Come on, lover boy," he whispered into his ear. With that they headed out, leaving Nina at The Black Jewel, James praying she wouldn't come across Kevin for her own good.

Chapter Fifty-Eight

Nina stepped outside and took a glance up at the sky. She could see the clouds rolling fast over the full moon. There was the smell of rain in the air. She unlocked her car and started to get in when she heard her name. Popping her head up, she peeked over the roof of her car at the figure in the dark. Nina drew in a sharp breath as she made out his face. The chiseled cheekbones and the dark eyes, the day old stubble she found irresistibly sexy.

"Hey," she breathed. Kevin walked toward her and the moonlight bathed his skin in a violet hue.

"Hi."

"Were you in there?" she asked, closing her door, walking around timidly to meet him on the other side of her car. She noticed she didn't see his car in the lot. He must have walked.

Kevin nodded and smiled faintly. "You look beautiful."

He looked her over carefully, studying the way the black satin clung to her. The way the black beads shimmered down one side of her, stopping along with the hem just above her knee.

"Yeah, it's a great dress. Earrings not required."

The sky lit up in a flash of lightning that caused both Kevin and Nina to glance up. Thunder rolled in the distance a few seconds later. Nina felt herself growing hot, knowing Kevin's eyes were now fixed on her. Everything unsaid between them had been building to this worrisome peak. Her heart had been crushed by him just months ago and yet each time she looked into his eyes, especially tonight, she was reminded just how much she still loved him.

"It's gonna rain. You want a ride?" she asked.

Kevin's smile became more apparent. "Sure."

The two of them got into Nina's car and lightning flashed again as a purple crack in the sky. The thunder was closer then, booming loudly. Nina put the key in the ignition and tried to start the car. The engine hummed and screeched. She tried again.

"Shit," Nina muttered as the car continued to deny her. She glanced at Kevin in the passenger seat and sighed.

"I'll take a look. Pop the hood," he offered.

Kevin began looking around in the guts of the car, twisting knobs and jiggling wires and Nina started to question whether or not he knew what he was doing. She was standing next to him anxiously tapping one high-heeled foot. Being near him was more difficult than she imagined and she regretted offering him the ride. There was a lot she regretted. The lightning was getting brighter, more aggressive with the thunder coming quicker behind the flashes. It was only a matter of time.

Suddenly he stood straight and looked her in the eye. She stared back at him with a look of exasperation and confusion.

"I made a mistake," he blurted.

The sky lit up above them and Kevin closed the hood of her car. He came toward her and her breath quickened. *Don't give in Nina*, she thought. Her eyes fluttered as the wind picked up and whipped the tendrils of her hair around her face. Her lips pressed together in a thin line, the devil on her shoulder forcing her to stay quiet so Kevin could go on.

"I can't keep passing you in the halls and not know when the next time is I'll get to touch you. I can't continue to be jealous of high school boys to the point where I want to fail them out of spite. And I can't keep having the same conversation with you. The one where I always lie." His voice was smooth and calm. He could have practiced it in a mirror for all Nina knew.

He'd gotten even closer to her, nearly pressed against her. He quieted himself and grabbed the hand that hung at her side. Their fingers interlaced and Nina felt a drop of rain hit her bare shoulder. Kevin reached up and smoothed over her hair then cupped her neck softly. A shiver ran down her spine as she was finally granted a wish she'd been begging for night after night. To be touched by Kevin again.

"Forgive me, Nina. I've made *a lot* of mistakes," he whispered as the rain started to fall on them. It was light and warm at first, almost soothing as it started to dampen their skin, hair and clothes. Nina's worries started to fly away on the wind. She tried to hold onto them for protection but his skin against hers and the impending storm that threatened their moment stripped her of her fears and she gave in.

His head started dipping down and he stared at her parted lips and for the first time, Nina didn't see the painful look in his eyes he'd worn for the past several months. She felt his hot breath tickling her face and then she felt the words as three little puffs of air on her lips.

"I love you," he said as he pressed his mouth against hers, wrapping his arms around her tightly. Thunder boomed loudly, almost shaking the ground below them and they pulled away from each other, staring into one another's eyes. A smile grew on Nina's face.

He watched as she bent over and hooked her fingers into the back of each of her shoes, slipping them off then holding them in one hand. His eyes narrowed on her, wondering what she was up to and soon her free hand slid into his and she tugged.

Before he had a moment to think, they were running hand in hand down the sidewalk to his house, rain pouring over them. Lightning flashed and thunder roared, the storm getting closer. Soon they were drenched, standing on Kevin's porch, out of breath and laughing at each other.

Nina slicked her hands over her hair, soaking wet and completely out of place. She laughed between huffs, catching her breath. Kevin did the same, chuckling at the absurdity of running through the pouring rain like carefree children. He shook his head like a shaggy dog, flicking water all around and on to Nina. She giggled, wiping the water from her face.

Suddenly Kevin's face fell, his eyes softened and he stared at Nina. Though he'd realized it long ago, telling her had changed him.

"I mean it," he muttered.

She bit her lip and smiled through it. "I know."

Kevin reached his hands out and took Nina's face between them and gently coaxed her nearer. His lips pushed against hers, the feeling he'd missed so much making him weak. Parting her mouth under his, she allowed him to kiss her more deeply. His hands loosened on her cheeks and his fingers began to slip into her hair. He pulled back to look into her eyes.

They were staring at each other nearly holding their breath for fear the moment wasn't real when the thunder boomed so loud Nina jumped. Suddenly it was raining so hard even the covered porch was getting drenched by the sideways pounding sheets of water. Kevin fumbled for his keys and opened the door ushering Nina away from the weather.

Kevin took her hand and stared down for a moment. His mouth twisted, not in discomfort but almost as if he was mustering up some kind of courage. Nina squeezed his hand and he looked up at her. Her delicate smile warmed him and his mouth stopped its contortion. Nina dropped her shoes and they clattered down to the hardwood floor. Simply and as graceful as she was when she was on stage, Nina slinked passed Kevin but didn't let go of his hand. His breath stuck in his throat as she took the first step upstairs. She looked back to see him.

Their eyes locked for an instant and nothing needed to be said. He saw in her eyes that it was all right and she saw it in his that he was terrified. So they made their way silently up to Kevin's bedroom.

As Nina stepped through the threshold, Kevin's hand fell from hers and soon his hands were gripping her waist from behind. She turned in his grasp letting him pull her close just inside the darkened room. Boldly he stepped into her, putting her back against the wall next to the light switch. His hands roamed the length of her, smoothing over the satin fabric of her dress, feeling her curves underneath. The silence of the room was broken by Nina's staggering breath as Kevin kissed her neck and collarbone. His hands slid up her thighs, under the skirt of her dress and rounded over the back of her.

Looking into her eyes, he slowly turned her with care. Nina's palms pressed against the wall and she felt Kevin's breath on her shoulder then the slow release as he dragged her zipper all the way down. He took his hands off her and she faced him again, the black fabric sliding and falling to the ground exposing her matching black strapless bra and panties.

Back in each other's arms quickly, they descended to the bed, Nina lying back comfortably with no hesitation. She pulled him to her and lifted his shirt over his head and off of him greedily.

The room lit up when a flicker of lightning struck in the sky. Kevin watched as the electric blue flash illuminated Nina's bare flesh and his craving for her grew more intense. Nina pulled him down on top of her, her hands caressing his back and chest, down to the rigid muscles of his stomach. He flinched under her touch when her hands moved lower in between them. The moment seemed so familiar and yet so different from that night. The clanking of the metal of Kevin's belt as Nina undid it hung in the air as did the sighs of breath each was letting go of.

Kevin laid soft kisses against Nina's shoulders and across her chest. Her fingers dug into his back and she arched herself up letting his hands slip under her to unclasp her bra. Kevin drew in a ragged breath gazing down at her covered in moonlight, the body of an angel, the young woman he'd come to love.

Nina's hands brushed his hair off his forehead and looked up at his awed face. She smiled at him and felt her heart, her thoughts, and her stomach finally ease.

"I love you, Kevin," she whispered with no fear.

She crushed his lips with hers. Her tongue slid against his and with her eyes closed, each kiss before this one seemed to flash behind her eyes. She felt him tracing his fingertips across her flesh, her trembling abdomen, the curves of her breasts, the crook of her slender neck all while they stayed locked in a kiss. He pulled away placing one small peck on her full lips before leaving a trail of kisses down her cheeks to her breasts and her navel before he stopped. The thunder and lightning had stopped and the only noise coming from the window now was the light tapping of rain against the glass. Nina felt shivers up her body. Kevin hovered over the top seam of her black panties. He expelled hot breath against her skin and when Nina could take no more, when Kevin saw her hips begin to fidget in intoxicated agony, he kissed her just next to the black fabric, high on her thigh, close enough to the place Nina craved him to touch to make her go insane.

Kevin came back up to meet her lips again and with his body meshed against hers, he reached over to the nightstand. The rest of their clothes came off in a rushed frenzy and then calm fell over them. Nina looked into Kevin's eyes as he held himself above her. A tiny gasp escaped Nina's lips as she melded to him, enjoying the weight of his body against hers.

Sweat was beading on Kevin's forehead and their breath became heavier and yet still in sync with one another. He was pushing her closer to the brink of ecstasy, pulling wild moans from her. Suddenly she was pushing up on him, forcing him to roll onto his back and allowing her to take control by straddling him. His hands gripped her waist as she moved against him. Then she took his hands, intertwining them with hers, looking deeper into his eyes as a shiver went up her spine and guttural noise flowed out of her before she weakened. Nina collapsed onto Kevin's chest and his arms wrapped around her tightly, feeling his own bliss take him over.

Sighing breaths were drawn out of Nina and into Kevin's ear as her lungs slowed. Her lips pursed against the hot skin of his neck, wanting to stay as connected to him as possible. He let his fingers drag up and down her back, soothing her. Soon she was on her side, cuddled in close to him, drifting off to sleep. Kevin held her tightly and watched her sweet face closely as she started to doze. She heard him say it once more, putting her completely at peace.

"I love you."

CHAPTER FIFTY-NINE

The sun peeked through the curtains and a slant of golden light was shining over Kevin's face awakening him. His hand lazily smoothed out over the sheet to the other side of the bed. With his fingertips he felt soft, warm skin and he started to come out of his sleepy state. With his eyes still closed, he attuned himself to the subtle feeling of the rise and fall of her breathing beside him. He heard her breaths slipping out of her and could no longer stay blind to the sight of her. Slowly his eyes fluttered open and he let a smile turn up on his face absently as he stared at her.

Her thick black hair pooled around her bare shoulders. Her lips were parted and ever so pink. Her dark lashes lay feather light against the top of her cheeks. She seemed so peaceful. Kevin was mesmerized by her beauty.

Just then she sighed heavily and her grey eyes blinked open. Kevin grinned, embarrassed to be caught watching her sleep. Nina smiled back at him and curled up closer to his chest, not saying a word.

"Good morning," he whispered into her hair.

She sighed dreamily.

Without hesitation, he caressed the length of her spine and pulled her close. The ease he felt with her now was frightening. For a moment before waking he'd clearly thought to himself it might have all been an amazing dream. But now with his arms wrapped around her, smoothing over her creamy white skin, he sighed a quaking breath, knowing it was all real.

"Are you alright?" she asked, her face still nuzzled into his chest.

"I'm fine. What about you?"

Nina moaned, flexing and arching her back like a cat, never leaving his embrace but pushing against it. As she relaxed she let out an unexpected giggle. Kevin grasped her arms and pulled her back to look into her eyes, concerned for the outburst.

Nina was failing to hide a grin. Kevin squinted at her, waiting for some sort of explanation. Looking at her sweet face, the laughter she was stifling, the Cheshire grin she wore, made Kevin's heart lighten and he, too, began to chuckle at the absurdity of it all.

"What on Earth are we doing?" she laughed.

Kevin pushed a strand of hair away from her face. "Whatever we want."

Nina's face fell somber and then a hint of sweet smile returned. Her eyes blinked in slow motion as she moved closer to him and pressed her lips gently to his.

Kevin fell back to sleep with new dreams of Nina to fill his head, more views of her body having just been discovered in the light of day. His eyes flashed open when he heard the sound of the shower being shut off. Stretching for a moment, he wondered how long he'd been asleep. As his languid mind struggled to focus, the bathroom door opened and there was Nina. With tiny beads of water on her skin and her wet hair black as coal, she stood with a fluffy white towel wrapped around her body and nothing but a smile on her face.

"Sorry, I needed a shower," she said, taking a seat on the edge of his side of the bed. He sat up, propped against pillows and made room for her.

"Of course, make yourself at home." Her eyes were on him in an instant and he felt his face growing hot.

"What I meant is you're welcome to …" Kevin was shushed by a sudden kiss and he nearly melted at the feeling of her damp hair tickling his face. Pulling away, Nina took a deep look into Kevin's dark eyes.

"Don't worry. I didn't think you were asking me to move in," she teased. With a soft laugh, Kevin shook his head.

"I should get going," Nina said as she stood up and searched the room for her clothing. Kevin watched as she struggled to keep the towel wrapped around her, bending to pick up her bra from the other side of the bed. She picked up her dress from the floor near the door and her face twisted. She stood still for a moment looking at the short black strapless garment. Not exactly a Sunday morning outfit.

"I have some sweatpants and a t-shirt if you want," Kevin offered.

Nina smiled graciously at him as he got the clothes for her. Nina was swimming in Kevin's black and gold Wexley Falls High shirt but managed to cinch the gray sweatpants tight enough with the drawstring that they didn't fall off her slender hips.

She folded her dress over her arms and stood in the doorway looking back at Kevin sitting on the bed. He had to laugh. She looked rather ridiculous in his clothes. Nina rolled her eyes at him and he hurried to her side to kiss her cheek in apology.

"You sure you have to go?" he whispered in her ear.

Nina shrugged nearer to him at the feeling of his head dipping down to kiss her throat as she moved her head.

"Gotta get my car looked at," she sighed.

Kevin pulled away and nodded, looking at her as his thoughts went anxious.

"Nina, what are we going to do?" he stammered.

Her eyes snapped up to meet his and he took in how white her face became at his question. What happened next? They'd crossed the line, they'd given in and thrown caution to the wind. But reality wasn't lost on either of them. Monday would come and the bell would ring and once again they'd be Nina the senior student and Mr. Reed, the English teacher.

"It doesn't matter," he said in reply to his own question. His arms pulled her in tight and he kissed her again. "It doesn't matter."

He repeated it, trying hard to convince himself.

CHAPTER SIXTY

Nina was standing next to her car in the otherwise empty parking lot of The Black Jewel, memories of the night before rushing through her head. She glanced around making sure she was alone before letting her smile grow wide.

She turned the key in the ignition to hear the noise she'd need to be able to describe to the mechanic. The ignition clicked once and started normally. The engine purred and the radio flipped on to the station it had been on when Nina parked the afternoon before. She sat stunned for a moment. Her eyes darted around again. She knew it hadn't been Kevin who fixed the car, not that she believed he had the know-how anyway. She shut off the car and tried again, thinking it might be a fluke. The car started easily once more and Nina let out a victorious laugh.

It was destiny, predetermined. But Nina questioned whether it was the angel on her shoulder or the devil who'd kept her car from starting. Was it fate that brought Kevin to see her, fate that gave him the courage to finally speak the truth? Or was it some series of mistakes and unfortunate steps they'd made that brought them to the parking lot and later to his bed?

As Nina drove home, she heard his timid voice in her head asking her *what are we going to do*. She had no idea. After wanting him so badly for so long, wanting his love and attention, she'd never thought about what might happen past that.

What would school be like on Monday? What would the weekends be like? Prom? Graduation? Another missing piece of the puzzle was what would happen when Nina was done with Wexley Falls High School and college bound.

She pulled into the driveway and felt her heart lurch at what she saw. Sitting on her front steps looking incredible pissed was James. He stood up as he saw her and she began to panic as he walked toward her, waiting for her to get out of the driver's seat. Nina slinked out and gave him an uneasy look.

"Where have you been? I've been calling and calling. No one's home. I had no way to get a hold of you. Do you know how scared I've been thinking something happened to you after I left last night? I've been up all night! I've been waiting *here* since five in the morning! Where the hell were you?" James yelled.

Nina's back was pressed against her car, startled by his outburst. She believed he hadn't slept, he looked ragged and like he'd downed more than a few cups of coffee. Her thoughts were racing, trying to pull something out of thin air to tell him. An excuse or a lie. Her eyes were wide and her mouth gaped as she stammered and struggled to find the words to explain.

James' eyes squinted and for a moment he seemed to be calm. He looked her up then down in confusion as Nina stood speechless.

"What are you wearing?" he asked skeptically.

Nina's mouth opened and a tiny squeak escaped in place of a reply.

Suddenly James' face grew grave as he drew in a breath before speaking. "Nina you didn't …"

Nina couldn't determine if it was a question, a statement, or merely a hope on James' part. But yes, she had and she knew her eyes, if not Kevin's clothes, had already given her away.

"I'm not sure what you want me to say." She was finally able to let her brain and mouth work in harmony.

James backed away from her a few steps and shook his head. He kept his gaze off his best friend and locked on the ground, clearly shocked by the reality setting in. Nina's stomach was churning and she wanted to reach out to James, calm him, make him see what was between her and Kevin wasn't wrong.

"I'm glad you're alive. I've gotta go," James said, walking off.

"Wait!"

He spun on his heels, feet away from her in the yard. "It's fine. It's your life. But it's not going to end well between you two and I don't want to see you get hurt."

"Who said anything about it ending?" she said, raising her voice, anger rushing to the surface.

"Well he got what he wanted so I imagine it'll be any day now," James spat.

Nina gasped and felt a burn in her chest. "You don't want to see me get hurt so you say *that*? God, weren't you the one who said you'd be having the *time of your life* sleeping with a teacher? You thought it was so exciting, so mysterious and sexy before you knew it was real. Well guess what James, he *does* love me, just like you suspected months ago. And I love him, too."

James stared at her, blank faced, unable to retort. Nina felt her blood boiling, angry at James for his unfair assessment of Kevin and for his cruelty. Her night with Kevin had been a dream come true but she hadn't imagined she'd be dealing with the fallout so soon.

"I'm really happy for you, Nina. See you at school," James' words were flat as he made his way to his car, not looking at Nina. "Guess I'll see your boyfriend there, too."

Before she could speak he was closed in his car and starting the ignition. He glared at her once more with a stone face before speeding away. Nina's stomach twisted but she tried to shake the feeling. She was happy. She forced herself to remember that.

Nina went up to her room and sat motionless on her bed for what seemed like hours. She thought of everything she'd ever been through with James. Every first they'd divulged to each other and every tear they'd shed with one another. Would it all be ruined? The sun eventually went down and she was yanked from her trance when her bedroom door opened. It was her father.

"Nina?"

Nina turned to him slowly, her eyes glazed and her mouth tight. She'd lost track of his travel schedule. She had no idea when he was coming or going.

"I'm back."

Nina nodded, annoyed by the unnecessary statement and the truth of the matter.

"And your sister just told me the most wonderful news. She and Blake are engaged to be married!"

Greta was in the hall behind their father with a smirk on her face, Blake just behind her. Nina's father turned to them and put an arm around each of them with a wide smile on his face. They were just out of her doorway when Nina heard her sister start asking about a date and a budget and of course a quickly thrown together engagement party.

As soon as they were out of sight, Nina dialed his number and waited for Kevin's voice.

"Hi," she whispered.

"Hey, you okay?" he asked.

"I am now."

CHAPTER SIXTY-ONE

APRIL

Nina was sitting in her room staring at her blank computer screen which should have been a half written assignment for her government class. Instead, her mind wandered to James and his icy stare as he drove off into the morning fog a week ago. The daggers he shot at her with his eyes in the halls at school. They hadn't spoken a word to each other since then. It was the longest they'd ever gone without talking.

Meanwhile, she and Kevin hadn't been able to get enough of each other. She was at his door as fast as she could be each afternoon when school let out and she was on the phone with him every night before drifting into dreams of his face. Kevin had become the ultimate escape from the rest of her life. When she was with him, in his arms or listening to him speak, she didn't have to think about the hatred that seemed to be building in James. She could let bliss envelope her and keep her mind off the racket her sister had been making talking about lilies and crystal, lavender linens and scalloped lace veils.

Her cell phone began to rumble, moving across the white wooden desktop. She looked down at the ID and smiled. "Hello?"

"Hey beautiful," Kevin gushed.

Nina sighed. "It's good to hear your voice."

"Why, what's going on?" Kevin asked.

"Just stressing a little. The engagement party is tonight. I've locked myself in my room with homework just to stay away from Bridezilla," she laughed.

Kevin chuckled and Nina's heart warmed, already more at ease.

"Maybe you could sneak away after the party and lock yourself in a room with me?" He mumbled the sentence and Nina grinned picturing him with a goofy smile.

"Maybe," she said coyly.

"Okay, try not to kill your sister and call me later."

Nina agreed to try and regretfully hung up which left her staring at the blank screen again.

With his voice gone from her mind for just minutes, thoughts of James crept back in and she felt a wave of dread flood her, thinking about having to see him at the party.

She could hear the festivities starting downstairs and knew she should join her family and put on a happy face. Taking a last look at herself in the powder blue shantung tea length dress, she slipped on her silver shoes and opened her bedroom door. She nearly ran right into the body that stood in front of her. He had his fist raised as if he were about to knock when Nina was suddenly staring into his eyes.

"Nina. You look amazing," Todd sighed, eyeing her up and down.

She huffed and forced a smile. Nina didn't feel like fighting, she just wanted to make her appearance at the party and find a way to sneak out to be with Kevin. "Thanks," she replied, moving past him.

Todd slipped his hand into hers and spun her around and back to face him again, closer now than before.

"I've been wanting a moment alone with you. Can we talk?" He made puppy eyes at her and she felt him smoothing his thumb over the back of her hand. It took all she had not to laugh in his face. Todd's delusions about rekindling their romance were enough to make Nina double over in hysterics, but she resisted.

"I really need to get downstairs, what kind of sister of the bride would I be if I missed the engagement party?" Nina pulled away again and started down the steps, silently praying Todd would take a hint and mingle with the rest of the family friends that filled her home.

"Later then?" he asked.

Nina turned around at the bottom of the stairs and smiled and nodded to him. Anything to shut him up. She rounded the corner to the large living room where the majority of the guests were and her eyes stopped on James. He was standing next to the grand piano with a smile on his face, talking to Nina's father. They were sharing a laugh when his gaze drifted and he saw Nina standing alone, staring at him. She lowered her eyes in shame and began picking at her fingers, holding back tears.

She looked up and he was before her, the same melancholy in his eyes.

"Wanna take a walk?" he asked, grabbing her hand, not waiting for an answer. Nina nodded and breathed deep to keep her tears at bay. The air on the back deck was cool but Nina could feel summer coming. *Summer*, she mused. *The end of it all.*

"James, I …" Nina started but he held a hand up to stop her. His eyes were soft as he leaned against the railing of the deck for a moment, collecting his thoughts.

"I was mean. I was really mean and I'm sorry," he said. He folded his arms across his chest and sighed. "You're my best friend and you've always accepted every part of me and I want to be able to do the same for you. But I can't be a part of what you're doing. Can we just pretend I don't know?"

Nina's face contorted and her mouth opened silently before she found her words. "Are you serious?"

He sucked in a breath and blinked slowly. "I love you Nina but I kind of think the less I know, the better."

She mindlessly let her head bob. "I understand."

"I knew you would. Now let's get back to that party," James' tone changed to his normal joking self and Nina continued to wear a mask of a smile. She was right back to the beginning, with no one to talk to about the most important thing happening to her, once again forced to be two separate Nina's.

The party dragged on with Nina glancing at the clock every few minutes wanting desperately to be at Kevin's side. Todd persisted with his attempts to get her alone but she successfully evaded him every time. She toasted her sister and Blake like a good girl and posed for family snapshots. All the while, her heart ached to be somewhere else. Guests were slowly trickling out the front door, leaving for the night so Nina took the time her father was distracted with good-byes to head outside, too. She glanced around and with cars pulling off the side of the street in front of her house, no one seemed to be paying any attention to her. She regretted staying in her heels but started walking down the street anyway. He was only a few blocks away. The weather was nice enough to walk and she figured she could use the fresh air to clear her head.

"Hey Cinderella! Running off from the ball so soon?" His voice sent a cold chill up her spine. *Shit*, she thought before turning to see Todd chasing her down the block.

"Just getting some air," she muttered. Her reached her and grinned from ear to ear.

"Why don't I join you?"

Nina huffed and shook her head exasperatedly. "Oh, why the hell not?"

"Nina, there's something I want to talk to you about." His tone suddenly changed and she sensed in him a shyness she was completely taken aback by. Todd was the most overconfident boy she'd ever known and yet now he was fidgeting at her side and looked as though he was struggling for words.

Nina stopped and turned to him with a confused look. She wanted to tell him to spit it out already. Todd stopped too and before Nina had a moment to ask him what his problem was, his arms were around her. His lips pressed firmly against hers in a sneak attack kiss that she couldn't shrug away from fast enough.

She managed to push him off of her angrily before he tried to deepen the kiss.

"What are you doing!?"

Todd stood with his mouth gaping and his eyes wide. "I love you, Nina."

Nina's face twisted in horror and she snapped. A fire grew in her eyes and she threw her hands in the air and began speaking to the sky.

"Are you fucking kidding me? It's just one joke after another, isn't it? Why can't you just leave me alone?" she screamed.

"Um, w-who are you talking to?" Todd asked dumbfounded.

She let out another angry rumble and started stomping back to her house. "I don't know! God. The Universe. You!"

Todd was close behind her, trying to keep up as she stamped her feet into the sidewalk getting home as fast as she could.

"It's not a joke, Nina. I'm in love with you. I want us to be together again. There could be a party for *us* someday, you know?" He choked the words out, still keeping a bashful sense about him.

Nina spun around to meet his eyes when she reached her front door again and he saw the rage filling her.

"There will *never* be a party for us. Go home, Todd!" she growled at him. Throwing open the front door, she snatched her car keys off the table in the foyer and yelled to whoever might be listening inside.

"I'm going out!"

She brushed past Todd, who still looked bewildered, hopped in her car driving off into the night to the one place she'd wanted to be all day long.

Chapter Sixty-Two

There was a knock at the door and Kevin bounced off the sofa to answer it. He'd been waiting for her for hours. He opened the door and let a wide smile grow on his face seeing her all dressed up. She was stunning. Her hair was in soft waves and she looked like she'd stepped off the pages of a vintage fashion magazine in the sweet party dress she was wearing. Her face however, looked angry. Without a word he grabbed her hand and pulled her inside.

"What's going on?" he asked.

Nina was quiet, her face flushed and she was flexing her hands into fists. Kevin cautiously led her to the sofa and took a seat next to her. Nina sighed and her head hung low as she finally relaxed.

"Are you okay?" Kevin whispered as he brushed her hair back from one side of her face. Nina made a weak attempt at a smile and nodded.

"You're all that I have," she said in a whisper.

Kevin felt his breath catch in his chest. He glanced at her. She looked tired, sad and heartbreakingly beautiful. He had no idea what to say to her. Guilt was flooding him quickly at the thought of young and beautiful Nina believing he was the only thing she had to hold on to. Had he created that feeling in her? Was their relationship cutting her off from the people in her life she really needed?

"That's not true."

Nina rolled her eyes at him. "My dad has no idea who I am and he doesn't seem to care to learn. My sister practically hates me. You know, she left me a note on the kitchen table *telling* me that I'm her maid of honor? If I didn't have my grandmother's eyes I'd swear I was switched at birth."

Kevin smiled a bit then grimaced at her. He and his father had been so close he couldn't imagine what she was feeling. He even found in his cousin Jeff the kind of brotherhood he knew he would've had if his mother had lived long enough to have more children.

"What about James?" Kevin asked.

Nina ran a hand through her hair and scratched at the back of her neck for a moment, deep in thought.

"Things between me and James have been … different lately," she said with a sigh.

"Right. It's got to be hard on you keeping a secret from him, huh?" Kevin touched her shoulder tenderly.

Nina turned to him slowly, deliberately. "Yeah, really hard."

"Well, what about Todd?"

Nina laughed loudly and glared at Kevin. "Are you kidding?"

Kevin chuckled back. "Not really. You told me he's your friend. Isn't he?"

"No. He's an asshole."

Nina's lips went tight and her face grew even more serious than before. Kevin felt like scooping her up in his arms and telling her everything would be all right. Her eyes came back up from the floor and met his. A smile curled on her lips and for a moment her eyes brightened.

"What's that smile for?" he asked, grinning back.

"I was *trying* to make you jealous when I said that about Todd. Couldn't you tell?" she asked.

Kevin snorted. "Well, I didn't know it was all a part of your master plan but it worked. I can't stand that kid."

Nina giggled and climbed into his lap with ease.

"He's nothing to be jealous of," she avowed.

"The thought of you in anyone else's arms …" He couldn't finish the thought.

It sickened him. Revolted him. The thought of Todd being Nina's friend was bad enough but if he were to ever be anything more than that again, Kevin would be disgusted by it.

"So what does next week hold for you?" he asked, trying to change the subject.

"Nothing, why?"

Kevin's brow furrowed. "You're not going somewhere?"

Nina gave him the same confused look and shook her head.

"I just figured with spring break you'd be going on a family vacation." His words trailed off as he saw Nina's face fall.

"Spring break. I totally forgot," she started to laughed breathily, her eyes squinted. "Dad's going back to London for work and I heard Blake telling someone at the party that Greta and his mother were going to Atlanta next week to look at some designer bridal gown boutiques. I guess I'm not invited."

Kevin's mouth twisted as he looked at her anguished face.

"Good." He stopped when Nina looked up at him. She batted her eyelashes and her pale pink lips parted ever so slightly, making him weak. "Do you want to go somewhere with me?"

Nina made a face at first and then lit up like a star. "Like a trip? You and me?"

"Yeah. I have a place in mind we could go just for a day or two. Do you want to?" he asked, his voice trembling a bit.

Nina slid closer to him on the couch and soon her hand was sneaking into Kevin's hair. She pulled him nearer and pressed her lips to his feverishly. He had his answer.

CHAPTER SIXTY-THREE

Nina peered out the front window taking in the sunrise. She couldn't remember the last time she was up early enough to catch it. She cringed a moment later when she finally did remember. It was Christmas Eve morning, when she sat on the beach telling James her secrets. It seemed so long ago now. Now that things were so seemingly perfect between her and Kevin.

Without hesitation Nina lied to her father telling him she was having a getaway with a girlfriend from school. He didn't ask where or how long or who this hypothetical gal pal was. He just gave her a simple yes and told her to take some cash out of the bank. It angered her that he didn't inquire further but she was so excited about spending time with Kevin she quickly forgot.

There was a brief honk outside and she popped out the door with her bag in hand and a cardigan slipped on over her t-shirt. Nina slid into Kevin's car and tossed her duffle bag in the backseat next to Sasha, giving her a quick pat on the head.

Kevin looked so handsome. He was in a black, long-sleeved cotton shirt and dark blue jeans. His hair was smooth, the chestnut waves still looking slightly damp from his shower. And his jaw was covered in just the slightest bit of stubble, just the way Nina liked it.

Silently he reached over and cupped the back of her neck. She leaned in and kissed him softly. The thrill of being able to kiss him when she felt like it gave her a surge of happiness.

"How long is the drive?" she asked.

"Less than an hour. Not far at all. You can sleep if you want," he said.

Nina thumbed through the visor attachment that held a sampling of Kevin's CDs. She found one that looked good and popped the disc into the stereo.

The music played with Kevin and Nina listening quietly with Sasha in the back, letting out tiny snores, a sort of whistling from her wet black nose. Nina sat with her head leaned against the window taking in the sight of golden wheat fields and tree covered hills.

"Hey," Kevin said.

They hadn't said anything to each other in a few minutes. It was the good kind of silence between them, a comfortable lack of words. Nina sucked in a breath and sat up straight. She hadn't been asleep, just peaceful. The sun coming in from the window had been keeping her warm and the songs coming from the radio had been keeping her mind at ease. She laughed, realizing she'd been singing along, probably annoying Kevin as he drove.

"Sorry."

"Louder please," he said. Nina smiled but ignored his teasing request. She turned the knob on the stereo, lowering the volume.

"Can you tell me yet?" she asked, putting a sugary whine in her voice.

Kevin huffed in playful protest. "Not a chance. But will you look at those directions for me?"

"The answer has been right in front of me the whole time?" she laughed.

Kevin shot her a smile and shrugged.

"What does it say I'm supposed to do after I pass through Harrisburg?"

"You don't know where we're going?" she exclaimed.

"I do. It's just been a while, okay?"

"Take Exit 34 South and then it's another twenty-eight miles. Which would lead us where exactly?" she probed again.

"You'll see."

Nina rolled her eyes but stayed quiet. If he wanted to have his fun she'd let him. Kevin pulled the car off onto the exit ramp and headed south. Nina turned the music up again and leaned back, letting her sleepiness finally set in, as she began to drift off.

"Baby?" Kevin said softly.

Her eyes fluttered open to see Kevin's face above her, the car door opened. She smiled dreamily at him and started to climb out of the car, stretching her arms and legs as she did so.

"How long was I out?" she asked.

"Just a few minutes. Come on, we can go inside and you can sleep some more." He took her hand and Nina glanced around noticing that the car had already been unpacked. She felt the crunch of dirt and sticks below her feet then turning to where Kevin was leading her, she saw the cabin. A small, dark log cabin tucked into a deep green forest, birds in the trees and the sun poking through the dense leaves from above. Sasha was investigating the porch, sniffing the two rocking chairs that sat just outside the door.

"Did you rent this place?" Nina asked as they walked inside.

It smelled a bit musty but the kind of smell that reminded her of her grandmother's house. The space was open, kitchen toward the back, the front was made up of a living room with mismatched furniture and a stack of quilts in the corner. There was an open loft above her, the bedroom presumably. She stepped inside further to see that above the fireplace in the living area was an assortment of photographs. A young boy and his father.

"I … uh, own this place," Kevin stammered.

He called Sasha inside and stood awkwardly as Nina examined the photos above the fireplace closely. It was an array of scenes, fishing trips and Christmases. Then a graduation, the young boy now closer to being a man was dressed in cap and gown and grinning adorably. It was the same adorable smile Nina had been enjoying for the past few months. Nina felt a strange sensation looking at Kevin as an eighteen year old just like her. She wondered if they'd met as fellow students would they still have fallen in love with each other. Turning to him, she tilted her head to one side with bright eyes.

"You were so cute."

Kevin laughed. "Yeah, what happened, right?"

"I bet you came here all the time as a kid. It must have been great," she said, swiping her hand absently along the mantle gathering a pad of dust on her fingertip. She wiped the dust on her pants and moved to Kevin who was still standing just inside the doorway.

He grimaced slightly and grabbed their bags. "Come on, let's go upstairs."

Nina followed him up the wooden steps and just as she suspected, there was the bedroom. Kevin dropped their things on the floor and ran his hand through his hair swiftly.

"Do you want to take a nap? The grocery store is about fifteen minutes away. I can run out while you sleep if you want?" he offered.

Nina patted the cream and blue checkered quilt that covered the queen sized bed and watched as a puff of dust filled the air above her hand. They shared a look and a laugh before Kevin quickly hopped off to the linen closet. Nina stripped the bed and Kevin was back with fresh sheets and blankets. They remade the bed in comfortable silence, the ease of being around each other setting in firmly. Once the bed was no longer a dust bowl, Nina took a seat, perched on the edge. Kevin walked around and stood gazing down at her curiously.

"You called me 'baby'," she remarked in a quiet voice. Her hand came up slowly and pressed against his chest, against his heart. Kevin's hand wrapped around hers and held it solidly as he nodded.

"Say it again," she whispered. He slid onto the bed next to her and let his lips move to her ear. He kissed the tender skin of her neck just below her earlobe.

"I love you, baby."

Leaning back against the soft quilt, she let Kevin position himself above her with slow, graceful moves as his kisses trailed from her throat to her collarbone. His hands were pushing up the material of her shirt, smoothing over her breasts. Nina moaned at the feeling and pulled her shirt over her head brazenly. She watched as Kevin did what he always did each time they made love. He took in the sight of her and his breath stopped as his eyes moved all over her. It was as if he was mentally photographing her flesh.

He helped her out of the rest of her clothes with a few rushed movements and she returned the favor. Skin against skin they explored each other with their hands. Nina reveled at the feeling of Kevin's mouth upon her. As he traveled further down her body, her hands slid into his thick locks of hair, gripping him. More noises were pulled from her as he tasted her in the place she most desired. With careful actions he took her to the edge then attempted to tease her but with her hands still in his hair, she wordlessly told him exactly what she wanted. And he complied.

CHAPTER SIXTY-FOUR

Nina woke up with her head against Kevin's bare chest, feeling the rise and fall of his breathing. She had the kind of rested feeling she'd only recently become accustomed to. It was the feeling of a sluggish body, worn out from love making and a tranquil mind from being so at ease with Kevin. She lifted her head and rested her chin lightly against the tight muscles of his chest.

"You're awake," he mumbled.

Nina nodded and smiled lazily. The loft was a dim amber shade, painted by the sunset through the trees outside. They'd been in bed all day, sleeping for at least a few hours.

"Should we go to the grocery store?" she asked.

Kevin cleared his throat and began smoothing his hands over Nina's hair.

"I was thinking we should go out to dinner. A date."

Nina propped herself up on her side and met his stare. "Really?"

His eyes were soft and his face, bathed in the orange glow coming from the skylights above them, looked angelic to her. "Yes really. Would you like that?"

She pulled her bottom lip in to her mouth and stifled a girlish grin.

"Yes, Kevin. I'd love a second date with you."

The restaurant wasn't very busy and it was a far cry from the fancy bistro where they'd had their first date. This place was a real barbeque pit. It was a hole in the wall, paper-towel-roll-on-the-table kind of place. But Nina was beaming sitting at the wooden table gazing across at Kevin.

"Are you going to tell me about the cabin?" she asked.

Kevin glanced down at the one page menu, the laminated edges peeling back and curling. "What do you mean? You saw it. What's there to tell?"

"Um, you said you own it, there's pictures of you and your dad all over the place but when I mentioned you going there as a kid, you made a face and shut up. So … are you going to tell me about the cabin?" Her face wasn't quite stern but she was determined to get an answer. He sighed and put the menu down.

"It was my dad's," he said.

Nina's eyebrows moved slightly inward, a signal for him to continue.

"I had no idea about the cabin until he died and I started going through the estate. He …" Kevin stopped when the waiter came over, a surly sight of a man with a bandana tied around his head and an apron around his waist. Nina gave a waning smile to Kevin and they ordered their dinner.

Kevin cleared his throat after the waiter stepped away. "The cabin was Dad's hideaway, I guess. This secret place he went to and never once told me about. When I first found out I was furious. Even when I saw it filled with pictures of the two of us, I was still angry at him. That he felt the need to hide a part of himself from me. Taking trips to get away from me. It hurt."

Nina reached across the table, humidity sticking her flesh to its surface. Kevin grabbed her hand and she felt a surge of excitement at the joy of holding his hand in front of others shamelessly.

"I get it now, though," his eyes lowered as he spoke and a subtle smile crept on his face.

"What do you mean?" Nina asked.

"I understand what it's like to have something you love so much that you don't want to share. And I also understand how hard it is to have a secret. I imagine whoever he shared that cabin with, whatever happened there, it was important to him and I have to respect that."

Nina smiled at him, her lips turning up ever so slightly. She squeezed his hand, still resting on the table.

"Tell me about him," she said.

"You read the book, you already know," he uttered.

Nina felt a pitch in her stomach as she remembered her icy words to Kevin about his father. She glanced back up at him and grimaced. She wanted to apologize but didn't know how. Kevin squeezed her hand in return and gave her a knowing smile.

"We were best friends. When I got old enough, I figured out just how much he sacrificed for me. You know, he was traveling the world having this grand adventure. The thing between him and my mom was just supposed to be a fling. I'm sure he had plenty of them. But then I came along. He didn't have to marry her, but he did. And strangely enough, he really loved her. It was clear to see that when she got sick. I was five years old and the cancer progressed pretty fast. God, but he loved her. He loved her until the day he died," Kevin sighed and absently smirked, lost in his own memories.

"After mom died he got a job at the bank in Detroit and we moved. He was an amazing father and he taught me everything I never thought I needed to know. He was teaching me with every simple word he ever said to me. I'm still learning from him." Kevin pushed his hand through his hair and then rubbed at his brow for a moment.

Nina caught a glimpse of his eyes, glassy with the threat of tears. She remembered the night Kevin cried to her on his father's birthday and felt her heart ache for him all over again.

Soon the waiter was back, carrying plates almost overflowing with baby back ribs and French fries. Nina laughed at the mountains of food placed in front of them. When she looked back up at Kevin he just smiled, the moisture gone from his eyes, a content look on his face.

The night was as close to perfection as Nina could have imagined. She and Kevin talked with ease about their lives and reminisced about what led them to this point. Neither made mention of the future. Nina left out James and Todd. Kevin kept quiet about college and the summer. They were still holding on to two different people, the one's living and loving in the moment and the one's dreading what was inevitably bound to happen.

CHAPTER SIXTY-FIVE

Kevin drew in a deep breath and rolled over expecting to let his arms wrap around Nina but the sheets next to him were cold. There was no clock in the room and it was almost too dark to see. It had surely been hours since they'd come home from dinner. Hours since she'd fallen asleep in his arms.

He sat up slowly and looked around the room, searching for a sign of her. Kevin climbed out of bed and started down the steps, calling out Nina's name in a whisper. The kitchen was empty but he saw steam coming from the tea kettle on the stove. A spoon sat on the wooden countertop with the remnants of sugar and warm tea pooled at its lowest point and Kevin smiled at the subtly sweet notion of Nina needing a midnight cup of tea.

From the front door he heard a noise and moved cautiously toward it. The screen door was open, letting the cool night air inside and he saw Sasha sitting next to one of the rocking chairs that was moving just barely, creaking. As he opened the rickety screen door, he saw her.

"Nina?" Kevin asked, moving to her side.

She was curled up in the large rocking chair, wrapped in a blanket and cradling her mug of hot tea with a blank stare on her face.

She shook her head absently. Kevin put a hand on her arm and waited for a reply, worried by the vacant look in her eyes. Nina didn't react to his touch, she only continued moving her head slowly back and forth, staring off into the distance.

"It's never going to be like this again," she whispered.

"What are you talking about?" Kevin asked.

"When we get back to Wexley, it won't be the same. We can't go out to eat. We can't stay the night with each other. We can never be a real couple."

He took her tea from her and set it on the table between the two oak rockers, a wrinkle set deep in his brow, his eyes locked on her porcelain face. His heart ached for her and the guilt he felt was only building each time he was faced with the truth regarding the amount of stress she was under. The back of his mind was screaming the answer to it all but he wasn't ready to lose her. To give her up.

"Come back to bed, we can talk about all of this later," he said, touching her hand, trying to coax her forward.

Nina snatched her hand back from him fiercely and shot him a look. Kevin stood stunned, holding his hands up in surrender. His eyes lowered in shame, Nina still stared coldly up at him.

"Don't do that," she growled.

"What?" His voice was barely a whisper.

"I know you're trying to protect me, but avoiding the topic is only making it harder. We're running out of time."

"We have all summer," Kevin retorted hastily.

Nina rolled her eyes at him and shook her head again. It was Kevin holding on to the fairy tale now.

"I got a call from Caldwell a few days ago. I've been accepted into the summer program," she evaded his gaze as she confessed.

Kevin sat down next to her once again, waiting for her to continue.

"My dad thinks it's a good opportunity …" her voice trailed off.

"But you haven't decided yet, right?" he asked.

Nina glanced at him and he knew.

"Well. Okay. Glad we talked about it," he spat. He stood and walked past her quickly going back inside.

"Kevin, wait …" Nina pleaded from behind him.

He turned, frozen in the doorway, gawking at her incredulously. Standing feet apart in the entryway of his father's cabin, he'd never felt further from her.

"This could be a really great thing for me. And we both knew I'd have to go at some point," she sighed.

"I know that. But we still have time together. What about the next few weeks?" Kevin asked, throwing his hands in the air.

"What about them, Kevin? Are you going to take me to prom? Sit with my family at graduation?"

Her mouth snapped shut as soon as she said it. Kevin blinked a few times and kept his eyes off Nina, scanning the dark cabin in silence. The quiet burned in Kevin's ears and he could hear the echo of her voice berating him.

"So that's how it's going to be? After everything we went through to be together, you're gonna push me away now? What was the fucking point?" he asked angrily.

He stared at the dark shadows moving across her face, a picture of the clouds rolling over the moon.

"I'm just … I shouldn't have said anything," she whispered.

Kevin's face softened and he came to her again, wrapping his arms around her instinctively.

"We can figure it out. We will," he breathed into her hair.

She let herself melt into his arms and Kevin's heart sank when he felt a shudder roll through her as silent tears begin to fall. Kevin could feel the moisture against his bare chest but he didn't say a word. He just held her and a few moments later he led her upstairs to bed where she fell asleep against him.

Kevin stayed wide awake, staring at the walls, his thoughts racing. The guilty thoughts he'd been having for weeks were still ever present. Guilt that he was keeping her from having a normal life with normal friendships and relationships. Preemptive guilt that it would indeed be ending soon. But now, a new feeling struck him—a new *idea*. It was different than the others, yet somehow still laced in guilt. It was crazy but he kept going back to it.

But it seemed simple enough. Leave the school. Quit his job then live happily ever after. Just as he thought it and felt a swell of excitement run through him at the notion, he snapped back to reality again. *Happily ever after for who*, he thought. What if Nina needed to be on her own? Needed that independence and carefree time in the big city to find out who she was and what she wanted. Maybe Kevin would be holding her back. With the idea of taking a huge step in the wrong direction for Nina sitting in his mind, he finally let his eyes close.

The next day was quiet between the two of them. A relaxing day spent outside walking some trails behind the cabin and making meals together. They didn't talk about what happened the previous night or what would happen when they arrived back in Wexley Falls. They tried to enjoy the time they had with one another before they headed home, knowing the final days of their relationship were about to unfold.

Chapter Sixty-Six

May

It was the end of the day, the day before the prom and Nina was gathering her books from her locker, ready to go home but not before she saw him. A pebble of sadness sat in the bottom of her stomach when she imagined her perfect prom. Kevin would show up at her door to watch her ascend from the stairs in her stunning, red-carpet-worthy dress. They'd dance together under strands of white twinkle lights and no one would stare at them. A kiss would be just a kiss, not a scandal or a secret. She sighed letting a slow blink of her eyes wash away the foolish fantasy.

Standing up to close the metal door of her locker, she felt a tender hand at the small of her back. Another sigh rolled out of her but this one had more of a shudder to it. Her lips spread into a grin as she turned.

"Happy to see me?" Todd asked with a smile as wide as hers. Nina's face fell and she pulled away from his touch.

"Oh, it's you. Hi," her voice quivered, bewildered by the unexpected sight of him.

Todd's brows crinkled together in the middle at the sudden distance between them. "Yeah … hi. Can we talk?"

Nina looked at him exasperatedly and nodded, leaning back against the wall. He smiled again and stepped slightly closer.

"I've been trying to ask you for a while now but I never seem to catch you in a good mood," he said.

His hand reached out to her for an instant but he redirected it quickly and scratched at the back of his neck instead.

"It's quite the trend when I'm around you," she snipped. Todd didn't notice the dig however and continued.

"Alright, I'm just gonna say it. Will you go to prom with me?"

Before she could think, a laugh escaped Nina's lips and with that Todd's face crumpled.

"Oh Todd, I'm sorry. I'm going with James. We've had it planned for a while so …"

"It's fine. I'll see you there I guess," he muttered, his eyes locked on the floor, his cheeks red.

Nina almost felt bad for him. She noticed how torn up he'd seemed lately but it didn't change the fact she could barely stand him. As she watched him bolt away from her, defeated, she shook her head at the strange moment before heading to Kevin's room.

Nina poked her head into B100 and grinned when she saw Kevin straightening desks. She waltzed inside and closed the door and the noise caused him to glance up.

"Well hello," he beamed.

Nina rushed up to him and stole a quick kiss.

"What's that for?" Kevin asked, still smiling widely at her.

Nina shrugged her shoulders and pulled her bottom lip between her teeth. She didn't want to tell him it was because she was trying to get in as many kisses as she could before she left. She didn't want to bring it up again.

"I'm glad you're here. I have something for you," Kevin walked to his desk and opened the lower drawer.

Nina watched carefully as he pulled his hand back out from the drawer with what seemed like nothing. He opened his hand to her and

Nina drew in a sharp breath looking down at the bracelet that sat in Kevin's palm. It was a beautiful weave of yellow and rose gold with tiny flower details along it. It looked old but it was so completely her style. Kevin latched it around her wrist and she continued to gaze at it.

"I found this at the cabin on our last day. It was my mother's and I want you to have it. I can't give you a corsage tomorrow like I want to but this you can have forever," he whispered.

Nina's eyes flashed up to meet his when he said that final word.

"I did something today and you can tell me I'm an idiot for it if you want," Kevin was stumbling over his words and laughing nervously.

She was waiting patiently for whatever his confession could be but then he glanced past her at the door. Nina turned to see what he'd stopped to stare at. James was standing in the doorway looking annoyed.

"Nina, come on. I've got to get home and Nick can't give me a ride," James said plainly.

Kevin cleared his throat and straightened up and away from Nina. "Well, I'll get back to you with that, uh, letter of recommendation," he forced a quick cover.

James snorted. "Man you've got that act down. Don't worry, Casanova, it's just me out here."

"James!" Nina nearly screamed. Kevin's face had gone blank and he shot glances back and forth between James and Nina.

"He *knows*?"

Nina felt her throat tightening as Kevin's eyes zeroed in on her. She heard James sigh from the doorway and she looked over at him as he hung his head in shame.

"I told him months ago over Christmas when things were bad," she said.

"So that somehow made it okay for you to tell him when things got better?" Kevin raised his voice and whipped his head back to glare at James.

"Kevin, he … he just knew. He figured it out."

She saw his hands clench into fists and she stepped to him to put her hand on his arm. Kevin pulled away from her violently and Nina flinched.

"Jesus, I can't believe how stupid I am. I don't know what I was thinking, you're just a kid," he growled.

Nina heard James gasp from the doorway. Her heart was stung by his words but she wouldn't let James see.

"James, get out of here."

"Why, Nina? He probably already knows everything we could possibly have to talk about. Let him stay," Kevin's voice was angry and growing louder with each heated word. James left without a sound and Nina was thankful for that.

"Can you please calm down so we can talk about this?" Nina tried to keep a steady tone but the quiver in her voice was overpowering.

"Don't you think I've wanted to tell someone? *Anyone?* Do you know how many times I've almost slipped in front of Jeff? It's been just as hard on me as it has been on you only you've had James to confide in this whole time and I've had no one. How is that fair? You lied to me, Nina. *Again*," he yelled.

Nina's chin trembled as she held back tears. She wanted to scream back at him that she hadn't had James. That James had forbidden her from speaking his name in conversation. She had no one as well. To her, James knowing and not caring was worse than him not knowing at all.

"You should go," he whispered.

Nina felt her heart lurch and she flashed back to the day she'd walked into the very same room months before. He had the same look on his face now as he had then. Nina's fear was filling her up overwhelmingly fast.

"What about us?" she asked in a voice quiet and shaking.

Kevin turned his eyes directly to her, his lips in a tight line. Nina watched in pain as he shook his head slowly and shrugged his shoulders. He said nothing. His face was cold and emotionless as he glared at her. Nina felt her eyes welling up when she flinched at the sound of another voice in the room suddenly.

"Oh Mr. Reed, I didn't realize you were with a student," Principal Andrews said as he stepped into the room nonchalantly. Kevin turned to him then looked back at Nina. A chill ran through her as his look was even icier.

Nina cleared her throat. "No it's fine Principal Andrews. I was just going."

The tall, pudgy man smiled at her and walked further into the room having no idea what he'd just walked in on. Nina took one final look at Kevin and forced herself to march out the door.

Kevin willed himself to unclench his fists and let his anger subside for the moment. He waited for his boss to say something, fearing if he spoke first he might scream.

"How are things, Kevin?" Principal Andrews asked, taking a leisurely seat atop one of the many beige desks.

His brow scrunched together in three perfect lines. "Uh, fine."

"Of course I'm asking because I'm wondering if there's something wrong. You've seemed to be quite a perfect fit here at Wexley. Taking over for Mrs. Oliver seemed to be a breeze for you. Your test scores are great, there've been little to no discipline problems in your classes and your students really seem to love you."

Kevin nearly winced at his words. *If you only knew*, he thought.

"So with all that being said, I was rather shocked to find your letter of resignation on my desk this afternoon," he folded his hands in his lap and gave Kevin a concerned, almost patronizing look.

"Yeah, I just … it's time for me to do something else. I wasn't planning on staying this long but I need to move on," Kevin stumbled over his words, his mind still with Nina.

"Well, you have to do what's best for you. You've been a great addition to our staff." Principal Andrews stood up and absently looked around the room before slowly heading out the door.

With his mind reeling Kevin started again. "Look, if it's okay with you, I've already written the final. A substitute could give it. I'd kind of just like to pack my stuff up now and be done," he blurted.

Principal Andrews squinted at Kevin and stayed silent for a moment. He slowly nodded after examining Kevin's face.

"Sure. If that's what you really want to do."

He thought about it for a split second. He might be making a huge mistake. He and Nina may not make it through this fight, let alone wind up happily ever after like he'd planned. He breathed deep and let his heart decide. Kevin lowered his eyes to the floor.

"It is."

Chapter Sixty-Seven

Nina's legs were shaking and her mind was blank. It felt like her head was filled with a blinding white light. She was nearly to the doors when she glanced at a table set up that had most likely seen quite a bit of traffic that day. Covered in a black cloth and sprinkled with glittering confetti, it looked out of place in the starkly lit hall of the high school. Nina let her eyes roam over the sign taped to the front of the table. *A Night to Remember* was painted in big cursive silver letters on a black poster board. She shut her eyes and breathed in for a moment then she heard a voice.

"What happened?" James's voice was soft. She opened her eyes to see him standing at the doors that led to the parking lot.

"I don't know yet."

"I'm so sorry Nina. I thought he knew you told me," James walked toward her but Nina stepped back and turned her face from her friend.

"He's gonna hate me just like before."

James tried again, getting close enough to touch her shoulder. "He never hated you. If he hated you then things wouldn't have worked out."

Nina's eyes flared up and pierced through James. "You don't know anything about us," she shouted.

"I'm sorry. I don't know what else to say," James breathed.

"There's nothing to say. The love of my life thinks I'm a liar and a child. It's over," she started to choke on her words and she pushed past James, heading to her car.

James followed quickly behind her. Nina slowly slid into the driver's seat. James waited outside the passenger side, hesitating as if he wasn't sure she'd be kind enough to still drive him home. As he let out a slow and patient breath, his door was unlocked and Nina was waiting for him to get in. They drove in silence to James's home.

She pulled into his driveway and was ready for him to finally be gone when he turned to her carefully.

"Do you really think he's the love of your life?" he asked in a whisper.

Nina's eyes tightened on him before she spoke. "If I thought you really cared, I'd tell you. And if you really knew me, you wouldn't have to ask."

Chapter Sixty-Eight

Nina's gaze hadn't left the mirror for minutes. She stared at herself for a long time, her eyes lacking the sparkle that a girl should have on her prom night. Fidgeting with the beaded halter strap of her dress, putting it perfectly in place, she started to feel a stinging sensation in her eyes. She blew air up from her mouth in effort to dry her eyes before tears had the chance to fall. Then there was a soft knock on the door.

"Come in."

James walked in holding a clear plastic box with a white orchid inside. His eyes swept up her slowly from her peep-toe heels, red lacquered nails showing through, to the shining champagne silk dress that hung in loose folds down her legs and clung tight to her hips, on up to the sweetheart neck and the sparkly halter strap. Her hair was pulled up in a twist, a jeweled comb placed in one side, shimmering gold next to her black strands. James took her hand and gently kissed the back of it. Nina didn't have the strength to pull away from him even when she saw his eyes lingering on the bracelet she'd yet to take off.

"Why are you here?" she asked.

"Because we made a deal in the eighth grade that we'd go to senior prom together no matter what."

She rolled her eyes at him. "I'm not sure our eighth grade selves could have realized the amount of shit that might be going down at the time."

He pulled her closer to him and she looked at him with sad eyes. It wasn't how she'd pictured it. Though James looked great in his black tux, a smaller matching orchid pinned to his lapel, she couldn't get into the prom spirit. The uncertainty of Kevin's next move was torturing her mind. She didn't even know if she wanted to go.

But as her best friend stood before her giving her an incredibly sincere look, she wanted nothing more than to be a teenager again.

"I screwed up. I don't know what I would've done if when I came out to you you'd said 'that's fine, just don't ever talk to me about it'. I'm such an asshole." His words were rushing out of him and Nina felt the tears coming back. She tried to shake her head and stop him but she couldn't.

"I'll spend the rest of our lives making it up to you. But for tonight, let's just go and dance and make fun of the people we don't like. The rest can wait for one night," James said.

She took another glance at herself in the mirror and let James place the corsage on her wrist gingerly. He leaned in close and kissed her cheek. With his face against hers, she felt a shiver run through her. James hugged her tight and she found the will to stifle her tears.

"It can wait for one night," Nina breathed. They headed downstairs to let James' mother take a ridiculous amount of pictures before they left.

The banquet hall had trees wrapped in twinkling white lights, glittery stars hanging from above and sheer fabrics draped strategically, transforming the room into the *Night to Remember* the students of Wexley Falls High were promised. Nina and James walked in and had their photo taken under the horribly cheesy arch of shiny cardboard stars and metallic colored balloons. Music blared and the floor nearly shook. She glanced around the giant sparkling room, hoping to see Kevin. James took her by the arm and they walked out onto the hardwood floor with some of their other friends and he coaxed the first few dance moves out of her. In no time she was swaying her hips and moving her feet in time with the music, letting go for one night.

Eventually the music slowed and Nina felt her stomach flip. James gave her a weak smile, not knowing whether to pull her into his arms for a dance or not. Nina saw his face suddenly light up and she looked behind her feeling a sudden anticipation that maybe Kevin would be there waiting. Turning, she saw a handsome young man who was eager to dance, just not with her. Nick stood in a black suit with a deep red vest and tie, smiling sweetly at James.

Without a word, Nina stepped aside and watched as Nick took James by the hand to dance. She went to an empty table covered in confetti and took a seat. As she watched James and Nick sway to the music, the other students looking on curiously at the pair, she felt bad that as little as James knew about the relationship she had with Kevin, it was about that same amount of knowledge she had about the progression of James' relationship with Nick.

Still sitting alone at the small table, she shook her head and smiled each time Nick and James tried to invite her back to the dance floor. She was content to watch two people enjoy their prom rather than only halfheartedly enjoy it herself.

It was almost an hour later when Nina felt a tap on her shoulder. Her heart leapt, thinking for a moment it had to be Kevin. She turned her head and looked over her shoulder sweetly. Her eyes shut in frustration seeing Todd standing beside her in his tux.

"Hello Nina," he said.

"Todd."

He took a seat next to her and scanned the room with his eyes. "Where's your date?"

"He's around. What do you want?" she asked annoyed by his presence.

He laughed and gave her a grin. "Just dance with me, okay? For old times' sake."

She glared at him blankly for a moment and thought about how pitiful it was that she hadn't danced a slow dance at her senior prom. Then she thought about how little she liked Todd.

Glancing around the huge space, she still saw no sign of Kevin. She'd been waiting all night. He hadn't even called. Suddenly Todd had a hold of her hand and was pulling her out onto the dance floor not caring to wait for her response. Nina went with it, though she immediately felt uneasy. She wished she'd checked her phone one last time before getting up but it was too late, Todd's arms were around her and they were swaying to the music.

Nina felt Todd's breath against her ear, causing a sickened shiver to roll down her spine. "Why won't you give me a chance, Nina?" he whispered.

She huffed and shook her head. "Drop it Todd."

"I know there's someone else."

Nina pulled back from him and looked into his eyes. Was he serious? Her heart began to race as Todd's eyes narrowed on her.

"It's easy to see it, it's written all over your face."

Nina opened her mouth to speak but nothing came out. She was stunned and afraid of what he might say next.

"The thing I can't figure out is, who is it?" Todd's voice was becoming raw and cruel.

Nina turned her eyes from him, she was about to shrug out of his grasp when she saw Kevin over Todd's shoulder in the distance. She wanted to smile but she knew what he was seeing. She must have looked so comfortable in Todd's arms on prom night from where Kevin was standing. His face was heartbreakingly handsome but sadness was painted in his deep brown eyes. He looked like her prince charming in his suit and all she wanted to do was run to him. Todd turned the two of them with the rhythm of the music and took a glance at who she'd been staring at. A tear slid down Nina's cheek, knowing Kevin's eyes must have stayed fixed on her.

"Him?" Todd said incredulously.

She sucked in a sharp breath and another few tears fell.

"Let go of me," she groaned, trying to pull free.

He held her tighter and forced her to look at him. "I could tell you had a crush, but—you're seriously crying over him?"

Nina beat her fists against Todd's chest and finally pushed herself away from him. Her eyes flew open wide when she realized she hadn't been the one to separate them. Kevin had Todd's shirt balled tight in his two fists, practically holding him off the ground.

"She said let go," Kevin barked into Todd's face.

Kevin let him go and took a deep breath, the entire room watching them. Other teachers and chaperones were on their way over but Kevin raised his hand to them, holding them off. The music kept on playing and it seemed as though their scuffle was over. James and Nick had pushed their way through the crowd and James caught Nina's eye from far away.

Todd began to laugh, smoothing the front of his suit where Kevin had ruffled him.

"Well I have my answer," Todd muttered.

Kevin glared back at him while Nina stood motionless, shaken by the scene. Todd took bold steps toward Kevin and Nina, sneering and holding back his laughter.

"Oh Nina, your hero's come to save the day. How sweet?"

Kevin came back at him, shoving him hard in the chest. Nina yelped and moved for the door. James hurried after her, keeping a hold of Nick's hand. Todd threw his hands up, a wicked grin on his mouth.

"You really want to fight a student? Don't you think sleeping with one is bad enough, Mr. Reed?"

His lips curled back in a snarl and Kevin lost control, pushing Todd once more, even harder than before. Todd lost his balance and flew back onto his elbows, separating a group of dancing students. The room turned to them again. Kevin stared down at him with fire in his eyes. He looked as if he wanted to kick him while he was down, or worse, pick him up and hit him square in the jaw. Kevin panted and glanced around at the crowd. Everyone was staring at the scene. He gave Todd his hand pulling him up fast, meeting him chest to chest.

"If you know what's good for you, you'll stay away from both of us," he said, his eyes still raging.

Kevin walked to the door with the whole senior class staring at his back. His eyes searched for Nina but he already knew she was gone.

Chapter Sixty-Nine

Up the stone steps to the front of his house he heard her sniff and it nearly broke his heart. Nina was sitting on the porch swing, rocking gently. Kevin had no idea what he'd say to her. Would he apologize? Tell her about his resignation? Or just sit down in silence?

"I didn't know where else to go," she croaked.

Kevin's brow furrowed and he nodded solemnly. Though the sky was dark, the lantern light outside his front door made it clear to see that Nina's cheeks were flushed and her eyes were wet.

"I'm sorry," he whispered.

Nina glanced up at him, her bloodshot eyes squinting on him.

"Me too. We have to talk …" her voice trailed off into the faintest squeak. Kevin's heart lurched in his chest for a moment. He took a seat beside her on the wooden swing and rested his hand on hers. Feelings of fear and regret filled him as he prepared for what he already knew was coming.

He could change her mind with a number of words. He could tell her there was no need to do what she was about to do because he'd quit his job at the school. They were no longer student and teacher. They could be just Kevin and Nina. He could tell her that the rumors and glares in the halls would blow over soon enough and then she'd be graduating. He could tell her he'd be able to find a job in New York. But Kevin held back because deep down he thought he needed to let her go.

He tried to prepare himself, he tried to remind himself of the thoughts and concerns he'd been stricken with lately, even if his love for her overpowered them most of the time. He had to let her go, let her move on. He didn't want to be responsible for holding back a young girl from a full life. She sat up, wiped a few tears away and looked him in the eye. His breath stuck in his chest as he waited for her to say it.

"I can't do this anymore," she said.

Her bottom lip trembled and his heart ached to see it. Drawing in a deep, calm breath, Kevin reached out and cupped her face in his hands. She leaned into the tender feeling of his thumb sweeping across the apple of her cheek, wiping her tears away.

Nina slowly pulled away and ran her hands over her face. "I'm leaving in two weeks. We haven't mentioned it once since our trip. How can this work out? Everyone at school will know now because of Todd. Oh God, you're going to lose your job."

Kevin chewed the inside of his cheek before letting his eyes graze over Nina's tortured face.

"It'll be alright. Don't worry about me," he said unconvincingly.

"Maybe we were never meant to be. What if it's too hard because we're forcing it?" Nina's words were now spewing out of her. Her shaking voice seemed to be keeping up with her undoubtedly racing thoughts but Kevin kept quiet, his heart feeling ripped in two.

"I love you so much. More than I think I might ever love anyone else but—" Nina stopped, a flood of tears welling in her pale eyes. She looked directly at Kevin for a moment. "I was crazy to think I could handle this. I can't. I just can't do it anymore."

Kevin nodded slowly, his lips twisting as he forced himself to hold back tears.

"I'm so sorry," she whispered.

She moved in close to him, sliding her hands in his thick dark hair, keeping his face inches from hers. He tried to avoid her gaze, looking anywhere but her eyes, tears streaming down her cheeks silently. But as

Nina held onto him he was forced to look at her. For an instant he took in her beauty, her dark hair, porcelain skin, heather gray eyes and perfectly pink lips. Her face mesmerized him from afar once then by pure luck, she'd become his for a time. He knew he'd never find anyone quite like her and maybe he'd never even try. But he had to say goodbye. He refused to keep her from being happy.

Kevin raised his hands and touched her face tenderly with his fingertips. Nina sighed at the feeling and with her sigh, Kevin's eyes brimmed with tears. Soon her lips were against his and he felt himself burning the memory into his mind. Panic set in when he thought it might be the last time they'd kiss. His last chance.

He pulled away and blurted, "Did I tell you how beautiful you look tonight?"

Her face was streaked with salty tears, her eyes red and bleary. Nina laughed unexpectedly and turned her cheek playing timid before kissing Kevin once more. His shoulders slacked and he melted in her arms, relieved he hadn't yet had his last kiss from Nina.

Their mouths separated again and Kevin felt a horrible tension in his chest. Once more she told him she loved him and his mouth went dry. His stomach was twisting in knots and he wanted to scream.

Instead his voice came out a soft, sweet whisper, his breath warm against her cheek. "I love you, too, Nina. I'll love you the rest of my life."

He prayed for another kiss, her hands gripping his hair, her heartbeat pulsing against him. Nina stood and let her fingers interlace with his and she pulled him to his feet. She wordlessly placed his hands on her waist. Her arms moved to his neck and they swayed to silence. Slowly her head found its way to his chest and Nina began humming a tune to which they had their first and perhaps final dance. He smelled her hair and memorized the curve of her hips under his hands and before he knew it, she was done.

The panic worsened quickly. "So this is it? Goodbye?" he asked as she stood ready to leave.

Her lips turned up at one side. "Well, I'll see you Monday—at school, right?"

Kevin's eyes tightened on her for a second. It was his last chance to be selfish. His heart and mind played a quick but intense game for the win. She'd be so angry with him when she found out. She'd question everything they'd just said. She'd forget all about how difficult everything had been if she knew they could be together. But would it really be easier? Would it really be better or as good? Worth it? He didn't know and he was scared to see. And his fear helped his mind win.

"Right. Monday," he lied. He pulled her in for a quick but soft embrace. "Goodbye, Nina," he muttered into her hair.

Nina turned to step off the porch and looked back over her shoulder with a weak smile. "Bye."

CHAPTER SEVENTY

Nina's weekend consisted of wrestling with the decision she'd made. Her nights were sleepless and her thoughts were consumed by the gravity of what she'd done. She'd ended the best—and worst—thing to ever happen to her. And why? Because she was scared? As she sat in class Monday morning, thinking about Kevin being in the same building with her, her heart starting to flutter at the idea. Everything she said on prom night, it all felt like bullshit. With only a few days left in Wexley Falls, she didn't want to be alone. She wanted to be with Kevin.

The bell rang and she was out in the hall fast, heading to her locker. The faster the day was over, the sooner they could talk again. Reaching in her bag she found her cell phone which had been lighting up in her first period class like crazy.

She had fifteen text messages since the start of school. Nina never considered herself very popular so she panicked. Maybe something bad happened. Then she remembered the prom incident.

The first round of messages were questions.

Is it true?

Is Todd lying?

Was it good?

Then there were congratulatory messages.

Way to go Nina.

Ur my hero.

Nina felt sick. She looked around after stopping at her locker and realized most eyes were on her. She tried to breathe deep, she knew this was going to happen but she still wasn't expecting the glares and whispers in quite the volume they were coming. Just as she was about to delete them all, James was in front of her, wild-eyed and frazzled.

Nina smiled at him. "Hey, what's up?"

James looked around frantically. "Have you heard?"

"Uh, that I'll be on the cover of any and all Wexley Falls tabloids? Yeah. It's ridiculous. But it should blow over soon," she teased, grabbing her Government text book. James' face fell and he stared at the floor in silence.

"Oh, it's fine. I'll be fine. It's just gossip. It's only a rumor, *remember?*" Nina pressed.

She'd prepped James and Nick over the weekend that should anyone ask, namely administration, they should just call it a juicy rumor.

"Nina, he's not here," James said.

She blinked. "What do you mean? Of course he's here."

"Hannah Bruckheimer is in his first period class. She said they had a sub and the sub told the class he quit. He's gone."

Her eyes stayed fixed on James, the wounded puppy look on his face, as she flipped open her phone and hit Kevin's number on speed dial. She listened to it ring, her blank eyes locked on James. Her heart leapt for a moment but she shoved the feeling down when she realized the voice she heard on the other end was only his voice message telling her to leave her name and number.

"Hey, it's me. I'm hearing some weird things at school and I'm just wondering why you aren't here to face the storm with me. I really want to talk to you. Call me back." Nina felt her throat getting tight as she finished her message. Something about James' face told her it was true and he was still looking at her cautiously as if he was waiting for her to explode.

"Look, I'm not going to worry about this right now. There's no way he would've let me say all the things I said Saturday without telling me he'd *quit his job*. It's just not possible." Nina slammed her locker shut and stared down the hall. Girls were giving her grins and raised eyebrows while boys were whispering to each other, slapping one another on the back with a laugh certainly at her expense. She put on a brave face and pushed the nonsensical idea of Kevin quitting to the back of her mind where it stayed until the end of the day. In her last class she was studying quietly at her desk when a student aid came through the door and handed her teacher a slip of paper.

"Nina. They need you in the principal's office," her teacher, Mrs. Felling said through a tight mouth. Nina could tell even the faculty had been talking about her. And now she was going to be interrogated.

The rest of the students in her class chuckled and ogled at her as she stood, grabbing her things, ready to follow the student who'd been ordered to summon her. She acted as if it were normal, no big deal but inside she was fuming. The walk to the office seemed endless. She envisioned an old pirate cartoon she'd seen as a kid, the evil captain forcing traitors and captured enemies to walk the plank. That was exactly how it felt. The ground beneath her felt unsteady like a thin wooden board off the side of a ship and soon she wouldn't even have that to stand on. Soon she would plummet to the sea, left to drown.

Principal Andrews was waiting for her, holding his door open to her with a solemn face. Nina smiled at him just to spite the office secretary glaring at her from the side like she had a scarlet letter emblazoned on her chest. Walking through the door to his tiny office, she thought she heard the distant sound of a splash in water as the door shut behind her.

"Have a seat, Miss Jordan," Principal Andrews said, sitting in his cushy leather chair behind his desk. Nina sat and folded her hands in her lap, relaxing, showing no signs of guilt or worry.

"Do you know why I've asked you in here?"

She felt like rolling her eyes. If this man knew anything about the students he presided over, he'd know gossip is the blood of the Wexley Falls High School vampires. The bigger the story, the better the feast.

"Of course I know. I've been stared at and mumbled about all day," she snipped. She immediately regretted her tone. Acting defensively would only show weakness.

"Well, I'm sorry about that. I hate for a student to be blathered about but what I'm more concerned about is, well, the story itself." His voice trailed off. Nina watched him roll a pen between his fingers in thought. She wondered what version of the tale he'd heard. The 'Mr. Reed and Nina fell in love over Shakespeare's sonnets' version or the more widely spread 'Nina the Lolita, hot-steamy-sex-on-the-desk' version? Judging by his reddening face, it was the latter.

"It's just that, Sir, a story. A rumor started by Todd Dawson," she said with confidence.

Principal Andrews cocked his head to the side, playing the part of the concerned authority figure. "Why would he say such things?"

Nina took a deep breath. "Todd has been bothering me since he returned this year. I've put him off and told him no at every pass. At prom, Todd made a pass at me when I refused to dance with him and he pulled me onto the floor anyway. I shot him down and tried to leave. He got aggressive. Mr. Reed saw it all and intervened. He helped me. Todd's ego must have been bruised so he started spreading garbage to hurt me. Todd told me once he didn't like Mr. Reed. Maybe he saw it as the perfect chance to ruin his career, too."

She waited nervously for some kind of sign that he bought the story and honestly, it really too far from the truth so it had to be somewhat believable. Principal Andrews started to nod slowly then he smiled at her.

"You know, normally I don't pay any mind to rumors like these but I guess the timing of this is what made me want to look into it," he said.

"What do you mean?"

"The fact that this rumor took over the school right when Mr. Reed resigned from his position just seemed odd. I suppose it was only a coincidence. An unfortunate one at that." He stood up and walked to the door to release her from her questioning leaving Nina's heart thudding loudly, pulsing in her ears after hearing the truth.

"Hopefully this will all blow over in a few days. Until then, chin up and if anyone gives you any serious problem, you let me know," he said, shooing her out into the hall. Nina forced a smile but her head was reeling.

The end of the day bell rang before she made it back to her classroom so she turned on her heels, mindlessly wandering to her locker. James was leaning against it, wringing his hands.

"Nina …"

"I know."

Chapter Seventy-One

She called and called, sent text message after text message. No answer, no response. It was as if he never existed at all. She was surprised her fear and anxiety had yet to make her burst into sobs. No, she hadn't cried. She was too panicked to cry. Nina drove straight to Kevin's house. Surely he'd be home. She'd bang on the windows as long as it took to get him to come out and explain himself.

She instantly noticed his car wasn't there but that didn't stop her from going to the front door. Standing on the porch, she felt a chill up her spine remembering how he'd said goodbye on prom night. He had really meant it?

She knocked until her knuckles felt raw. She peered in the windows and saw all of his things just as they'd been the last time she'd been inside. Pulling out her phone, she dialed his number.

"It's me again. Why are you doing this? Why didn't you tell me about resigning? Why did you let me end it? I love you. I'm *in love* with you, Kevin. Now where the hell are you?"

Each message had been similar but she couldn't stop calling. She was determined to find him. A thought flew into her mind and just as quickly she was back in her car and on to another house, knocking on its door.

The door opened and Nina saw the look of disappointment right away.

"Mrs. Benson, I'm really sorry but I didn't know where else to go.

Do you know where Kev ... Mr. Reed is?" Her voice was quaking as she kept her teacher's gaze timidly. Mrs. Benson's face was blank. Her eyes shaming.

"I think you should go home," she said gravely.

"It's not how you think. He's a good man."

Jennifer scoffed and rolled her eyes, folding her arms across her chest. She glared at Nina from inside her doorway, waiting for Nina to turn and leave. Defeated, she did, hearing the door slam behind her. She felt the breakdown coming and then she heard another voice.

"Nina?"

She whipped around, the tears starting to well. She prayed it was Kevin and that his voice only sounded different. But as her eyes cleared quickly she saw Jeff, Kevin's cousin, before her. She'd only seen him a few times but the resemblance to the man she loved was undeniable and almost made her heart leap. He was halfway down his front yard when he ran his hand though his hair. Her stomach knotted, missing Kevin even more.

"You won't find him."

She opened her mouth to ask why, to ask a million questions, but nothing came out.

"He didn't tell me much but he's not in Wexley. I think he just wants to let you go," he said.

"*He* wants to let *me* go? What about me? Don't I get a say?"

Jeff didn't answer, he only shrugged. Her breath started to feel like it was being ripped from her, sucked out of her by some unknown force. Nina hung her head and her eyes brimmed with tears again as the reality hit her hard. She heard the front door open again. Mrs. Benson stood angrily in the doorway and Jeff looked back at her with a pitiful face.

"Nina, I'm really sorry," he muttered quickly before heading back to his house.

She didn't really remember the drive. She didn't know how many traffic laws she may have broken but she made it back to Kevin's house, her breath still heaving out of her. Reaching into her book bag in the backseat, she found a notebook and a pen and did the only thing she could think of. She wrote him a letter. She said everything she might've said had he been face to face with her in that moment. When it was all written, when every word was on the page, she signed it with a heartfelt *I love you.*

Putting her body back on autopilot, she eventually ended up at her own house, in her room, on her bed, a pillow clenched in her arms. That's when the sobs took over. As tears rolled down Nina's face, she felt lost and alone. Confused as to why Kevin would do such a thing to her and angry that she didn't have the chance to make him change his mind.

There was a knock at her door and she tried to compose herself enough to tell whoever it was to go away but she couldn't and her sister walked right in.

"What do you want?" Nina growled.

Greta didn't fire back. Shutting the door behind her, she took a seat on the edge of Nina's bed.

"You know Blake's little brother Cameron? He's a freshman at your school. He heard something today and … well, I just wanted to see if you were okay." Her voice was soft and sweet. It was a genuinely concerned tone Nina had never heard out of her sister. She sniffed and looked over at Greta whose eyes were sober and patient.

"What do you care?" She couldn't bring herself to believe Greta's sincerity.

Greta sighed and scooted closer to Nina on top of the comforter. "I know we don't always get along but you're still my sister. And whether it's true or not, you shouldn't be alone right now. Especially if it's true."

Nina glanced at her, giving her a look that told her quickly it was indeed true. Greta's face fell at the look and Nina was overtaken with sobs again. Without a word, Greta slid even closer to her and wrapped her arms around her and began stroking her shiny black hair as she cried.

"It's all gonna be okay, Sissy," Greta whispered down at her as she curled up near her, now nestled in Greta's lap, letting her tears flow. Greta hadn't called Nina 'Sissy' since they were children, when they liked each other. Before their mother left and their father played favorites. Before school and friends had changed them. Nina relaxed under her sister's touch knowing even with all of the ugliness between them, when it really counted, she had a sister who loved her.

He let two weeks pass before returning to his home. Anxious still that she might see him or come by the house, Kevin acted like a ghost in his own home, never turning on too many lights and keeping all the blinds shut. But he saw the folded piece of notebook paper stuck in the front door.

It was her handwriting and it had his name on the front. His heart was already too weak from walking away. Leaving her. He hadn't yet had the courage to listen to her voice on his cell phone. She'd left him countless messages. Even scanning through his text messages was a testament of his will for not running to her and changing his mind.

He remembered the agony he felt pushing her away in November, when she'd first professed her love for him. It was the same but different. He wasn't scared for himself. He wasn't hiding from his feelings. He was protecting her. Or he thought he was anyhow. But as the days went by he began questioning his decision. Still, he held as strong as he could. *It's the best thing*, he tried to convince himself.

At some point, he finally gathered the nerve to read her note. He was afraid of what her words could do to him but he couldn't wait any longer. He took a deep breath, sat down on his bed where they'd first made love and unfolded the letter.

Dear Kevin,

I don't know where you are or why you left but I don't care. This has been the greatest year of my life.

I'll survive without you. It doesn't feel like it in this moment but I know I'll go on. I'll go off to Caldwell and I'm sure I'll find happiness there. Because I don't need you to have a life.

But I want you. I want to be in your arms. I want to see your smile every day and I want to hear your laugh.

You were worth fighting for and you still are. You're also worth waiting for. You need to know I'll be waiting. Patiently as I can, without judgment or anger, I'll wait.

I love you,

Nina

The conniving whispers and tormenting glares from Nina's classmates dissipated in the few days before the end of high school. Nina gracefully walked across the stage of the auditorium that bared her name, receiving her diploma and thinking to herself the whole time how hard she'd worked to get there. And she wasn't thinking about grades.

She sang one last time at The Black Jewel, praying Kevin would breeze through the front door at any moment. Through each song she squinted to see the very back corner near the bar, hoping he might be waiting. He never showed. Eventually she stopped calling him, stopped texting and emailing. Still having too much to say, too many questions, but no more will to survive without answers.

Her life was packed up in brown boxes and clear plastic tubs, ready for college. But as she settled into Caldwell and her New York City apartment, ridiculously overpriced but an expense not spared by her overindulgent father, she continued to think of Kevin. She started her summer program and excelled with ease. Unbeknownst to her professors her passion for music, her talents in writing and performing, were all fueled by her emotions for Kevin.

Greta and Nina became closer than ever as they planned Greta's wedding countless hours over the phone. Greta and Blake even flew to New York to celebrate Thanksgiving with Nina, bringing James along as well. She suddenly felt blessed in her life to have them. A misfit family maybe, but they were her family nonetheless and she often thought she wouldn't have been able to get through it without them.

As hurt as Nina still felt, confused and even enraged at times, she continued to miss Kevin. She always asked about him, if anyone had seen him or heard anything. And it wasn't until Nina met up with everyone again on the family Christmas trip to Florida that she got some information. James and Nick had seen Kevin working at Wexley Falls First National Bank. Neither of them spoke to him but James told Nina he'd clearly made eye contact. James said something about giving him the evil eye because he still felt like kicking his ass. Nina scolded him, telling all of them to be nice if they saw him.

She made new friends at school, fell in love with her classes, and even took up a part time job singing a few nights a week just like she had at The Black Jewel. New York suited her and gave her a new found confidence in herself she'd only thought she already possessed. Everything seemed right. Good friends, good family, school, work, life in general. Everything was falling into place. There was just one thing missing and it had been an aching hole in her heart since the Monday after senior prom.

CHAPTER SEVENTY-TWO

AUGUST

"Kevin, it's been so great meeting you. We'll be in touch," Angela said.

She was a petite brunette woman who didn't look much older than Kevin. He'd only spoken to her a few times on the phone, mostly emails as they finalized plans and finished up the editing process on his book. He shook her hand and thanked her again for all she'd done then he was on his way to the hotel he'd spent way too much money on.

His book was going to be published. He could hardly believe it. He felt nostalgic for a phone call to his father as he walked down the busy streets of New York City. There was another phone call he was nostalgic for as well. He was in New York and he knew she was, too. Somewhere.

Kevin sprawled out on the California king sized bed and flipped through the channels, finding nothing of interest as he finished the last of his room service French fries. He walked over to the window and pulled the nearly-sheer drapes to either side, exposing the view. It was breathtaking. Times Square lit up at night could make anyone want to live in this city forever. He sighed. *Damn.* There was her face again in his mind.

It had been over a year since he'd seen her but just minutes since he'd thought of her. There were days when all he wanted to do was call her, explain and apologize. He'd let a myriad of calls and messages from her come and go without responding. Would he look like a total jerk speaking up after all this time? Kevin cursed himself almost daily for running away. At the time his heart had been in the right place. Letting her go seemed like the only logical thing to do. Otherwise he would have forever felt like he held her back from something greater than what they had.

He winced at the thought, wondering if *he* would ever have anything greater than what they had. *Never,* he thought. Kevin tried to return his life to normal. He got a job at the bank and motivated himself to finish the book and it really paid off.

Nina filled his thoughts pretty regularly. Certain songs on the radio or something as stupid as scores from the high school sports teams on the news would put her in his mind. He'd seen her friends and felt sick to his stomach, knowing how they must hate him. But he wouldn't dare rush over and try to defend himself.

Once her calls and texts stopped, he felt the weight of the world sitting on his shoulders. *She might never call again,* he'd thought. Maybe he'd never have the chance to tell her how much he really loved her.

He heard his phone ringing on the bedside table and he sprung over to answer it.

"Hello?"

"Hey man! How'd it go?" Jeff asked.

Kevin shut his eyes and shook his head. He forgot he told Jeff he'd call. He sighed letting the hope the phone call might have been from her, for whatever unrealistic and fateful reason, float away.

"Great. I met with Angela and we signed the paperwork. Kinda surreal, you know?"

"That's so awesome. Jen and I are super happy for you," Jeff replied.

Kevin nodded as if Jeff could see him accept the pleasantry. His eyes wandered back to the city lights through the large pane of glass.

"So … are you gonna call her?" Jeff asked in a hushed tone with his words drawn out cautiously.

Kevin let out a snort of a laugh. "I had a feeling you were going to ask me that. To tell you the truth, I've been asking myself the same thing all day."

"You should at least tell her you're in town," Jeff offered, still in a whisper. Kevin knew Jeff was probably hiding in a corner of his house, keeping this portion of the conversation secret from Jennifer. She'd been curt with him since she figured out what happened. Things hadn't been the same.

"She's probably busy. Hell, she probably has some trendy boyfriend," Kevin mused.

"Or she's dating one of her professors."

"Jesus Christ, Jeff," Kevin started angrily.

Kevin grimaced at the thought even though he knew Jeff was kidding. Or maybe he wasn't kidding. Kevin wondered so many nights about what she was up to, figuring out who she was and what she wanted to be. He barely thought of her dating, much less dating someone he wouldn't like. He thought about her letter, telling him she'd be waiting. He wondered how long those words were good for.

"I think I'm just gonna go down to the bar, have a few drinks and call it a night," Kevin said. He and Jeff said their goodbyes then Kevin was in the elevator headed down to the swanky lounge he'd passed when he checked in.

"Scotch and water," he said, taking a seat on a black leather stool. The bartender nodded and fixed the drink quickly. There wasn't much of a crowd and Kevin was surprisingly happy about that.

As his eyes lowered to his drink, taking in the first swig, he caught a glimpse of a woman in the lobby for a split second. Her pale skin shown out of the back of her strapless dress. *Pretty fancy for a Tuesday night*, he thought. Then again it was New York; she could have been doing anything in a dress like that. Something about the way she walked though … He shook his head and took another sip of his drink.

Not a moment passed and he glanced back at her again, strangely curious. Now she was standing amongst the cluster of chairs and tables in front of a baby grand piano. Her back was to him and she was chatting up a woman with a hotel name badge. He watched the light glinting off the subtle beading of her midnight blue dress. Kevin's eyes slid up her legs just as she was turning toward the bar. He scanned her body from the floor up and soon was looking right at her beautiful face. His breath caught.

Even from a few feet away he could see her eyes were gray. Her jet black hair was now painted with caramel highlights. It was luscious looking, pulled into a ponytail swept over one bare shoulder. Dark curls cascaded down the front of her. Her hair had grown.

Her eyes met his and he watched her face go blank. She looked at the woman she'd been talking to and muttered something to her before maneuvering through the tables and chairs to get to him. Kevin felt paralyzed in his chair. She was coming at him quickly, with marked determination. His mind raced through their final conversation, the messages he'd listened to and the text messages he'd never answered. That letter. With the sound of his heart pulsing hard in his ears, he braced himself for her rage as she approached.

Nina stood in front of him silently looking into his eyes, her face emotionless. Then in an instant her arms were wrapped around his neck and her body was against his in an unexpected embrace. Kevin hesitated to put his hands on her bare back, but he couldn't resist the artlessness of it. He breathed in the scent of her skin, shutting his eyes as his head reeled. She pulled back and dropped her arms to her sides, laughing nervously.

Both were at a loss for words. Her smile widened and she opened her mouth to speak but a breathy laugh was all that escaped. Kevin was bewitched staring at her. Her eyes stayed fixed on him.

"Nina?" a voice called from behind her and she turned to look. It was the woman she'd been talking to. Her pianist.

Whipping her head back to Kevin, she finally spoke.

"I have to go on."

Now Kevin breathed the same sort of laugh and shook his head a moment. "Oh my God," he sighed in astonishment, realizing she was about to sing. It was fitting, for fate had haunted the two of them since day one.

"Don't leave," she blurted.

Any other person saying it to him and he wouldn't have felt such a heaviness in the words. Kevin shut his eyes slowly, guilt seeping into his heart. She turned to walk onto the hardwood square where a microphone and a piano stood waiting. The dreamlike occurrence of Nina standing right in front of him had his mind swimming and he knew he needed to let her get on stage. As she started to move away from him, he couldn't stop himself from grasping her wrist. Kevin spun her back around to meet him. A little too close.

He looked down at the slender wrist he held in his hand and he saw the bracelet he'd given her just a day before the fallout. A fire burned between them that had been only glowing embers seconds before they realized they were in the same town, in the same building. He leaned in next to her ear, the smell of Nina's skin making him dizzy and he whispered, "Ladies and Gentlemen, Miss Nina Jordan."

She shifted back on her heels and looked deep into his eyes silently before pulling her bottom lip between her teeth, letting a sultry slow smile creep through. Kevin beamed back tenderly and watched as she headed to the microphone. It was a dream he'd had a million times. Nina sang out only to him, her eyes locked on him, her smile just for him. Her voice wrapped around Kevin like a warm silk blanket and he shut his eyes for a moment to truly enjoy it. It was the most stunning performance he would've never expected. Nina smiled shyly but belted out to him just like all those nights at The Black Jewel.

A few songs later after light applause from the diminutive crowd in the lounge, the piano continued on without Nina's voice over top of it. Kevin watched with more anxiety as Nina made her way back to him. She perched on a barstool next to him, her ankles crossing and sliding to one side. The bartender seemed to know her and asked her what she wanted. She took water with lemon. No words had been exchanged since her last song ended.

Abruptly she faced him, a look in her eyes he couldn't name. "How are you here?"

It wasn't the first question he was expecting but he found the answer anyway.

"I'm getting the book published."

Nina's face lit up and she took her first sip of water. "That's fantastic,"

"You look beautiful," he uttered the words hastily but with sheer conviction.

Her smile stayed but it softened and her eyes lowered. Kevin watched her black lashes brush the tops of her rosy cheeks and nearly stopped breathing. She was a vision.

"It's so weird. I was just thinking about you today," Nina replied.

Kevin's brow had risen at her confession and he waited for her to go on. The soft lights of the lounge bounced off the bit of sparkle in her lipstick and the strands of amber in her hair looked more like gold thread as she ran an absent hand through the ends. He watched her sigh and avert her eyes. *Here it comes*, he thought.

"Where did you go?" she whispered.

"The cabin. Just for those two weeks."

Nina laughed a bit. "I knew it. I just didn't know how to get there. My own damn fault for sleeping in the car."

Kevin tried to smile but his heart felt gripped tight.

"I'm sorry," he whispered.

"I know."

She'd kept her word. *Without judgment or anger.*

He felt her hand reach out and rest on his arm. He could have keeled over from the oddity of it all. His hands were trembling, his breath quaking, as he waited for her to punish him. Scold him and curse him.

Instead, he looked into her stunning gray eyes and saw a smile lighting her up from the inside. "Would you believe me if I told you Greta and I are more like best friends than sisters right now?"

"Nina, that's great. What changed?" he asked, shifting on his seat, leaning closer to her. It felt so natural, her talking to him again, like nothing had changed, like no time had been lost between them. She breathed a minute and continued to gaze at him almost lovingly.

"I guess I finally needed her," she said, her eyes flitting away from him for an instant. "She and Blake are getting married on Saturday. I'm actually headed back to Wexley tomorrow to start the festivities. It'll be my first time back since I left."

Kevin sighed slowly. *Is she still waiting,* he wondered.

"I'm going back to Wexley tomorrow, too," he replied softly, his voice trailing.

She lowered her gaze to the ground and mumbled bashfully. "We should go together."

"To Wexley or the wedding?"

Nina snapped her head up and saw a smirk making its way onto his lips. She could feel the blush in her cheeks and the heat radiating off of her skin. Looking at his handsome, unchanged face gave her goose bumps. The ease with which they spoke, the magnetic force she felt pulling her closer to him, it was all making sense. She'd wanted this chance for so long, maybe longer than she realized, and now it was hers for the taking. Screw the small talk, apologies and explanations. There was only one thing that needed to be clarified.

"So you came all the way here to sign some paperwork?"

Nina sipped her water through a straw and peered at Kevin with doe eyes, trying to melt his heart. She prayed for him to touch her.

Boldly, gracefully and just as Nina had imagined he would when he came around eventually, Kevin reached out and brushed a loose strand of hair behind her ear, cupping her cheek in his palm.

"I guess I just had a feeling I'd like it here."

A shudder rolled through her. Kevin smiled and gave her a look she was sure was telling her it wasn't over. With his hand still against her face, Nina felt one last urge to be convinced he was there for her and her alone.

"And do you … like it?" she asked and waited with bated breath for his reply.

"I *love* it," he said.

A smile as bright as the sun spread on Nina's lips and she gave in once again.

Not caring who saw, knowing there were no repercussions, Kevin and Nina each leaned closer to each other and shared a tender kiss much like their first, back when they were just two people who'd found each other. After all of the months of fighting and yearning, hiding and denying, loving then leaving, they were just two people in the end. Two people—at the beginning.

Acknowledgments

First, I'd like to say that since the original publication of this book, my world has changed dramatically. I never knew what amazing things would lie ahead when I first put my fingers to the keys to write the story that had been in my head since I was seventeen. The readers, fans, bloggers, and fellow authors I have connected with during my short time as a published author have impacted me each in their own way. Thank you to everyone who read and reviewed the first edition of *The Low Notes*. I will never forget all the firsts that Kevin and Nina brought me.

Thank you to my husband Adam, the love of my life.

Thank you to my loving family. My parents, sister, brother, mother and father-in-law, sister-in-laws, brother-in-law and my lovely nieces and nephew.

Thanks to Sammy for putting up with the laptop for so long and still loving me unconditionally.

Thank you to the women of Bliss for encouragement, curiosity and courtesy while I typed away back in 2008.

Thank you Julie Young, my teacher, friend, sounding board and the Paula I need.

Thank you Jana for being a part of the brain child that eventually became this story and a dear friend.

Thank you Amanda Neighbors for reading and encouraging me along the way.

Thanks and an abundance of love to Maggie Mahurin, my best

friend for 17 years. You've inspired me more than you know.

Thank you Laura for helping me to find the strength within myself to make this dream a reality.

Many thanks and much love to Britni Hill. You are a confidant, a reader, an editor, a partner, the cheerleader I often need and so beyond an incredible friend.

Thank you to all of my amazing friends who supported me along the way.

Thank you to all of the beautiful clients of KRB

Quite simply, thank you K.D.

And lastly, no thanks are in order but I must acknowledge a seventeen year old Katie Cole, for whom this is a love letter to. Look at us now.

ABOUT THE AUTHOR

Inspired by music, film, art and the wealth of stories she has heard through her career as a professional hair stylist, Kate Roth has been dreaming up love stories since junior high.

The Low Notes is Kate's first novel, originally published by Rebel Ink Press in 2012 and now in its second edition. Her other works include the paranormal romance, *Reckless Radiance* and the contemporary adult romance, *Natural Harmony* (book one in *the Confession Records collection*). She is currently working on the second book in the *Confession Records* series as well as another new adult romance set in Wexley Falls. She is a small business owner and lives in Indiana with her husband, Adam and their dog, Sampson.

You can stay up to date with all of Kate's news by following her on Facebook www.facebook.com/authorkateroth. To find out more about her books as well as exclusive extra content pertaining to *The Low Notes*, go to www.katerothwrites.com .

28207228R00172

Made in the USA
Charleston, SC
04 April 2014